# A Mother's Survival: Finding Balance through the Storms

HOPE BROOKS

Cover Design by Zoey Diamond

Publishing
Directions


Publisher: Publishing Directions
ISBN: 978-1-928782-92-6
Library of Congress Control Number: 2016934827

# Preface

THE YEARS OF my life have passed so quickly. Now in my retirement from thirty-eight years of teaching, I seek a new meaning for each passing day. As a teacher of young children, my work enabled me to touch lives and make a difference. But in retirement, I no longer have the opportunity to experience that indescribable joy and satisfaction. An emptiness dwells within me, and I have been asking myself how I can continue to leave a mark in this world.

Today I had my awakening. I am driven to share my story with you. It is the story of the hardships I endured through a traumatic childhood, a marriage to a man with mental illness, and the impact of bitter divorce on my children and stepchildren. During the course of my journey, I struggled to balance the joys and adversities of both my personal and professional life, as I became empowered to conquer the endless challenges to happiness. Traveling the path that I did opened my spirit to wisdom and enlightenment, as I came to find the key to survival in this world.

Reading this book will shed the light on your life, enabling you to walk the road through the obstacles to a better, happier place.

In Honor of My Children and
Stepchildren

# A Mother's Survival: Finding Balance Through the Storms

By Hope Brooks

# Contents

# Chapter 1

## A Trip Back In Time

"Mom, you have to help me. I told you the last time we talked that my dad had just been diagnosed with terminal pancreatic cancer. He's declining rapidly, and I'm the only one he has to help him. I just don't have the time. It's impossible. He needs to be driven to and from the hospital for chemotherapy, and must be monitored every minute. With the pills he's taking, he often doesn't even remember where he is. Could you please leave for Michigan today and stay with Dad until I can make other arrangements?"

My thoughts ran rampantly through my head. Here was my married daughter Allison calling me in a state of panic. What? She wants me to take care of Drew, my ex-husband, who had left me thirty-five years ago for another woman? The man who wouldn't speak to me while our daughters grew up, because fighting over child support and college tuition seemed more important? And what would Ray, my present husband, think of this plan? Would he agree to my leaving home for an undetermined period of time to be with Drew? I just wasn't prepared to do this.

"Allison, I don't really know what to say, I need time to think about it."

"How could you say that to me? When have I ever asked you to help me? You're never there when I need you, and you just don't care! I'm never speaking to you again, Mom."

She slammed down the phone and hung up on me.

Ok, I thought, she's so angry now she probably hates me. I don't think I have a choice. I have to do this. I have to go, and I hope Ray will understand.

Ray had not yet left for the office, and I found him in the den, watching the morning news. It would be difficult for me to tell him where I was headed. I had to get his attention, so I turned off the TV and confronted him, face to face.

"Ray, listen to me. Allison just called with an emergency, and I'll be driving to Michigan as soon as I'm packed and ready."

"Why, what happened?"

"She needs help with Drew and his illness. There's no one else to assist with his medical needs. Can you deal with this? If I refuse to go, she'll be upset and angry with me, and I just couldn't bear those consequences."

Speechless, Ray stared at me. "Drew?" he questioned. But after observing my expression, he shrugged his shoulders and said, "It's alright, whatever you need to do. Hope, just be careful."

I gave him a quick hug of gratitude, then ran to find my suitcase. Within fifteen minutes I stepped into the car, feeling fearful and alone. I did not look forward to spending time with my ex, or seeing him suffering. Undoubtedly, this had to be one of the most difficult tasks I had ever faced. Yet I realized that the concern of this day must take precedence over all others.

As I traveled for hours on the highways, my thoughts drifted back to the beginning of my life, and the journey that I have taken through the years. It all began with my childhood, and as I continued the drive, I began to relive all the things that had brought me here today, at this time, and in this place.

*******

# Chapter 2

## *My Childhood*

**1946 - 1959**

I GREW UP in a part of Brooklyn, NY, called Bensonhurst. The world was a different place at that time. Mothers stayed home with their children while fathers went to work, and family life and values were the most important part of daily living.

We lived on a tree-lined street with semi-attached houses near the corner of 78th Street and 12th Ave. The houses had been built close to each other, and adjacent homes shared use of a common driveway for their cars. Every house had a front stoop, and on warm pleasant days, neighbors sat outside on their steps, waved to each other, and took time to talk. The neighborhood children often played together on the block, and organized baseball games in the street, taking turns to look out for ongoing traffic.

In the spring and summer, a truck carrying fruit would stop in the middle of the block. The driver would ring a bell, summoning all residents to come out of their homes and buy his farm-fresh products. Twice a week, the milk truck would be seen delivering milk to almost every family. The friendly driver would actually carry the milk to our back door with a smile.

Italian, Irish, Jewish and Norwegian families composed most of our neighborhood. All of my grandparents had been born in Italy and immigrated to this country in their youth. While growing up, I often listened to the Italian language spoken at home, but never had an opportunity to study it. If you wanted to take a long walk from my house to 13th Ave., you would find numerous Italian delis and the most delicious freshly baked Italian bread. I remember that day when my mother sent me on an errand and asked me to buy her a loaf. The aroma of the bread was so tempting that I actually ate half of it before returning home.

I was the middle child of my family. My older sister Tracey had an outgoing, friendly, and assertive personality. My baby brother Steven, five years younger than me, also came into this world with boundless energy and a fearless zest for life. But I was like neither of my siblings. Quiet and shy and rarely talking, somehow I learned early in life to never tell people how I really felt about anything. My parents saw me as the "good" child that could be seen and not heard, while my sister and brother always had to be disciplined.

My mother, Maria, a stay at home mom, devoted her time and energy to caring for the home and family. I never left her side until the day I reached six years old and started first grade at the local public school. I clearly remember my first day of school. My father, Frank, tightly held my hand and led me into the school cafeteria. All of the first grade students entered the room, accompanied by one of our parents. Silence reigned as a teacher called out our names, one by one, directing us to our newly assigned classes. I finally heard my name announced.

"Hope Cavelli, please line up in Mrs. Rogers' class."

As I walked to the line of children, I kept my eyes focused on my dad. I couldn't believe that in a matter of minutes he would be leaving me there. I gasped to take my next breath, as my eyes filled with tears and fear overcame me. I wondered what would happen to me next, as I obediently followed in the footsteps of that strange lady.

I made it through first grade and progressed through the years. School was different in those days. When the lunch bell rang, the teachers led their classes to the side door and dismissed the children to their mothers. My mom, pushing Steven in his carriage, would meet my sister and me, and walk us home to the lunch she had waiting for us on the kitchen table. When we finished eating, she would walk us back safely to the school yard to complete the afternoon of our school day.

During these years, the student-teacher ratio in the public schools was usually thirty-five to one. Yet there was not a sound to be heard from the students' lips, as we had all been indoctrinated with the concepts of respect and obedience for our elders. And if our principal, Mr. Delaney, happened to walk into our classroom to speak with the teacher, the entire class would stand up together and greet him with, "Good morning, Mr. Delaney." We would return to our seats only when given permission.

I vividly remember the weekly assembly periods that each grade attended. The girls wore white blouses and blue skirts on assembly days, and the boys wore their white shirts and blue trousers. (Girls were never allowed to wear pants in those days.) The assembly always began with the salute to the American flag and the singing of the National Anthem. Then Mr. Delaney would stand before us on the stage and read a passage from the Bible. Although the auditorium was filled with several hundred students, every eye and ear focused on him.

It's hard to believe that the principal of a public school in New York fearlessly spoke about God. During one of my fifth grade assemblies, I made a terrible mistake. In the midst of the reading of Mr. Delaney's Bible passage, I unconsciously cracked my knuckles. That sound resounded throughout the room and seemed to be heard by everyone. Mrs. Maguire, the tyrannical, religious Irish teacher, glared at me mercilessly and said, "Heathen."

I didn't know what a heathen was, but as soon as I got home, I looked up the word in the dictionary. Apparently, she had thought of me as an irreligious pagan.

Both of my parents attended college. They met at the St. John's University School of Pharmacy, from which they graduated together.

It was unusual for a woman in my mom's generation to earn a college degree, but she chose to remain a homemaker until I began high school. And in the true Italian tradition, she took care of my dad's needs, served him, and obeyed all of his commands and wishes. I remember my parents sitting in the living room together watching TV. My dad called out to my mom,

"Maria, I'm thirsty."

Without a word, Mom rose out of her chair, walked to the kitchen, and returned with a glass of cold water which she presented to Dad.

We all recognized Dad as our dictator, the commander-in-chief, the one who made all the decisions and established all the rules. He spoke in a loud and overbearing voice, instilling in me a great sense of fear and anxiety. His yelling permeated our daily lives, and I often questioned in my mind why he chose to treat us this way. Having no answer, I withdrew more and more into myself as my childhood years continued, and often sought solace within the lonely boundaries of my bedroom walls.

I never had any classmates as friends, or interacted with any of the other children in my class or neighborhood during my elementary school years, except for Richard Corolla. He was a handsome boy who lived three houses away. Sometimes my parents allowed me to play outside with Richard, and I can recall the joy that we shared, watching and capturing ants as they crawled up the tall maple tree that stood on the sidewalk in front of our houses. Looking back, I realize that nothing can replace the joys of nature in a young person's experiences.

My parents valued the concept of the extended family. My mother and father both had two brothers who married, so my sister, brother, and I had many aunts and uncles, and cousins of all ages involved in our lives. My father's brothers lived nearby in Brooklyn, and his mother, Grandma Camilla, who only spoke Italian, would come every week to visit and spend a day with us.

My mother's parents, siblings, and their families lived on Staten Island, so it became our tradition to travel to Staten Island from Brooklyn every Sunday. My mother's mother, Grandma Rosa, would prepare the Italian Sunday dinner, and invite all her children and grandchildren.

Getting to Grandma Rosa's house was a time consuming journey, since the Verrazano-Narrows Bridge had not yet been built. We had to take the Staten Island ferry in both directions. This usually involved sitting in the car on lines for hours, waiting for our turn on the next available ferry. My dad, who loved mysteries, would turn on the radio while my family intently listened to the old-time radio series called *The Shadow.* The Shadow was an invincible crime fighter who could defy gravity, speak any language, and become invisible. He spoke in a voice that frightened me, and I would sit in the back seat of the car, hugging my brother and sister in fear of the impending danger.

I had a favorite cousin named Ryan, who always had a happy, lovable disposition. He was one of those rare people who I felt connected with, and could relate to. As the years passed, he became not only my cousin, but also a valued friend. Ryan and his family would often join us at our Thanksgiving, Christmas, and Easter celebrations. My parents had insisted that I take piano lessons starting from age six, and as I played the usual holiday songs at the keyboard, Ryan and his father would sing the words and fill the air with spirit and treasured memories.

My most favorite aunt in the whole world, whom I admired and loved, was Aunt Ava. She was married to my father's brother, Scott. Aunt Ava, an elementary school teacher in Brooklyn, dedicated her time and energy to caring for the needs of her students and inspiring in them the love of learning. Like my mom, she regularly hosted family parties and served homemade food and delights that had taken hours to prepare. But her home reflected warmth and compassion that I had never before experienced, and her generous heart reached out to all who crossed her path.

When I was ten years old, Aunt Ava and Uncle Scott made a decision to purchase a country home in New Jersey in a town called Lake Hopatcong, and they often invited my family to spend time with them and visit. Usually we spent several weeks of the summer there, and my dad would commute back and forth from his job in New York, or just come to the Lake for the weekend. My sister, brother, and I found Lake Hopatcong to be a place of great excitement and novelty. Being city children, we had never before been exposed to living near water. The first time our dad took us for a walk at the edge of the water, Steven became mesmerized by the large carp visually swimming before us and shouted, "Dad, this is what I want to do. Please, please can we go to the store and buy a fishing rod so I can catch them for dinner?"

My sister stared at the people in the small canoes, using their oars to float over the placid water. Her excitement erupted as she tugged on Dad's sleeve. "Hey guys, let's all go canoeing. I'm not even afraid of going into the deep water."

I happily watched the goldfish swimming in the nearby pond, and quickly reached down into the water, trying to pick them up with my bare hands. I managed to touch them, but they easily escaped from my fingertips.

Dad watched us intently as we became fascinated with our interests. For the first time in a long while, he smiled and laughed with us, and seemed to become a changed man.

Another memorable day when we returned to the Lake, Steven arrived with a supply of worms to hook onto the end of his newly acquired fishing rod. He stood without movement, staring at the end of the rod as he held it over the water. Without warning, something began to pull on it, and Steven grasped the handle with all of his strength. Startled, we all stood up and silently watched.

"Dad, Dad, I think I have a fish!" shouted Steven.

He continued to pull until the fish rose out of the Lake and we saw it, a carp, more than twelve inches long.

"Keep pulling it son," shouted Dad. "You could do it! Hurry, don't let it get away."

Steven did it. He slid the fish onto the land, and placed it into the large bucket we had brought along. We never did eat that carp. My father experienced so much pride over this event that he had that fish stuffed and mounted. It remained on the living room wall for as long as I can remember, for all to see and admire.

One night at the Lake, Mom and Dad and Aunt Ava had a social engagement, and asked Uncle Scott to stay home and babysit for all the children. He agreed, and that's the night that my world as I knew it came to an end. My siblings and cousins decided to hang out on the outdoor porch playing board games. But I had wanted to watch my favorite TV show, so I walked alone into the living room, located on the other side of the house. That's when Uncle Scott came in and sat down next to me on the couch. He placed one arm around me tightly, and with the other hand, began to fondle my private parts.

I tried to pull away, but he overpowered me, determined to have his way. He grabbed my arms and held them tight, preventing me from getting away. After a while, he spoke to me in a quiet, secretive voice.

"Hope, do you like this?"

Traumatized, I couldn't answer.

"Did you ever do this with anyone else before?"

I just shook my head, no.

"Well, I'm going to let you get up now. But you have to promise me that you will never tell anyone what happened tonight between us. This is going to be our secret forever. Do you promise?"

Terrified, I would have said anything just to escape. I nodded my head and agreed. But I did not understand what had happened to me. My parents had never told me the facts of life, and I had not been prepared to defend myself against him. So when a grown up told me to keep a "secret," I obeyed.

The molestation continued over the next two years, whenever we visited the country house, and my uncle became more aggressive each time. One night with the entire family at home, he pulled me into the master bedroom and locked the door. He threw me on the bed and began to massage my breasts, kiss me on the lips, and force his tongue into my mouth. Another night when I slept alone on the small front porch which had been converted into an extra bedroom, a disturbing sound awakened me. I opened my eyes and Uncle Scott suddenly appeared on my bed in the darkness, sliding his hand underneath my blankets to again gain access to my private parts. This time I cried and whimpered, "No! No!" Miraculously, he left my room, and for the first time he didn't have his way.

These events impacted me in every aspect of my home and school life. I became more isolated as the thoughts of the "secret" never left my consciousness. Sitting at my desk in school, my thoughts would wander off as I relived the experiences with Uncle Scott in my mind. The thoughts would return and haunt me at night. They would awake with me and shadow me wherever I went and in all that I did.

I wanted to cry out and tell someone about it. I wanted it to stop, but I had nowhere to turn. One Friday afternoon, our family was driving back to the Lake to spend another weekend there. I remember sitting in the back seat of the car for the two hour trip, imagining what might happen to me next with my uncle. I wanted to scream out to my dad every second of the long drive, but instead I suppressed my thoughts and fought back the tears. Then I realized that if I told my father, he would be angry at his brother, and our family would be torn apart. And most important of all, if I told my father, then Aunt Ava, whom I adored, would find out about it and she would be devastated. She would have to leave her husband. Her children would know about it, her life would be destroyed, and it would be all my fault. Aunt Ava deserved better than that. I couldn't bear to see her hurt, and vowed to myself that Aunt Ava would never know. I would take my secret to the grave, and leave her the gift of peace and serenity in return for all that she had given to me. So I said not a word and quietly exited the car when we reached our destination.

Finally, in eighth grade, I succeeded in sharing a friendship with another girl, Rita Burnstein. Her father owned a small grocery store in the neighborhood, Burnstein's Mini Market. My parents met her parents and approved of them. I had a play date and visited my friend at her home, an apartment located above the store. Rita, bright and vivacious, also had a great sense of humor. She gave me a gift, as she brought laughter, kindness, and intimacy into my longing soul. As the eighth grade school year progressed into the autumn months, Rita and I became more and more comfortable with our friendship. We began to share our thoughts, experiences, and dreams. With Rita, I feared nothing, and I knew she would love and accept me no matter what I said or did. So one afternoon after school, while doing homework together in Rita's bedroom, the haunting thoughts returned and took power over my being. Tears began to stream down my cheeks, followed by my sobs. Not understanding the reason for the onset of my grief, Rita instinctively pulled me close and hugged me with her warm, caressing arms.

"Hope, what's the matter? Do you feel all right? Did I do something to offend you? Why are you crying?"

Feeling safe, I at last revealed the "secret."

"Rita, can I tell you something?"

"Of course you can, that's what friends are for."

"It's my uncle Scott. He did something to me."

Rita, puzzled at first, just looked at me. Then suddenly her eyes lit up, and she knew.

"Oh, no. He didn't."

"He did."

She hugged me again, and in that moment a great weight was lifted from my heart. For the first time in so long, I felt free.

After talking for a while, Rita gave me her advice.

"The next time it happens, allow nothing. Fight back with all your strength. Kick him in the balls, bite him, slap him, and scream in the loudest voice possible."

Her enthusiasm for helping me find justice, and her description of this possible scenario led us both to laughter and relief.

Then came the final incident. Again, my family went to the Lake. While my parents and Aunt Ava prepared the barbecue dinner outside in the yard, I became actively involved nearby in a badminton game with my brother, sister, and cousins. After a while I needed to make a quick trip into the house to use the rest room.

As I approached the rest room, Uncle Scott lay in wait for me in a dark corner near the living room wall. He quickly swirled through the hallway, grabbed my arm, and pulled me into the rest room, locking the door behind us. He began to squeeze my breast with one hand, and attempted to slide the other hand down into my underwear. My thoughts became scrambled as I remembered all that Rita had advised me to do. No, I'm not a fighter I told myself. Seconds passed as I limply surrendered to him once again. It would take courage to stand up to him and fight for my freedom. I doubted I had any. What if I screamed and my family heard me? They would all come running and everyone would know. I couldn't do it. Our family vacation time together would be an unforgettable disaster.

Suddenly, something within me said don't be afraid, and you can get through this. Instinctively, I kicked his private area, then fiercely bit his arm with my teeth. Shocked, he backed away. Grabbing his bleeding arm in pain, he stared at me.

"What do you think you're doing?"

In response I screamed with all the strength within me, "No, no! No more!"

Terrified that I would be heard, he let me go. I opened the door and escaped, running outside to join the other children in play. When I saw them, I wore a smile and pretended nothing had happened. I had buried my fears and triumphed at last.

Uncle Scott never again attempted to take advantage of me and my innocence. Looking back to that day, I realize that Rita's advice and friendship influenced my life greatly, and rescued me from further harm. If only in the 1950's there had been sex education at school, or if only I had parents who openly discussed those issues, I might have been spared my suffering. It took years for me to realize that I had been a victim of a horrendous crime.

Today, with computers and modern technology, I have tried to find Rita to thank her for her deed of friendship and love. But I have been unsuccessful in my searches. Rita, if you ever read this book, please know that I have reached out to you, and you are in my thoughts and prayers forever.

***

# Chapter 3

## *High School*

**1959 - 1961**

Although I had attended a public elementary school, my parents felt it important for all of their children to attend a private Catholic high school. Their high school of choice for my sister and me was the Academy of Sacred Heart.

The Academy had a small but beautiful campus. Run by the St. Joseph's order of nuns, it was a private school for girls. The school held a strict uniform policy, with the girls wearing pleated skirts, mandated white gloves, and hats. My first year as a freshman led me into a new world, a place that carried the message of Jesus into every subject, and where each class began with a prayer. This new world swept away my heart, my soul, and my identity. I changed into a different person as I grew in admiration and respect for those dedicated nuns, our teachers, who had sacrificed their lives for what they believed in.

Still in recovery from the trauma of my earlier years, my days at Sacred Heart became a time of peace and tranquility. My academic subjects became my focus, as I enjoyed the challenges of algebra and became fascinated with the language of Latin and the conjugation of the Latin verbs. We often celebrated Mass in the gymnasium of the school, and soon I was able to join the other girls (who had attended Catholic elementary school) in reciting the Latin responses of the Mass without needing to read them from the Mass booklet.

At this time of my life, I remained quiet and withdrawn. My parents began arguing a lot, as my mother began to assert her independence from my dad. When I started high school, she gave up her role as full-time homemaker, and launched her teaching career as an elementary school science teacher. To avoid their confrontations, I would have dinner with my family each evening, and then I would isolate myself upstairs in my room, spending the night hours studying. Soon I began to realize that with all my effort, I had become a very successful student. For the first time, I began to feel that I had personal worth, and that I could achieve my dreams and make my parents proud of me. I could make the honor roll, be accepted into college, choose a career, and in time, make my way to independence.

By the second month of freshman year, I began to interact with the other girls in the school setting. We exchanged phone numbers and consulted on homework assignments, and solving algebra problems. I still had no social life outside of school, as my dad continued to be protective and considered it inappropriate to allow his young daughter out of his sight. But during that moment in time, I was happier than I had ever been, and accepted his rules without complaint.

My love of knowledge and learning quickly expanded in this new setting. My sister, who already played the flute in the high school orchestra, became my idol. Thinking about joining, I questioned her about her experience there.

"Tracey, what made you join the orchestra and decide to play the flute?"

"Sister Bernadette, the orchestra leader, got me interested. She came into our class one day and asked for volunteers interested in playing the flute. I agreed to participate, and I'm so glad I did, Hope. I just love playing songs with all the instruments together. If you're willing to be part of it, we can practice together at home. It would be so much fun!"

After speaking to Sister Bernadette, the clarinet became my instrument of choice. Every Tuesday and Wednesday afternoon we stayed after school until 5:00 p.m., and practiced with the other aspiring young musicians. Then my dad would pick us up in his car, and drive us home.

Being part of an orchestra proved to be an amazing experience. The sounds and the tones of the flutes, clarinets and saxophones blending together with the string instruments bonded us together as we created a work of beauty. Our music permeated the air and reached out to all. I came to perceive Sister Bernadette as a very special woman. As the months passed, I viewed her as the shining light of all that I wished I could ever be. Her presence became a gift from God. It was a blessing for me to know that despite the evil in the world that I had experienced, goodness and virtue existed as well.

In one of my classes, a student named Emily sat next to me. I hesitantly began to share with her my reverence for my favorite nun.

"Emily, I think Sister Bernadette is the most awesome person that I've ever met. She always smiles, and has the kindest heart. She's dedicated to all the girls here, and I think that God sent her to earth to let us experience the meaning of love."

Emily responded with a surprising revelation.

"You're not going to believe this, but I feel the same way about her. I'd like Sister to know how much I adore her, but I'd be too embarrassed to tell her in person. Do you have any ideas?"

We developed a plan to send an anonymous letter to her at the convent. Together we composed the letter, fearfully walked to the nearest mailbox holding hands, then took time to decide which one of us would have the honor of dropping the letter into the box.

A few days passed. Emily and I wondered if Sister had ever received our mail. How would we ever know? How could we find out? If she did receive the letter, did she guess who had written it? A few days later, Sister Bernadette made an announcement in class.

"Girls, today I have a message to give you. Sometimes being dedicated to the religious order of St. Joseph is not an easy task. When you become a nun, you give up the idea of having your own family. You make sacrifices, and dedicate yourself to the beliefs of the Catholic Church. There are some students in this room who, by their written inspirational words, have reminded me why I chose this path in life. Whoever you are, I thank you from the bottom of my heart."

I am grateful for the opportunity I had as a young girl to express gratitude to this memorable woman. I hope that in some way, as the years of my own life pass, I could do for others what she has done for me.

I continued on the path of excelling in academics. At the end of my freshman year, I ranked second out of 133 students on my grade level. I couldn't believe my success. The only girl who surpassed me and maintained an incomparable average of 99% was Shirley Delarosa.

At the beginning of sophomore year, I came home from school one day, collapsed on my bed, and woke up the next morning with a raging fever. My parents called the family physician, who in those days routinely made house calls. Dr. Lynch diagnosed me as having a severe case of mononucleosis, and ordered me to bed rest until the illness ran its course, which could take several months. My high school principal arranged to provide a home school tutor four days a week to bring me the homework and class assignments that I missed. This was a difficult time for me, especially since Dad added to my stress when he decided that the onset of my illness must have been caused by a chill from inclement weather conditions we had had. He believed that rain and water, the dangerous culprits, should be avoided at all costs.

I remember feeling frustrated and asking him, "Dad, can I please, please take a shower and wash my hair? I feel so dirty and my hair is greasy and stringy."

"No, Hope. I'm sorry, but in order for you to recover from this, you must avoid all showering, bathing and wetting your hair during the length of your illness. Maybe I can get you some powdered shampoo in the pharmacy that would absorb some of that grease."

You could never reason with my dad about anything.

Finally, during a home visit, Dr. Lynch announced that I could return to school. I had been absent for the entire first marking period. My first day back turned out to be report card distribution day, and I opened my report card with apprehension to see my grades. To my amazement, despite my prolonged absence, I had again earned the second highest average of all the girls in sophomore year. Of course, the highest achiever continued to be the invincible Shirley Delarosa.

The year continued, with the demands of Sacred Heart directing all of my thoughts, dreams, and ambitions. As I entered into my junior year, I became increasingly preoccupied with following the teachings of the Catholic Church. I believed that missing Mass on Sunday or eating meat on Friday was a mortal sin, which would cause my soul to be cast into the burning fires of Hell upon my demise. My faith in God soared as I prayed throughout the day, and repeating the incantation of the Hail Mary we recited in class, bonded me with the other girls in a way that inexplicably made us one forever.

One day in religion class, the teacher introduced a new topic.

"Do any of you know what the Index of the Church is?"

In response, most of the students lifted their hands in the air, but I had never heard of it.

"The Index is a list of books prohibited by the Catholic Church, which means we are forbidden to read them. These books have been selected by the highest ecclesiastical authorities in the Church because of their message of evil in many forms. I'm going to give all of you a copy of the most updated list of these books. Please look over their titles to see if you recognize any of them."

I sat quietly and scanned the list. Unexpectedly, I recognized the title of a book that I had often noticed on a bookshelf at home, *Les Miserables*, by Victor Hugo. This book was part of an expensive collection that my parents proudly displayed in the entry room of our home, and they had always hoped that their children would someday read every one of them. But once I believed that having that book in my home violated the will of God, I knew I had to act. Hesitant to discuss this with my parents, I secretly removed the book from the shelf. I tore the pages into tiny pieces, and hid the rest of it in my bedroom closet.

I hoped that no one would ever find out what I had done. Surprisingly, within a week, my mom found the remnants of the book, and my parents convened a family meeting. Tracey, Steven and I sat mesmerized at the kitchen table. Dad began speaking.

"I'm very disappointed in one of you or all of you. Your mom found *Les Miserables* destroyed and thrown into Hope's closet. I need to know right now who did this and why. Was it you, Hope?"

My siblings stared at me, believing that I had been the culprit.

"It was me," I confessed.

Before anyone had a chance to react to my confession, I threw myself on the floor, crying hysterically. Through my sobs, I tried to explain.

"You don't understand! You can't allow that book to stay in this house, it's on the Index. We would all be committing a terrible sin if we allowed it to stay on that shelf. We would be punished. I had to do it to save us from the wrath of God. I learned all about it at school."

After gaining control, I made an announcement.

"When school ends this year, I want to leave high school and enter the convent. I want to be like the nuns I've come to know, and devote my entire life to Jesus."

None of this sat well with either of my parents. They gazed at me, and my father spoke firmly.

"That's not going to happen, Hope, not at age sixteen. You will stick to our plan, complete high school, attend college, and hopefully become a teacher someday. Say not another word, and go up to your room."

I obeyed, while Mom and Dad remained downstairs to discuss my actions and analyze me. I think they finally began to realize they did not really know their daughter.

While thinking alone in my room, I questioned why the religious teachings at Sacred Heart had impacted me so deeply, and dictated my behaviors. In my reflections I came to understand that I felt safe here, safe from the trauma I suffered with Uncle Scott. Here existed a new world, a world based on honesty and decency, and love for your fellow man. A place that showed me a better way to live, with faith, and an opportunity to learn how to survive. With my new found power of prayer, I could reach out to God, who would stand by my side and enable me to rise above the trials that stood before me.

## 1961 - 1963

I made it through my junior year. In a way, it turned out to be a thrilling experience. At the end of June, the glee club and orchestra performed at a school concert after hours of practice. Hundreds of people attended the event. At the end of the presentation, the principal walked to the microphone to thank the performers and make announcements. Surprisingly, I heard my name called.

"I would like to announce the recipient of the scholarship for having maintained the highest average in this year's junior class. Hope Cavalli, would you please join me here on the stage?"

I walked from my orchestra seat and stood speechless before the crowd. I couldn't believe it. At that moment I realized that miracles could actually happen. Maybe Shirley Delarosa wasn't so invincible after all.

Until the beginning of my senior year, I had never dated a boy, and never wanted to. But when I became friends with Samantha, things began to change.

I could never understand why Samantha liked me. She possessed an engaging, outgoing personality. Her smiling eyes communicated her joy of life to everyone she met. She instinctively loved boys, and on the days that we took the city bus home from school together, she flirted and chatted with every cute young man that crossed her path. In return for her interest, the flattered young men smiled back, and it seemed that every one of them enjoyed her company and wanted to spend time with her. Her make-up and colorful lipstick, items of beauty which I had never considered or been allowed to wear, made her even more attractive. I considered myself unworthy to be her friend. I had limited social skills, and no idea how to interact with a boy. But Samantha and I, with our opposing personality types, always seemed to support each other. Although Samantha introduced me to many boys, none of them ever expressed any interest in me. As the months passed, I continued to be simply an observer of her success with the opposite sex. Finally, an opportunity arose which opened a new chapter of my life, and introduced me to a new part of myself.

Every year Sacred Heart held dances for the senior girls, and invited the boys from the nearby Catholic High School to attend. I had never before been in a social setting with teenage boys, and the dance began with most of the girls shyly huddling together in small groups. We all wondered if any boy would approach us to begin some kind of conversation. Sometimes we gathered the courage to smile when we thought one of the boys might be gazing at us from across the room.

Then an unbelievable thing happened. Three of the boys approached our group together, and one of them walked up to me.

"Hi, my name is Brandon. Who are you?"

"Oh, hi, I'm Hope," I replied.

"Hope, it's nice to meet you. Would you like to dance?" Nervous, I stumbled, unsure of my footsteps. But Brandon, with his poise and confidence, guided and directed my movements, and together we gracefully glided across the floor of the school gymnasium.

Brandon smiled. "You're a really good dancer. Did you ever take dancing lessons?"

"No, it's just that you're a very good leader."

"This is the first dance I've ever been to. I was a little nervous about coming here today, but my two friends agreed to come with me. How about you?"

"I've never been to a dance before either."

We talked for a while. I can't explain why, but from the moment we met, I felt comfortable with him. I didn't have to pretend anything about myself. Before the dance ended, Brandon shyly moved closer to me and asked, "May I have your phone number?"

Amazing. A boy liked me. Before the evening ended, I ran into Samantha in the ladies room. Filled with delight, I hugged her and exclaimed, "Guess what?"

She gazed at me with a smile and raised her eyebrows.

"He asked for my phone number, and wants to see me again."

"Awesome!"

We laughed together until the dance ended, and it was time to go home.

Within a few days, I received the first phone call. We made an afternoon date and hung out for a while at Hinsch's Ice Cream Parlor on 5th Ave and 86th St. We enjoyed our time together, and made plans for the following weekend. I just had to make sure that my dad never found out I had a date with a boy.

Brandon, tall and handsome, swept me away with his fascinating blue eyes. The more I learned about him, the more I admired him. An only child, he lived near me. He did well in school, and seemed to know how to balance his life with school and friendships. As the weeks and months passed, Brandon became an integral part of my life. I came to consider him an endeared friend, and gradually, my social life began to expand. With time, I found myself emerging from the protective shell that had isolated me from the world for too long. I now belonged and felt accepted by my peers. I held a place in society, and my best friend, Samantha, remained at my side to share the precious moments.

As the end of senior year approached, I asked Brandon to be my date for the senior prom. I shopped at the mall for hours, looking for the most attractive dress. On the night of the prom, the evening began with Brandon, Samantha and her date, and a few other couples gathering in my living room for Dad to photograph a moment to remember. At least he didn't object to this formal, supervised event.

At last, life was good! Now I could laugh, and share my thoughts and feelings with others. I came to understand that this was the meaning of happiness and I did have value as a person. Memories of Uncle Scott began to fade and be replaced by positive and rewarding experiences.

***

# Chapter 4

## *My College Years*

**1963 - 1964 Freshman Year**

SENIOR YEAR OF high school proved to be a busy time, submitting college applications and making choices. Samantha and I yearned to attend college together. Best friends, we couldn't bear the thought of being separated. But Samantha's parents had already made plans to send her to Brown University, the well-known Ivy League college located in Providence, Rhode Island. My father completely rejected that idea. In addition to the high cost of private school, he considered it inappropriate for a young girl to live away from the safety of home. My dreams shattered as he announced that I would only attend a local college. Nothing else to be discussed.

The end of the year approached. I had been accepted into several colleges, but my parents postponed their final decision. A week before graduation, a letter arrived in the mail deciding my fate. I had been granted a full, four-year scholarship to St. John's University, located in downtown Brooklyn, New York. My parents, ecstatic, presented it to me. They never expected my response.

"Mom, Dad, you don't understand. I'm not going there. I don't care what you say, or what you think. Maybe I can get a student loan. I want to go to Brown University with Samantha. St. John's is a big school, with a long commute. I'll have to travel hours every day and ride the city buses and subways to get downtown. I don't want to do that. I hate you!"

I ran upstairs to my room, and out of control, slammed the door behind me. I didn't know what to do. I contemplated running away, far away, where no one could ever find me. But before I contrived my plan, I heard my dad knocking on my door. I opened it. He spoke in an unusually calm voice.

"Hope, I'm sorry you feel the way you do. You have to remember that sometimes you can't always have what you want. Give it a chance, and I bet you won't regret your decision. Accept the scholarship, and major in education, so that someday you can become a teacher. That is the best career you can have as a woman."

I had no control over my fate. Free college for my parents meant St. John's University for me. Now Dad was also trying to determine my career, telling me to be a teacher. Standing there, drained of all my energy, I just couldn't defy him any longer.

With lowered eyes, I reluctantly murmured, "Ok, I'll do it."

I gave my word, but mourned the loss of a lifelong dream. I had worked so hard in high school, didn't I have the right to choose my place of higher learning? I'll be an adult soon, shouldn't I follow my chosen path to independence? In my daydreams I visualized what life would have been like at Brown University with Samantha. I saw myself walking from class to class, building to building, carrying my books on the gorgeous 146 acre campus. I would have spent time with my best friend, and most of all, I would have earned my freedom from Dad.

Two days passed before I found the willpower to reveal my status to Samantha. Facing her with the reality of my plight would not be easy. At the end of the school day, I told her I'd like to discuss something. She replied, "Sure, let's go to Hinsch's. We'll have some ice cream and talk."

We took the city bus to 86th Street and arrived. We ordered our ice cream and began with small talk. When my delicious vanilla sundae appeared before me, I realized I had no appetite. My eyes turned directly to Samantha. She stared back with a look of realization and dread.

"Hope, what is it? What's wrong?"

This was the moment I had to tell her. "Samantha…in the end, my dad has made the final decision for me. I won't be going to Brown with you. I'll be living at home, attending St. John's in Brooklyn. You'll be far away in another state, and we probably won't even have time to see other. I can't believe this happened to me. I'm so sorry. It's all my fault. I have no strength to stand up for what I want and need. But thank you for being in my life. Knowing you has been a blessing and a gift."

Samantha reached across the table with compassion. She grabbed both of my hands and held them tightly. After a moment of silence she said, "Let's not give up. We'll try. It will never be the same, but we'll stay in touch as much as we can."

"Ok, we'll try."

Each day I tried to analyze the meaning of it all. Would it always be like this? Do people come into the fiber of our lives, and then they fade and disappear? I internalized that anger toward my father once again, as feelings of worthlessness returned. During family dinners, I sat respectfully at the table, speaking only when spoken to. Then I removed myself and regressed to my previous state of seclusion, returning to be the person I had been before my experiences of friendship and love. I hid in my room as in the past, when the pain and shame that I carried had overwhelmed me. I wasn't ready to change. I had learned to cope with life by escaping.

I continued to date Brandon during the summer before college. One beautiful summer day we met in the park, and he gave me the most surprising news.

"You're not going to believe this, Hope. I'm so excited, I can't wait to tell you. I've decided to attend St. John's, too. We're going to be classmates. We can see each other every day, as much as we want. We can even meet at the subway station in the morning, and ride on the train together. What do you think?"

Suddenly, everything changed. Maybe St. John's wouldn't be that bad after all. I would see Brandon every day, but then I wondered if this would be an unsettling situation. Would we just remain friends at school, or become lovers? Would he become interested in other attractive girls in his courses and reject me? I became a little nervous thinking about the possibilities, but decided that only time could reveal the outcome.

Fall came and college began, along with a new chapter of my life and adjustments. St. John's was a huge school, with an environment of several thousand students. As a beginning freshman, I barely knew anyone, except Brandon, so I often sat alone at the lunch tables, intimidated by the large crowds and high noise level. The University maintained a strict policy for dress codes in the 1960's, both for men and women. The young men were required to wear jackets and ties, and the girls had to wear only dresses and skirts. Even on the coldest winter day, slacks or pants would not be tolerated. A security guard would meet everyone at the entrance door of the building, ensuring that everyone admitted had followed the rules. Sacred Heart's uniforms became a memory of the past.

Brandon and I spent more time together, usually meeting for lunch. By the beginning of the second semester, we remained intensely involved.

"Why don't we register together for the same required courses for the spring classes?" Brandon asked me. "Don't all students have to take the basics, like algebra, American history, and English literature despite what majors they've chosen?"

"That's interesting," I replied. "Let's look in the course bulletin, and see if that's possible. In the same class, we can share note taking, study together, and do research in the school library. Maybe – I'd like that." As I considered the scenario, I became convinced that I would feel comfortable with it. The longer we knew each other, the more I began to feel that Brandon was not only a person in my life, but a part of me as the person I had become.

In time, Brandon, who sat by my side in the classes we chose, who shared my endeavors and newly found world of knowledge, became my soul mate. One day over lunch in the school cafeteria, he made a disclosure. "Hope, as I sit here with you, I realize something today. Something I've been thinking about for a while. Hope, I love you. It's not just infatuation or romance. I love everything about you, the person I see on the outside, and the person I know on the inside. Having you in my life has altered my outlook on the world. Being so young, I never thought I could experience these feelings."

I looked at him, a young man with a work ethic who attended college full time, and worked part time after school to help his family with tuition bills. He never drank alcohol, never asked me to have sex with him, and had totally gained my admiration.

"Brandon, I love you too."

Suddenly drawn to each other, we kissed passionately, not even noticing or caring about the shocked expressions on the other students around us.

Things had changed for me so much over the past two years. I no longer desired to enter the religious life. Still too young to consider marriage or commitment, I just longed to enjoy the moment and be thankful for what I had.

Settled in at last at St. John's, my father continued to be my major challenge. He still objected to my dating anyone. Although he held nothing personal against Brandon, he obsessively attempted to shelter me from him. He monitored our phone calls and whereabouts, always hoping to prevent us from being together. I never really knew how my mom felt about this. She rarely voiced her opinion, knowing this was the best way to get along with her husband. One night, Brandon asked me to type one of his course assignments for him. I agreed, and invited him to my house where the typewriter had been set up in the den. Brandon rang the doorbell, carrying his handwritten work. We walked into the den and sat down next to each other. Dad followed us, intent to watch our every move.

"Hello, Brandon," he began. "I see that you've brought some work along with you. Is there some reason why you're not able to type your own assignments?"

"Good evening, sir. I do have a typewriter, but the ink has run out and I don't know how to replace it. I'm thinking that I'd rather buy a new one, but I haven't had time to work on that project. School and work have been keeping me busy."

Dad didn't respond, but he stood steadfast in the den for more than an hour, ensuring that nothing but typing happened when we were together. I took a moment and looked at him. Here he is, I thought, wasting all his energy for nothing. He keeps trying to protect me from Brandon, but where was he when I really needed him? I wanted to say, "Dad, why didn't you protect me from Uncle Scott. He's the one who hurt me, didn't you know?" But as always, I said nothing.

I finally sat down with my mother one day and questioned her about my dad's controlling temperament.

"Mom, I just don't get it. Why does he always treat me like a child? Why doesn't he trust me? I've never done anything wrong."

My mother discerned my anguish, and decided at last to reveal the traumatic childhood that my father had suffered.

"Your dad's parents married at a very young age in Italy. They immigrated to the U.S., but surprisingly, your Grandma Camilla never learned a word of English. When your dad and his older brother Scott were young children, their father ran off with another women, leaving your Grandma Camilla pregnant, with no job. Having no money to feed her new baby, she surrendered him to an orphanage."

"Mom, that's a terrible story. How come no one ever told us about it? How did they all survive?"

"Somehow, they did. But your dad experienced poverty, abandonment by his father, and trauma in the loss of his newborn brother. I believe that with his own children, your dad is reliving his past in his own way. Maybe he's just trying to be the caring parent he had yearned for throughout his entire life, but never had. Maybe he's overprotective because he imagines the bad things that might happen to you, Tracey, or Steven."

My mother's heart seemed warm with understanding.

"Hope, now that I've shared this with you, are you ready to forgive your father and accept him as he is? Can you move on to another place?"

I realized my dad certainly had a terrible childhood, and I felt compassion for his years of suffering. But my life would take me on a journey of many more years before I could release my anger and find the path to peace.

"No, Mom. Not yet. Not today."

## 1964 - 1965 Sophomore Year

I began my sophomore year with the determination to improve two aspects of my life. My grades during freshman year had been acceptable but not great, so I decided to work harder to earn a higher grade point average. I also wanted to improve my social life and develop some friendships with other girls. St. John's had several active sororities on campus. I became interested in joining the sorority called the Squaws, with the hope that I could find a group of friendly girls who would accept me. To join a sorority, you had to be formally interviewed and voted for by its existing members.

When the moment for my interview arrived, the stress that accompanied it seemed more that I could handle. One of the Squaws led me to the front of a classroom, where I stood, while the sorority sisters sat before me. The interrogation began, but when asked the first question, I found myself taking rapid, deep breaths, and my voice became barely audible.

"Why are you interested in joining our sorority, rather than one of the others?"

"You're all well known around the campus as intelligent, confident girls with great potential for successful careers. I admire everything you stand for. I would consider it a privilege to be accepted into the Squaws."

"Are you willing to commit to attending our weekly meetings and participating in our extracurricular activities both on and off campus?"

"Yes I am."

"What are your academic goals and plans for the future?"

The interview continued for the next thirty minutes. At the end I left the room, and believed in my heart that they would vote against me. I just could not have measured up to their expectations.

Within the next twenty-four hours, I received a call from one of the Squaws, Anne.

"Hi Hope, I'm calling you with some great news. You've been approved by our members. Welcome into the Squaws!"

"Oh my God, I can't believe it. Thank you so much for calling me."

"We're going to meet at 7:00 p.m. on Friday night to discuss the plans for hazing. See you then."

Awesome. I found out later that several of the other candidates had been rejected, but not me. Hazing? What exactly was that? I had heard many stories, both on campus and in the news, about questionable activities that had occurred during fraternity hazings at other colleges around the country. But I would not allow any of my doubts to stand in the way of my acceptance.

Hazing began on a Friday afternoon and proceeded through the weekend. The Squaws drove up in a large van in front of the University and picked up all the candidates. We were ready and excited about our forthcoming adventure. Anne stood up in the van and made an announcement. With the tone of her voice, she did not seem friendly at all.

"Girls, hazing will begin right now, here in this vehicle. Please understand that you are going to be blindfolded, and we will be transporting you to an unknown location, far from the streets of Brooklyn and civilization."

She wasn't kidding. Within a few minutes, the Squaws proceeded around the van and covered our eyes, preventing us from seeing or knowing where we were going. A few hours passed. As darkness approached and night prevailed, I could hear the birds, and other sounds of nature. My other senses told me that we had been brought to an isolated cabin in the middle of some rural area. Anne continued with her instructions.

"Ok girls, each of you will now be given a guide who will bring you to various locations in the woods where you will remain until someone returns to get you. You will be separated from each other and remain in your private, designated place. You will stand tall and repeatedly recite the refrain:

> I'm a Squaw pledgee and that's all I'll ever be,
> I'm a Squaw pledgee and that's all I'll ever be.

Hazing turned out to be a nightmare. I must have recited those words thousands of times. I remained abandoned in the freezing cold for hours by my so-called new friends, terrified of the hooting of owls and other unfamiliar sounds. I needed a rest room. I thought my bladder would burst, but no one cared. Finally, one of the Squaws came to find us about 4:00 a.m. and led us back to the cabin. Physically and emotionally exhausted from the trauma of the experience, I needed several days to recover.

Perhaps I shouldn't have taken it all personally, but I did. Each time I attended the weekly afternoon sorority meetings, I became more aware that this was not where I belonged.

Eventually I stopped participating in the Squaws meetings and social events, but I did not give up on my resolution to find meaningful friendships with other girls. By the beginning of the spring semester of sophomore year, I found myself hanging out with Megan and Emma, two girls in my sociology class. Emma was tall, sophisticated and beautiful. Megan, always smiling, had already decided to become a social worker and devote her career to helping the less fortunate, needy people in our society. In a short time, she earned my respect and admiration, and I felt blessed to have connected with such a special person.

While devoting much of my time to these other issues, my relationship with Brandon continued to be solid and strong. We moved together from adolescence to adulthood. We were known and recognized everywhere we went, on campus and off, as the inseparable couple. My dad continued to object to my relationship with Brandon. He just couldn't let go of his old-fashioned, Italian ideas. One night he confronted me and began yelling, almost out of control.

"You're too young to have a serious relationship. You need to date other young men, not just him. And anyway, your main focus now should only be your academics and career plans. Forget the boys!"

Luckily, he never really knew how much time I spent with Brandon at school. Although I never would have had the courage to openly defy my father, this had become the first time in my life when I lived by my own decisions, and thrived on my feelings of personal triumph.

## 1965 - 1966 Junior Year

When junior year began, I felt that I had achieved the two goals that I had set out to accomplish the year before. My grade point average during sophomore year had improved to a B+, and I had maintained my ongoing relationships with Megan and Emma.

The next important goal was to decide my major field of study. After being influenced by Megan, I became interested in being a social worker, a psychologist, or some type of guidance counselor. Whatever I chose, I wanted to be involved in people's lives, and to learn the needed skills for helping them deal with their problems. My interest in these fields intensified as I recalled the many first-hand situations in my own life that I had survived, without the advice and support that would have benefited me.

When I told my dad of my plans, conflict immediately ensued.

"We've already had this discussion, Hope. I told you the only acceptable choice for a woman is to be a teacher. With your teaching certification, you'll be home from your job by 3:30 p.m., with time to prepare dinner and take care of your children. After retirement, you'll collect a New York City pension. There's nothing else to be said. You're going to major in elementary education, and become a New York City teacher."

I couldn't believe it. Time after time, I had been forced to relinquish all power over *my* dreams into the hands of my relentless father. And now it would happen again. I couldn't see myself taking charge of a classroom filled with children. Although I had grown in confidence over the past few years, I was still dominated by a shy, insecure disposition. Teaching was doomed to be a failure. My heart beat rapidly as I tried to suppress my rage. Finally I spoke with a quivering voice, hoping to thwart my father's conviction.

"Dad, I have a great idea. I should set up an appointment with a St. John's career advisor to gather information about other possible options for me."

His voice escalated.

"End of discussion! I've already told you what you will do!"

I ran to my room, threw myself on the bed, and cried. I felt like a victim, as if some terrible crime had been committed against me. Why did he have this one-sided way of viewing the world? Why did he need to control all of my life's choices? But now, as always, the die was cast. I would satisfy my father and work toward my Bachelor's degree in elementary education.

On Dec.31st of 1965, my sister Tracey decided to host a New Year's Eve party in the basement of our house. My parents gave their approval. They planned on periodically checking on us to make sure everyone's behavior was appropriate. I invited Brandon to the gathering, thrilled to spend my first New Year's Eve with him.

The party began with music of the most popular songs of the Beatles, Bob Dylan, and the Rolling Stones. The mood of the evening was quiet and serene, with feelings of warmth and comradeship. Tracey and I worked together to serve trays of antipasto, eggplant, and pasta salad. When Brandon and I decided to sit down, there were not enough chairs to accommodate everyone. Thinking nothing of it, Brandon sat on the nearest chair, with me on his lap. A short time later my father walked into the basement. He observed us seated together on the chair.

"The two of you, come upstairs to the living room. Now."

Oh no, big trouble ahead. We quietly obeyed and positioned ourselves on the couch, waiting for the confrontation.

"Brandon, I do not like your inappropriate behavior with my daughter, and I will not tolerate this in my home. Please leave the premises now, and understand that you are no longer welcome here."

"But…" he began as he tried to defend himself.

"Get out, NOW."

Brandon remained speechless as he exited the front door. He was reluctant to call me at home, so we didn't see each other until school resumed after the holiday weekend.

"Hope, we have to talk."

"I know we do," I replied, as we looked into each other's eyes. Reluctantly, he whispered, "We can't go on like this. Think about this. Your dad is intent on breaking us up, and I feel like he hates me. We have to make a choice. You could declare your independence and marry me now, or we need to say goodbye and end our relationship."

His ultimatum took me by surprise. No, no. This couldn't be happening. I couldn't hold back the tears as they streamed down my face. I looked away from him as I processed his words. Didn't Brandon love me? If he really did, how could he leave me? The image of my father flashed before me. If he causes our break-up, my anger toward him will turn into hatred. I can no longer deal with him controlling every aspect of my existence. Why, oh why, is he doing this? I'll never understand.

Brandon had decided to abandon me. But was I ready for the moment to rebel against Dad? This became the most difficult thing I had ever done. We reached out to each other with a final embrace.

"I'm so sorry, Brandon, but I just don't have the courage to defy my father's wishes and marry you now. Besides, how would we live? We have no money. We'd have to quit college and get jobs to support ourselves. But neither one of us wants to do that. Maybe we could break up until we graduate, then get back together. Is that possible?"

"Maybe."

We sadly walked away in separate directions, and parted forever.

The next morning I began my usual weekly routine. Standing on the busy Brooklyn street corner, waiting for the city bus, I noticed a mother and her two children. The children were busy observing a colony of ants that had built a home in the sidewalk cracks. Their faces reflected fascination, as they found wondrous pleasure in the discovery of life.

As I watched the children, a transformation overtook my mind and spirit. Crowds of people waited with me at the bus stop, but I no longer saw them. Noisy cars and trucks drove past me down the street, but I no longer heard them. My thoughts took me to a place far away. And in that instant, I came to realize what I was meant to be. Like the dawn of a new day that brings daylight into the horizon, I knew I was meant to be a mother. Someday I wanted a child of my own, to hold and to treasure, to nourish and adore. But with Brandon only a memory now, the dream for a family of my own seemed impossible. I became consumed by the overpowering sense of loss and plummeted into deep despair.

## 1966 – 1967 Senior Year

Along with the last year of college came new concerns. During the upcoming spring semester, I would complete my student teaching assignment in a local public school. I would prepare lessons, present them before the students, and be evaluated by the classroom teachers and professors. At the end of the semester, I would receive a grade based on my performance. Besides my academic commitments, I still had not recovered from the loss of Brandon. It would take a long time, and I had no interest in meeting another young man or starting a new relationship.

I'm so thankful that I had found Megan for support. She was always there to listen and walk me through the difficult days. One afternoon she had an idea.

"Have you even been to any of the Friday night fraternity parties?" she asked.

"No, Megan. Have you?"

"No, but maybe we should try going to one this weekend, and hook up with some new, handsome guys."

I considered it. A new experience, I had never been in a fraternity house before. It might be fun, just what I needed.

Thinking of it made me giggle. "Ok, I'll go."

Friday evening arrived. Megan and I had perfected our makeup, and bravely entered the building. The atmosphere seemed friendly and vibrant, while the alcohol flowed rampantly. At age twenty, I still had never even tasted an alcoholic drink. I walked over to the bar where the fraternity brothers served beverages, and I timidly asked for a ginger ale. The young man serving me gave me a suspicious grin, then handed me my drink.

The evening turned out to be a blast, especially when a number of boys seemed interested in me. When one of them asked me to dance, I turned my attention to Megan and saw her actively engaged in her own conversation. It seemed as if our decision to embark on this new adventure had been a good one.

After a while the fraternity house seemed quite warm, so I approached Megan.

"It seems to be so hot in here, I'm feeling really thirsty. Do you want to come with me to the bar while I have another drink?"

"Sure."

I ordered my second ginger ale, then another. In a few minutes after my third, I began to feel dizzy and disoriented. I grabbed onto Megan's arm.

"Megan, there's something terribly wrong. The room is spinning around in my head, and the music keeps fading away. I think I'm going to faint."

She grabbed me, and with the help of one of the fraternity brothers standing nearby, slid me onto the nearest chair. I could hardly keep my head erect.

"Hope, what's the matter?" yelled Megan, concerned.

Another one of the fraternity brothers walked up to us and turned to Megan.

"I know what the trouble is. The guy behind the bar has been heavily spiking your friend's ginger ales with vodka. Right now, she's wasted. You should probably just take her home."

Megan and I left the fraternity house, never to return. After arriving home and collapsing, I finally opened my eyes after eighteen hours of a deep, rejuvenating sleep. I stepped out of bed, feeling nauseous and still slightly hung over. I headed for the phone to call Megan.

"Megan, how could this have happened? What an experience. I've never been drunk, ever. That guy violated me in a way I never thought possible."

"I know, Hope. Luckily, we left right away and avoided any horrendous consequences that might have occurred. I guess we learned the true meaning of life in a fraternity house."

"Yes, and I can promise you that after only one night, I've had enough of fraternity houses to last a lifetime."

Weeks passed uneventfully, then one afternoon I got a phone call from my cousin Ryan.

"Hi, Hope. How are you doing? It's been a while."

"I know, my schedule is so busy!"

"My life's been like that too. But I'm calling to ask you a question. A good friend of mine, Drew, saw a high school graduation picture of you that I've kept in my wallet. He's interested in meeting you, and wants to know if you would agree to a blind date."

"A blind date? Are you serious? I don't know, I've never done anything like that before."

"Come on, he's a really good guy. He's tall, handsome and bright, currently working on a B.S. in Science."

"Well Ryan, I'll do it, just because I trust you and would feel safe with any good friend of yours."

I had no awareness at the time, but this date was destined to bring me to the entrance of another world that I knew nothing about.

Drew lived in the borough of Staten Island, but had a driver's license and use of his father's car. I had never dated anyone with a car before, and surprisingly, my father allowed me this privilege. At last, in some way, I felt I had made my first small step toward long desired independence.

We both enjoyed our first date. Drew had amorous blue eyes, a mostly serious and quiet disposition, and at times, a phenomenal sense of humor that made me laugh. He easily towered over me with his incredible six foot, eight inch stature. We both agreed to see each other again. Within a month, he declared his love for me and began to pursue me passionately. One evening during dinner, he made promises that every young woman would want to hear.

"Hope, you are the most beautiful girl I've ever met. I feel so attracted to you that I've been visualizing what it would be like for us to spend the rest of our lives together. We'll both graduate from college in a few months, we'll easily find jobs and jump into our careers. It's not too soon to ask. Hope, will you marry me?"

"Marry you? Are you serious?" I couldn't believe what I heard. I felt like I hardly even knew him.

"I want you to think about it. You don't have to give me an answer now. I know you've had a lot of issues and problems with your father over the years. I promise I will be good to you. I will rescue you from him. I'll become a research scientist, and I'll have a good income. I'll support you and our family, and you won't need your dad for anything. Together, we'll be happy and free."

"Drew, this is all too soon. We both need more time before we commit to marriage. I'm not ready to say yes, but some day, maybe, with time.

I went home that night feeling both desired and confused. Marriage? How could I? Deep within me still lived the dream that after graduation I would reconcile with Brandon, and things would work out. We occasionally ran into each other in the hallway or cafeteria, either ignoring each other or making small talk. On one of these occasions, Brandon unexpectedly invited me to lunch.

"Would you like to have lunch with me, today? There's something I'd like to talk to you about. My treat."

I felt somewhat uncomfortable about it, but couldn't resist the opportunity to be with him. Also, I wondered what he wanted to discuss.

"Sure, Brandon. We're still friends, it would be nice to have lunch together."

The conversation began with impersonal questions. We shared updates about our courses and professors, families, and plans for our futures. Then the bombshell hit.

"Hope, I asked you to lunch because I wanted to tell you something. I wanted you to hear about it from me, in person, and not from someone else." He paused, choking, trying to find the words.

"I know we had some wonderful years together, and I will never forget what we shared. But now I'm moving on. I have a girlfriend.

She's pregnant, and soon I will be marrying her and starting a family. I just wanted you to know."

As he spoke, he kept his eyes focused on his lunch plate.

I couldn't believe it. I had always believed that Brandon and I were meant to be together. Only the factor of time delayed our reuniting. But in reality he had betrayed me, made love to another woman, and planned a life without me. I had been forsaken, and he would move on to have and enjoy the family I had dreamed of with someone else. All of this seemed beyond my comprehension. I wanted simply to walk away, or to run and hide somewhere, so that no one could find me. But I managed to brace myself despite the inner tension I experienced, and responded with truth from my heart. "Brandon, I just want you to know that I had always hoped we would get back together. I guess now I realize it will never happen."

I took a deep breath. "Good-bye, my friend. May you find love and fulfillment in all of your days."

At least Brandon's revelation represented closure for me, and led me to open my mind and consider other options for myself. Perhaps now I could move forward, I thought, and contemplate whether or not I wanted to marry Drew. As the next few months of senior year passed, Drew continued to declare his passionate love for me. Feeling adored, my ego soared. Gradually, he became the new focus of my plans and aspirations.

On occasion, I became perplexed by Drew's strange behavior. He often seemed sad and depressed, avoiding social engagements with friends and family whenever possible. I remember one evening when he pulled over and parked the car in a remote area of Staten Island. A despondent look overcame him, and he gazed at the silhouette of a nearly apartment building.

"Look up there to the top of that building," he said. "It's really tall, isn't it?"

"Yes. But why are you so interested in the building?"

"I've thought about it lots of times. If I could climb to the top, I could jump off the roof, and the nightmare of my existence would be over at last."

He kept staring into the darkness, as I sat there.

"Drew, I don't want to stay here any longer. This place is too depressing. Let's go now."

I was young and unaware that Drew manifested the symptoms of mental illness that night. The next time I saw him he seemed just fine, so I dismissed what he had said, and continued our relationship as if that event had never occurred.

The last semester of college began in January. I received my assignment as a student teacher to Public School 201, an elementary school in Brooklyn. I was thrilled, since my favorite Aunt Ava still worked there as a first grade teacher. I looked forward to the opportunity of spending precious time with her during the school day. For the first ten weeks of student teaching, I was assigned to work with a teacher in a fifth grade class. Interacting with these pre-teen students proved to be a discouraging experience. I would ask the students to perform a task, but they would often respond with a defiant attitude. Beginning to feel insecure once again, I feared that I would never succeed in this profession.

During the second ten weeks, my position changed to a first grade class of five and six year olds, right across the hall from Aunt Ava's classroom. This setting turned out to be a much more rewarding assignment. At this age, the children viewed their teachers as people very important to them. One day I stood in front of the room holding a supply of reward stickers in my hand. I asked,

"Who can come to the blackboard and point to the word cow?"

Many children raised their hands in response. I called on Louis, who walked to the board and correctly located the word. I said, "Good job," and handed him a sticker. He returned to his seat with a captivating smile. He loved that sticker, a symbol of his success, which he instantly attached to his shirt for all to see. The process continued, with my naming words and students wildly raising their hands to be chosen and granted a sticker. I now considered the possibility that maybe I could actually be a teacher of children in this age category and succeed.

My most treasured moments in P.S. 201 included exposure to Aunt Ava. I observed the unforgettable influence she had on her students. They frequently ran up to her and hugged her, thriving on her attention and inspiring words. Sometimes we would have lunch together in the teacher's room, and sometimes I visited her in her classroom to observe her in action. Her presence, whether with co-workers or students, emanated compassion and a joyous zest for life. My admiration for her soared, and I was more grateful than ever to have her as the model of the person I wanted to be.

On weekends I continued to spend time with Drew. Although sometimes I had my doubts about a commitment, I finally agreed to marry him. After my college graduation, I knew I had to break away from Dad's domination somehow. Soon I would be twenty one, old enough to make my own decisions. It took me a long time to gather the courage to break the news to my parents, but I finally did.

"Mom and Dad, do you have a few minutes to talk to me? There's something I've got tell you."

"What is it, Hope? Is there a problem?"

"No, not a problem, but something really important. I decided I want to marry Drew."

I definitely captivated their attention. A moment of silence.

"Marriage? When?" asked Dad.

"Some time in the summer, after graduation."

For the first time, my usually reticent mother joined in the conversation. "I think Drew is a decent young man, highly intelligent, with a bright future ahead. But before we approve, Drew must follow the Italian tradition and formally ask us for your hand in marriage. Also, we must meet his family to be sure they are decent, caring people with values."

My dad finally announced, "I agree with everything your mother said. Let's make some arrangements and invite Drew's family over for dinner. That would be a good beginning."

I had witnessed a true miracle. Both of my parents accepted my marriage plan with Drew. In a while, I would be free at last. I would find my path to independence and control over my own decisions. My feelings of exuberance overcame me. After a moment of thought, I ran to my parents and for the first time in years, hugged them.

"Thanks for supporting me in this. I love you."

* * *

# Chapter 5

## *Marriage*

**Summer of 1967**

AFTER FOUR YEARS of hard work, I earned my B.S. in Education as well as my New York City and New York State Teaching Certifications. Drew and I planned our wedding for the end of August, and decided to settle on Staten Island, near his family. Each day seemed filled with endless tasks and preparations. Our first priority would be finding jobs to pay the rent and expenses. Drew, now employed as a microbiologist, decided that working with exposure to germs and bacteria might be a dangerous career. Instead, he considered becoming a teacher and mailed out resumes. He accepted a position in a private high school for girls, teaching math. For an inexperienced young man, this was a beginning. With my certifications, I wanted to secure a job as a teacher in the New York City public school system. Bewildered, I did not know how to begin a job search. But then I had a surprising encounter with Professor Howard, one of my former professors on the St. John's campus. He recognized me, and stopped to talk.

"Hope, nice to see you. How are you doing? Do you have a teaching job lined up for the fall?"

"No, not yet. I don't really know where to begin. Do you have any suggestions?"

"Actually, I have a friend who is a principal of an elementary school on Staten Island. I know she needs to hire a teacher for a first grade class in September. If you're interested, I'll give you her contact information and I'd be willing to give you a letter of recommendation. You definitely have the potential for a successful teaching career."

My heart began to beat rapidly. "I can't thank you enough, Professor."

We shook hands and parted. I took the information, made the phone call, and had my first interview ever. The principal hired me, and school would begin that September, immediately after the wedding and honeymoon. I became ecstatic, having so much to look forward to. With our plans settled, I looked forward to a new beginning with the man that I had come to believe in.

The most wonderful thing that Drew had to offer was his family. His mother Patricia, also known as "Nanny," had come from Ireland, and spoke with remnants of her Irish accent and traditions. A simple woman without much education, she asked for little in life. She was a homemaker, always clad in a housedress, smiling and enjoying every moment. As the months passed and we spent time together, I realized she was the heart and strength of her family. She became enamored over the years for her frequently used expression, "God love ya," to all who crossed her path. Drew's father, a quiet man, had served his country for many years in the U.S. Marine Corps. He worked hard, devoting his time and energy to his family. Then there was Drew's younger sister, Grace, a high school student when we met. I looked forward to welcoming her into my life as my sister-in-law.

A career opportunity, an upcoming marriage, independence from Dad, and a new family that I cherished - what more could a young girl ask for? I started to believe that all my dreams would become a reality after all, and only days of bliss and contentment lay ahead.

Friday night came, and Drew picked me up with his car. As I seated myself beside him, I noticed his sad, depressed state of mind.

"Drew, are you all right? You seem distracted."

"I have leukemia."

"What do you mean? Have you been to a doctor?"

"No, I don't need to see a doctor. I know what's wrong with me, and I have leukemia."

The conversation continued incessantly along these lines. Too upset to drive, he burst into tears, sobbing uncontrollably, insisting that he had leukemia and death was imminent.

Frazzled by the unexpected, I sat in my seat and said nothing. He finally calmed down, but continued with this obsession over the next week. If there was the possibility that Drew was indeed gravely ill, I needed to discuss this with both our parents. I summoned my courage and approached my father first.

On hearing the news, he became extremely distraught. He and Mom sat down with me and advised that if Drew had leukemia, the wedding must be cancelled. I could not begin my life caring for a terminally ill person. My parents proceeded to contact Drew's mother and father, who scheduled an appointment with a physician highly qualified in the field of blood disorders. My father and I accompanied Drew to Dr. Young's office for blood work and medical testing. When the reports became available, Dr. Young called to inform us that Drew was in perfect health and did not have leukemia, or any related illness.

I thought that with this news, the crisis of the moment would pass. But it didn't. My parents summoned me for another family conference. My mom sat quietly and intensely with tears in her eyes, while my father, as usual, dominated the meeting.

"I don't understand it exactly, but I see that there is something wrong with Drew after this leukemia episode. He's just not right. You can't marry him, and we're calling off the wedding."

Inside my head my thoughts ran rapidly. No! Not again! He will not ruin my happiness and rob me of a life with another man who loves me! When I finally spoke, the words erupted uncontrollably from my mouth.

"Yes, I will marry him, even if you cancel the wedding reception. I'll run away and elope and this time you can't stop me."

I ran up to my room crying hysterically, and lay motionless on my bed until the dawn of the next day. Eventually, my parents agreed to proceed with the wedding plans after all. But as the day drew closer, I became increasingly aware of Drew's depression, fears, and frequent misconceptions of reality. I remember the time when we had planned on attending my cousin's engagement party. An hour before the party, he called to say he didn't feel well and had to spend the day in bed. When I asked what was wrong, I couldn't get an answer. I never really believed he was sick. He just couldn't face meeting new people in a social environment.

Sometimes I thought I didn't really know this person at all. The week before the wedding, I considered calling it off. But I managed to convince myself that my concerns were irrational, probably just normal anxieties related to growing up and taking on adult responsibilities.

Finally, my moment arrived. It was the moment that every young girl imagines in her mind from the early days of childhood. I dressed in a beautiful white gown with a flowing train. My long brown hair had been professionally styled and fell softly over my shoulders. I was a young, twenty-one year bride and felt radiantly beautiful.

As I stood at the back of the Church ready to begin my descent down the aisle to the alter, I gazed across the seated guests and the light from the colorful stained glass windows. The organ began its entrance song to begin the ceremony as I stared across the room at Drew, who in a matter of minutes would be my husband. There was only one problem. I had stayed awake all night thinking, and feared that this marriage was destined to be a big mistake. Before taking my first step down the aisle gripping my father's arm, I closed my eyes and my thoughts drifted into the past. The image of Brandon appeared before me, and suddenly I knew he was the one I wanted to be with, the one who had won my heart. When I opened my eyes, I remembered he was gone.

I continued my walk down the aisle, and Drew and I were united in wedlock at Our Lady of Angels Catholic Church in Brooklyn. I took the solemn vow to be his partner in sickness and in health, in good times and bad, in joy as well as sorrow. Although no one can realize what these words mean until you live them, I promised myself that they would be the foundation of my life with Drew, from that moment forward, and forever.

# Chapter 6

## *Reality*

**Fall of 1967**

I NEVER REALIZED that marriage meant hard work. As a wife, I had to learn all the skills needed to maintain the household. I had never before used a washer and dryer, cleaned the house, or cooked dinner. Upon arriving home from my new job each day, I either called my mom or my older sister Tracey to get advice on a new recipe or the ingredients needed for a particular meal.

My role as a classroom teacher progressed amazingly well. The first grade students began the year with an alphabet review. After they could recognize all twenty-six alphabet letters, we began using phonics books and daily lesson plans to learn the sounds of all the letters. Most importantly, we concentrated on the short and long vowel sounds. After learning the skills, the children began to combine all the sounds to create words, and could actually read them aloud. Just a short time later, they mastered the skill of reading books for beginning readers. With time, I began to understand that I held a powerful influence over these young lives. My actions and efforts would impact their self-esteem and futures. Their enthusiasm for what they learned touched my heart and replenished my spirit.

Another responsibility that I assumed as a newlywed was taking courses to earn my Master's degree. Beginning in 1967, a new law required all elementary education teachers to earn their Master's within five years, to maintain their permanent teaching certification. So one night a week after work, I attended my graduate class at Richmond College, and resumed the tasks of studying and writing research papers. Living close to Drew's family, I visited them often. We sometimes spent hours together, sitting on the spacious deck in the front of their home. I became surrounded by new people to love, and I treasured my blessings.

But as the first few months of marriage passed, I became more concerned about Drew. His depression and fears often dominated his thoughts and actions. Every day, all day, he manifested a great fear of illness and germs in the environment. His comments often intruded into our daily living. One day he noticed some dust on the dining room table, and swiped his finger over it.

"Look, I told you, this dust is dangerous. Germs are all around us, and we're breathing them in. If we get sick it's going to be your fault. Why don't you ever clean this place enough?"

"Drew, can't you stop obsessing about these things? Nothing here will hurt you."

But he remained convinced that germs lived not only in our home, but everywhere. One day he came back from the pharmacy with what he considered a solution to the problem.

"The greatest thing just happened to me. I browsed around the shelves of the pharmacy and found this liquid soap called Phisoderm. It says on the back of the container that if used regularly, it cleanses the skin and kills all bacteria that we come in contact with. I'm going to shower right now and begin using it."

Drew jumped into the shower and began meticulously scrubbing every crevice of his body with Phisoderm. When done, he walked out smiling and relieved.

"I did it, Hope. I've killed every possible threat! This is going to be a great day." From that day forward, this hour long ritual became the most important part of his daily routine.

Drew also spent much time alone, secluded in our home office, studying mathematics, both for his teaching job and for pleasure. He avoided friends and visits to my parents, but found contentment in pursuing his solitary interests in the confines of his own personal space. Periodically, he would begin a conversation with me, then experience an outbreak of tears and sobbing, describing the many reasons for his unhappiness. At times his complaints related to social issues at work.

"None of the other teachers there like me. At lunch no one seems to want to have anything to do with me. I sit away from them at the opposite end of the table. I'm a reject."

"That's not true, Drew. Why don't you reach out to them? Have you tried initiating conversations?"

No words of encouragement or positive support on my part could help him. His needs became the center of my universe, and I gradually found myself abandoning friendships and spending all my time with him. I began to think about the concerns that my father had expressed about my marrying Drew. Maybe he had been right after all. In a way, I had finally escaped from the dictatorship of my father, but assumed a similar role with my new husband in marriage.

I decided I could make this marriage work. I still loved Drew, and I just had to understand him more. Yes, he was different, but with a little more time and adjustments, we would have the life and family together that I had envisioned.

**Summer of 1968**

I completed my first year of teaching successfully, and passed my graduate courses. I looked forward to working a summer job in a vacation day camp to earn extra money, and my marriage to Drew seemed to have settled down. I had been so busy with work and school that I hadn't noticed Drew's frequent late nights out, with no explanation of where he had been. In addition, Drew had decided not to work that summer after his first year of teaching. Once my summer program began, I left the house early each day, wondering how he spent his time with no job and nothing much to do.

Then one evening, reality confronted me, as Drew and I sat talking. Suddenly, without warning, he began one of his crying episodes.

"Drew, what's the matter? Why are you crying?"

"I don't really know, but I have a terrible problem," he sobbed.

"What is it? You can share it with me, I'm your wife, remember? I'm here for you. What's getting you so upset?"

"Hope, I'm sorry. I'm so sorry."

"Sorry for what?"

"I'm in love with her. I didn't mean it to happen, but it did." He covered his eyes with his hands, wet with tears. I just couldn't believe what I heard.

"Who, Drew? Who are you in love with?"

"It's one of my students, Heather. She's a senior. We just got involved. I know that I love her, but I love you too. I don't want to break up our marriage, but I don't know what to do."

I tried to suppress my feelings and remain composed for the moment.

"Does anyone else know about you and Heather?"

"No one. We don't want anyone to know about it." The sobbing continued.

Disillusionment, disenchantment, disappointment. My husband had fallen in love with a seventeen year old high school senior, when we were married less than a year. I needed help. I could never tell my parents because they probably would hate Drew forever. Shame kept me from sharing my sorrow with my sister or friends, as I had not yet learned the skill of opening my heart to another. I had no information about counselors or support groups, or how a professional could help me in this time of crisis. Alone, my world shattered in pieces around me

## Fall of 1968

September came, and a new school year began. Each new day I gathered the strength to smile and face my co-workers and students, despite my inner turmoil. As the weeks passed, I began to realize that teaching those precious little children was my salvation. Once in that classroom, my problems momentarily disappeared, and I found myself in a new place. The place where I belonged. Here I would always be needed and important, respected and loved, for years to come. During these difficult times, my thoughts again drifted back to my childhood, with memories of my Uncle Scott. With eyes closed, I heard him slip into my room that night at the Lake, while I had screamed, "No, no," not wanting him to hurt me. I had been powerless then, and felt powerless now.

I had stayed with Drew throughout the summer, waiting for him to make his decision about our marriage. Finally, we talked.

"Hope, will you give me another chance? I promise you this will never happen again. I don't know why I ever got involved with her. I beg you, please don't leave me."

"Alright, we'll try," I agreed, but hesitantly.

He threw his arms around me and held me tight, but I stood motionless, not reaching for him in return.

Forgiveness would not come easily, and I often looked at Drew and thought that he was not the man that I had believed him to be.

***

# Chapter 7

## *My Little Miracles*

**1969 – 1972**

WITH OUR RECONCILIATION, Drew re-committed to the agreement we had made before marriage. We would both work for a few years and save money. At some point, he would find a better paying job which would enable him to support a family. Then we would be financially prepared to have a child.

While working on these issues, we got an unexpected call from Drew's mother. The tenant that lived in the rental apartment of her home had given notice that he would be leaving. The apartment would be vacant, and my mother-in-law asked if we wanted to live there. Thrilled at the idea, we relocated from our one bedroom apartment into the gorgeous, two-story townhouse that had become available to us.

Life proceeded without incident over the next two years. I enjoyed living in the same house with Drew's family. Each Sunday morning, Aunt Tina stopped at the bakery on her way home from church. There she would buy us some tasty treats which we found waiting for us behind our entry door. On other days, I would return home exhausted from my teaching job to find that my mother-in-law had washed and folded all my laundry, carried it up the basement steps, and deposited it in our living room. I know I will cherish their kindness without end.

Also during these years, I bonded with my sister-in-law Grace, who became my soul mate. She had married, conceived a child on her honeymoon, and now had a beautiful two-year-old son, Billy. She visited often, and watching my little nephew grow and develop renewed my passion and longing for a child of my own.

In March of 1971, Drew began to explore better paying employment opportunities. After speaking with a college friend, he had an idea.

"My friend told me about job opportunities working for the Federal Bureau of Investigation as an agent. This would be a high paying government job with a secure pension. It sounds exciting. If I am asked to transfer from New York to another state, are you willing to travel, and maybe give up your teaching job?"

"Wow, that's a lot for me to consider, Drew. You might as well apply and see if you would be offered a job."

Drew applied, and took the FBI entry exam. Two months later he received his acceptance letter. He had attained the highest possible score on the exam in all areas, including language skills. Now it was time for major decisions.

"I really want to do this, Hope. But just as I thought, they want to transfer me to Tampa, Florida to begin my career. I'd be in training there as a first office agent for a period of one year. After that, I don't know where they'll send me. What do you think, should I do it?"

"Sometimes opportunity strikes just once. It would be a whole new way of living, far from our families. But yes, do it."

I took a leave of absence from my teaching position and accompanied Drew on this venture. I interviewed for jobs in Tampa, and began working in a day care center. Being exposed to the Southern culture of our country, and meeting people from various backgrounds proved to be an enriching experience. Drew worked an intense schedule with overtime hours, and became consumed with the challenges of his new career. At the end of that first year, the FBI offered Drew the opportunity to move to Monterey, California for the next nine months to attend the Defense Language Institute and learn the Romanian language.

He accepted the offer, and I extended my leave of absence from the New York City public schools for another year. Then we drove together to California to begin another thrilling phase of life that we had never anticipated.

While traveling, Drew and I had been trying unsuccessfully to conceive a child. I feared that I would never become pregnant, never be a mother, never experience the joys that come with the creation of new life. I tried to be patient but as the months passed, my thoughts of motherhood became obsessive.

"Drew, I feel so frustrated. What if we could never have our own family? My life would be so empty. That's all I could think about now."

"Stop worrying. Everything comes in time."

## Spring of 1973

As we drove into the Monterey peninsula, I believed that I had entered paradise. Monterey, located on the Pacific Coast next to the gorgeous Monterey Bay, had an amazing coastline and stunning beach, surrounded by seagulls silhouetted against the bright blue sky.

Leaving the car, we walked to the rocky landscape to view the ocean waves. The sound of the rippling water and the beauty of nature brought into my spirit a serenity which I had never before experienced. We stood there in awe as a group of California sea lions suddenly appeared before us. And in the distance we observed a pod of gray whales bobbing up and down as they migrated past the Monterey coastline to their summer feeding grounds in the Bering Sea.

We rented a house on the famous road called 17 Mile Drive. Following this road from our new home led us through a scenic, forested area along the oceanfront, passing three golf courses, and luxury hotels. Each morning a fog covered the land and forest, then lifted by noon. The fog moistened the environment, and gave life to the trees and plants, eliminating the need for rain in a world that thrived without it. Each day brought a deep satisfaction to my mind, and living in Monterey made me grateful that God had created this beauty.

Drew quickly became a fluent Romanian speaker, admired greatly by his teachers and fellow agents. But despite the beauty of his new surroundings and his success in his new endeavor, he began to have difficulty settling into Monterey. As the weeks passed and we continued our transition, his fears and paranoia began to re-surface once again.

"I'm sorry we chose this house to live in. I just hate living in this place with the carpet covering the floors."

His eyes intently scanned the room.

"I can't prove it, but I know there are unseen fibers emanating from the carpet into the air, contaminating our environment. Sometimes when the bright sunlight is casting its rays through the open window and into the house, I can actually see the fibers floating before me. If we stay here for the full length of my assignment, we're going to be poisoned. We will die."

"Drew, are you sure you can't just deal with this? I lived in a house with carpets during my entire childhood, and nothing ever happened to me. We just got here a short time ago. We signed a lease and made a legal agreement. I don't want to endure the trouble and expense of moving all of our furniture and possessions again. Isn't there another solution to this problem?"

We talked for a while about all the possibilities, but Drew could not let go of his obsession. He finally decided that there would be only one other alternative.

"Ok, Hope, I'll remain in the house if you agree to my plan. We'll purchase rolls of large, plastic sheeting and install it over all the carpeted areas. We will tape the ends of it to the walls, and then maybe we will be safe and protected from the unknown."

Having lived with Drew for almost six years now, I easily gave in to his needs and wishes, whether they seemed rational or not. This made life easier than arguing about things I couldn't control. Since I found it embarrassing to explain the reason for the plastic sheeting to anyone, I refrained from inviting guests or new acquaintances to visit, and we remained sheltered from the social life of the other FBI agents and their wives.

I did not plan on working in California. I remained intent on having a child and made an appointment with a fertility specialist who would evaluate me for pregnancy issues. Secondly, I needed to complete my last three-credit graduate course to earn my Master's degree from Richmond College. Since I had moved out of state, my professor had allowed me to submit the last required assignments by mail.

At the end of April I received a letter advising me that my Master's degree would be granted on May 14, 1973. At last, I thought, school is over forever. I excitedly called my parents in New York to tell them of my achievement, and they decided to come and visit us in California to celebrate the event. Although I looked forward to my parents' visit, a part of me dreaded dealing with my father. In his eyes I would always be his child, and he would never change. He thought I would always need his unwanted opinions, that he always knew what was best. On the day they arrived, I had other news to announce.

"Mom, Dad, I'm so excited, I can't wait to tell you. I'm pregnant! You're going to be grandparents!"

"Oh my God," screamed my mother, her eyes filled with joy. All three of us joined together and hugged.

"When is the baby due?" asked my dad.

"January. I might be back home to give birth. Drew's assignment in Monterey will be completed by then."

Surprisingly, by the end of my parents' two week visit, I realized I had enjoyed my time with them. Of course, things had not gone without incident. One afternoon when my mom and dad were alone with me, reiterating concerns about Drew's mental health, my father's questioning began.

"Why does your home look like this? Why is your entire living area covered in plastic sheeting? I can see the beautiful carpet underneath it. What is going on? When I asked Drew about it yesterday, he ignored me and wouldn't reply. Are you alright?"

"Dad, don't worry about it. Everything is fine, and the plastic is not important."

I tried to make our conversation of short duration, attempting to shield my parents from my deep worries about Drew's paranoia. Distracting them, I shifted our discussion to the mystery and joy of the new life that I carried within me.

"Ok, so do you think I'm carrying a boy or a girl?"

They both laughed, and I had successfully achieved my goal.

## Final days of 1973

As the months passed, I continued to adjust to my life in Monterey, and at some point it became my home. Each day brought perfect temperatures in the 70's, and time to sit on the rocky coast, listening to the splashing of the waves and pondering my future. I gradually reached out to some of the other wives and enjoyed their friendship. Drew's assignment in California was scheduled to be completed at the end of December, then he would be transferred back to New York. That would give us time to return home to Staten Island in time for the birth of our baby in January. We planned to move back into the townhouse next to Drew's family.

I flew home on December 26, more than eight months pregnant. I can't imagine how the airline allowed me to fly in that condition, but no one questioned me. The next day, I had an appointment with my new gynecologist who would deliver my baby in New York. He said that I was dilated several inches, and to expect the onset of labor at any time.

On the morning of December 30, childbirth began. Drew had just left for work, already on the subway headed for Manhattan. In the year 1973, cell phones had not yet been invented, so there was no way to contact him. I called my mother-in-law next door.

"Nanny, it's time. My water broke, and I'm home alone. I called my doctor, and I need you to be with me."

Becoming part of my moment, she caressed my hand as we walked together across the street to Staten Island University Hospital.

My little angel Allison came into the world at 11:53 a.m. What a wonder when I met my child, as I realized she will be part of my life forever. I became fascinated with her radiance. She had the brightest blue eyes, a thick head of straight dark hair, and unusually long and slender feet. I knew immediately that some day she would grow up to be tall and beautiful. As her mother, I made a promise to her from my heart.

"My child, I pledge to give you a wonderful life, filled with love, family, and opportunity."

Drew was thrilled with Allison, and together we brought her home to experience the joys and the novelty of parenthood. On the weekends when he didn't work, he played, laughed, and bonded with Allison. We watched her grow and become aware of the world around her. Soon she recognized and cried for us, and sought comfort in our caring arms.

Again I extended my leave of absence from my New York City teaching job, this time taking child care leave. I loved being a stay at home mom, able to witness my child sit up for the first time, reach for a toy, say her first word, and take her first step without holding on.

## 1974

At this point in my life, I was thankful for my good fortune. My family of loved ones began to expand as Drew's cousin Linda, who lived down the block from us, also gave birth to a baby girl. So Allison had another cousin who would be in her life as she grew up.

Linda and I often walked our babies around the neighborhood in their carriages as they took their naps. When they started to walk, we set up a sandbox in the yard, and Drew's sister Grace and her son Michael would join us. Then we had the idea to hook up a giant gate across the large front deck of our house. With this safe enclosure, the mothers talked while we watched the little cousins crawl, run, and play together.

Occasionally, I thought about having another child, a sibling for Allison. But when I discussed this with Drew, he seemed reluctant, and said he wasn't ready for more responsibilities. So I put the idea on a shelf, and remained content with the child I had.

The day Allison turned eleven months old, I remember feeling tired and nauseous. I thought I had the flu, but as the day progressed, I became aware of some unusual cramping that felt familiar. I put her in the car and we drove to the nearest pharmacy for a pregnancy test kit. It tested positive. Yes, I was going to have another child.

The realization of my condition brought mixed feelings of joy and apprehension. I wanted this child more than anything, yet feared disclosing the news to Drew, being unsure of his reaction. Would he happily accept our growing family, or would he resent the added responsibility and financial demands of a second child?

Several weeks passed while I quietly carried my secret, revealing it to no one. Finally, an appropriate moment arose when Drew seemed relaxed on the living room couch. Out of nowhere, I blurted out that I was pregnant. I waited for the response of approval, and the hug that I longed for. But my worst fears materialized as Drew's mood changed to anger, and he stormed out of the room with raging words of blame.

"This is all your fault. I don't want another child crying and keeping me up at night! Everything has to be your way. I'm sorry I married you."

**January - September, 1975**

From that moment forward, my relationship with Drew would never be the same. During the next nine months, he remained distant. Depression began to dominate his world. He spent his time at home alone in the den, showing less and less interest in me, Allison, or family life.

I reacted to the situation with sadness and pain, as I questioned the path of my marriage. I considered having an abortion, hoping that this would restore things to what they had been. But how could I do that? My dream of having children had finally become a reality. Could I possibly take away the life of my child, just because of Drew's problems? No, I knew in my heart that my love for this unborn baby would surpass all other fears or concerns, and I quickly dismissed ever considering this option again.

***

# Chapter 8

## *The Crisis*

**October 10, 1975**

MY SECOND LITTLE miracle came into the world on Oct. 10, 1975. Reliving the experience of her arrival always brings a smile to my lips. My parents had arranged a Sunday family dinner with me, Drew, my siblings, and their spouses. Drew, moody and depressed, chose not to join us for the event. My mom had prepared a home cooked meal using her favorite family recipes. I remember taking my first bite from the platter of hors d'oeuvres and feeling a strange pain in my lower abdomen. I ignored the discomfort and continued enjoying mom's feast. Next I devoured the plate of homemade raviolis, followed by the cauliflower pancakes. The pains returned at five minute intervals, and I suddenly realized that I must be in labor. I called my doctor who instructed me to report to the hospital as quickly as possible.

My brother Steven drove me over the Verrazano Narrows Bridge at top speed to the hospital. I remember lying across the back seat of his car during the trip, as the contractions became more frequent and intense. I squeezed my legs together, struggling to keep my baby from pushing her way into the world as we drove over the bay, back to Staten Island.

"Go faster Steven, or we're not going to make it in time!"

We finally arrived at the emergency room entrance, where a nurse greeted me, settled me into a wheelchair, and whisked me away into the delivery room. Within seconds, Rebecca came into the world and made her entrance known with a loud, permeating cry. Soon she was washed and wrapped in her warm, pink blanket. When I held her in my arms for the first time, I knew that no matter what may lay ahead for me, having her would be worth it. Thinking of Drew at this moment, I hoped that despite his apprehensions, he would come to love and accept her with time.

## Winter of 1976

Caring for a newborn and a twenty month old twenty-four hours a day certainly proved to be an exhausting challenge. Rebecca woke up several times each night, crying for her bottle and keeping me awake. But in time, the girls both settled into their daily schedules, and as my body recovered from the trauma of childbirth, I felt confident that I had regained control of my life once again.

With two young children demanding my attention, I had little time to focus on Drew or the difficulties in our marriage. Things were not improving as I had hoped. After Rebecca's birth, his depression deepened. He displayed little or no interest in knowing her, rarely picked her up, and often seemed to gaze at her with disdain and contempt. I knew not what to do or where to turn for help.

Again, I mastered concealing my feelings and torment. Shame and disappointment kept me from telling anyone. During the cold winter months of 1976, I rarely left the house with my two babies, except to shop for groceries or needed baby supplies. My contact with Drew's sister and cousin became limited. They both were occupied dealing with new pregnancies, and the freezing temperatures and winter storms kept us all isolated in the warmth of our own homes. Also at this time, my brother Steven, a brilliant young entrepreneur in the field of engineering, decided to accept a job opportunity in Dallas, Texas. He relocated with his wife and children to a place more than two thousand miles away. It would be years before I ever saw them again.

## April, 1976

Spring had arrived, and I looked forward to taking my girls to the park, resuming our daily walks through the neighborhood in my newly purchased baby stroller for two. The days lengthened, and my spirit lifted as the world became filled once again with the light and sunshine of my favorite season.

Although still a married woman, in reality, I faced each day alone. I had learned to expect nothing from Drew, and to accept my ongoing situation. But inside of me always lived the hope that things would improve, and that Drew would someday learn to appreciate what we had built together. I still saw myself as the Italian-American wife whose role it was to cater to the needs of her husband, to tolerate his mood swings and temper tantrums, and to make him happy in any way he desired.

On the second Sunday of April my mother-in-law invited us over for a family dinner, and had prepared her special pot roast for the occasion. The visit went well and warm, encouraging words and laughter surrounded us all. My children thrived in this loving family environment. I never expected what happened next.

After dinner, Drew and I returned home and I put the girls into bed for their afternoon nap. They fell asleep instantly, and the house became quiet. Suddenly I heard a loud, moaning sound coming from the living room. Worried, I walked into the room and found Drew lying on the couch, grasping his stomach in pain. He told me that he had a terrible stomach ache and that he never before had experienced such distress. I offered to get him some Pepto-Bismol or antacid from our medicine cabinet to calm his symptoms, but he rejected the offer.

Within minutes, Drew's behavior escalated and became out of control. He began to scream that he had been poisoned from his mom's pot roast.

"Yes, it was the pot roast. There was something lethal in it. I can feel it in my stomach! It's going to kill me! It's going to kill us all!"

I tried to reason with him, explaining that I felt just fine, and I made a quick phone call to his parents to confirm that they also did not experience any adverse effects from our meal.

"Drew, I've just spoken to your mom and dad. No one has become ill from eating the pot roast. None of us have been poisoned. Is there something I can do to help you calm down? You're obsessing on this idea, and you need to let it go."

But nothing I could do or say could change his mind, and shortly afterward he began gasping for breath, shouting that he was unable to breathe. Feeling so helpless, I again called his parents. When Drew's father arrived and saw his condition, he sat Drew up and walked him across the street to the emergency room of Staten Island University Hospital. A short time later, I received a call from a doctor in the hospital. Drew had been sedated, then moved to the psychiatric wing.

"This is Dr. Roberts. I am the treating physician for your husband Drew."

"Do you have an update on my husband? Has his condition improved?"

"My colleagues and I have diagnosed Drew as suffering from bipolar disorder. His brain is not functioning properly. His inability to breathe had been caused by hyperventilating, brought on by his belief in oncoming death. Drew needs medical treatment and help to have a normal life."

I listened intently. In a way, this was good news. At last, a reason for Drew's episodes throughout the years. Now with a diagnosis, maybe he could improve with proper medical care and medication. After his release from the hospital, we discussed making an appointment with a psychiatrist to begin a treatment plan. But Drew refused help and rejected the idea of taking any drugs that were available for his condition during the 1970's. After the pot roast crisis, I allowed myself some quiet moments to contemplate what lay ahead for me. I still wanted this marriage to work. But with each day that ensued, his rages became more frequent, filled with verbal attacks. I began to live a life of fear and dread. One evening he complained about the dinner I had prepared, bellowing, "You don't know how to cook. This meal is disgusting. Can't you do anything right?"

Other times he focused on my appearance. "You gained so much weight during your pregnancy, I'm not attracted to you anymore." Or if the children cried, he commanded, "Take them out of here, now, they're so annoying!" To protect them, I would quickly carry them upstairs to their bedroom and close the door.

## June 13, 1977

On the morning of June 13, 1977, I experienced the inevitable. Drew woke up in a state of uncontrollable anger. He angrily approached me in the kitchen and raised his voice.

"I'm sick and tired of hearing about nothing but the children every time I'm with you. They're your whole life and you never have time for me anymore. You never wear pretty, attractive clothes like you used to when you worked, and all you do is sit around the house with baby throw-up all over your shirts. I've had enough of this life and I want a divorce."

"You want a divorce? Tell the truth. Is it that I am a terrible wife or have you been cheating on me again?"

"Ok, you'll find out the truth anyway, so I'll tell you. I met someone through work. She's a Romanian, and her name is Cosmina. She's smart and attractive, and knows how to dress. She can offer me a better life than I have here, so I'm leaving you."

I raised my usually quiet voice for the first time ever, and the girls began to cry in response to the commotion. Drew physically overpowered me and threw me on the floor. Frightened for my life, I grabbed my purse, jumped into my car, and escaped. I drove away like a maniac, not knowing where I was headed. I knew I needed to distance myself, so I ended up at one of the Staten Island beaches. Like a crazy woman, I pulled up onto the sand and parked my car in a spot where I could see the ocean. I remained there for an hour, listening to the waves and considering my next course of action. I needed a place to go, someone I could talk to. And I needed to know that my girls, whom I had left at home with Drew in my frenzy, were safe.

After gaining control of my emotions, I decided to drive to my sister-in-law Grace's house. I turned on the ignition, and realized that my wheels were stuck in the sand. Now what would I do? How could I end up like this, I thought. Alone in the world and abandoned on the beach, with no way of reaching out for help. With no idea where the nearest pay phone could be found, I sat behind the wheel of my motionless vehicle, and began to cry. Seemingly out of nowhere, a man appeared. He had been sitting nearby on the beach observing my predicament, and offered to help. Although I noticed that he had a prosthetic leg, his arms looked strong and muscular. Within seconds, he amazingly pushed my car off the sand and onto the solid pavement.

As I drove away towards Grace's house, I observed that man following me in his car along the highway. He honked the horn and motioned for me to pull over. Fearing that he had noticed a problem with my car, I complied with his request. I rolled down my window as he approached. He introduced himself as Peter and said he would like to see me again. Then he asked for my phone number. I don't really understand why, perhaps I was just desperate for love and someone's attention after feeling so rejected. But I gave him my number and continued my journey to Grace's, more traumatized than ever.

I rang Grace's doorbell. She answered the door with a look of surprise.

"Hope, what are you doing here?"

Before I could explain the reason for my visit, the tears resumed.

"Your brother doesn't love me anymore, and he wants a divorce. I had to leave the house and had nowhere to go. I left the children behind with Drew, but I'm frantic about their safety. He was out of control and I'm just not sure what he'll do next."

At that moment, Grace became the template for stability and strength. She calmly called her mother and asked her to go next door and check on Drew and the girls. Nanny, bewildered by the recent turn of events, called back within a few minutes to give us an update. The girls seemed fine and she agreed to stay with them until I returned home. She told me Drew packed a suitcase and stormed out the door without saying good-bye.

Grace continued to talk to me in her tranquil manner. Extending her friendship and concern, she offered me a place to sleep that night in her basement. Strangely, she asked that I remain quietly in the basement throughout my stay, without making her husband Michael aware of my presence. At first I questioned her request in my mind, but gradually I rationalized that Grace, in her own way, was not ready to discuss with anyone the emotional impact of my announcement on her own life, children, and family.

I made myself comfortable on the couch in the basement, but soon realized that with so much on my mind, falling asleep would not be easy. Looming in my thoughts were my parents and how I would present my situation to them. I dreaded facing them in person, so decided to write them a letter and leave it on their doorstep the next day. That way, they would have time to assimilate my words and be in control of their turmoil by the time I saw them.

## June 14, 1977

I stayed awake for what seemed an eternity in the basement, thinking of the words to write in my letter. I finally fell asleep for two or three hours, and woke up ready to face my day and implement my plan. At 5:00 a.m. I quietly exited the house with my letter in hand, got into my car, and began driving to my parent's house. When I arrived, I ran up to the front door and slid the letter into the mailbox. The deed had been done, and I knew that within hours I would be facing my father's wrath and my mother's sorrow. I tried to convince myself that telling them would be the start of a new beginning for me and the acceptance of my future as a single mother. But fear, anxiety, and feelings of loss overwhelmed me as I gripped the steering wheel and headed back home to my children and life without a husband.

I spent the morning playing with Allison and Rebecca, until the anticipated moment arrived, and the phone rang. My parents had read my letter and were coming over to discuss my situation. When my parents arrived at the door, my mother looked at me sternly and was the first to speak.

"Hope, today is my birthday, did you forget? Your news made this the worst birthday I've ever had."

I looked at her, not understanding at first. Wrapped in my own problems, I had forgotten her special day. No words could express my regret. "Mom, I'm so sorry. Can you forgive me?"

Of course, I predicted what my dad would say.

"I knew it all along, you should never have married Drew. If only you had listened to me and cancelled the wedding, you wouldn't be in this predicament."

Was there nothing I could do in my life that was right?

## June 21, 1977

One week had passed since Drew moved out. While the girls napped, I sat quietly in the living room gazing out the window, pondering my life. I felt angry because things hadn't turned out as they should have for me. My father had always told me while growing up that if I got my college degree and completed my education, my future would be wonderful. What he should have told me is that life is difficult and filled with endless disappointments and challenges that we must boldly face and conquer. But he didn't, and I did not yet understand that the path to wisdom and knowledge was something that I had to find myself.

I tried to call my sister-in-law Grace repeatedly during this week. Although I left her several messages, she never returned my calls. When she finally did answer the phone, her voice sounded cold and distant. She spoke only briefly, and I wondered if I had done something to offend her. The next morning, I brought Allison and Rebecca outside to play and ride their tricycles. Nanny and Aunt Tina had already settled themselves on the front porch, relaxing and talking. Upon seeing us, they hugged and kissed the girls but seemed to avoid me. As I walked away, I suddenly realized that they all had taken sides in my separation from Drew, and they had chosen to be against me. I had not only lost my husband, but the family that I treasured as well. With this loss, sorrow and darkness once again dominated my thoughts. Once again I closed my eyes and envisioned Uncle Scott come into my room, as if it were yesterday. I had been unjustly robbed of my childhood, and now I wondered if I would be doomed for failure forever. I prayed for the strength to accept my new life and raise my daughters successfully.

***

# Chapter 9

## The Single Life

**Summer of 1977**

MY DAUGHTERS WERE one and a half, and three and a half years old when their father left. The impact on Allison, who had strongly bonded with him and thrived on his attention, seemed the most serious. It had always been the highlight of her day when her father came home from work. She seemed to have an inner clock which told her when evening approached, and each day she would run joyfully to the front window in anticipation of Drew's arrival. Drew would never come home again. Yet, each evening Allison anxiously looked out the window, waiting for him.

"Mommy, where's Daddy? When is Daddy coming home? Where is he?"

Her words were like a knife that cut deeply into my heart, because I could do nothing to make things different or alleviate her pain. Weeks passed and Drew finally came to visit the girls. I had opened the window to enjoy the warm, fresh summer air. When Drew walked into the room, Allison hugged him, ran excitedly to the open window, and called out to the neighbors.

"Daddy came home and he is going to live here again!"

Obviously, she did not understand the situation. Rebecca had the opposite reaction. She did not seem to remember Drew, distanced herself from him, and ran across the room for safety into my arms. With Drew's entrance that day, I became instantly aware of the problems the girls would be facing as they grew up. Allison would always be longing for a father that wasn't there, and Rebecca had a father who had never really been a part of her life.

## September, 1977

I soon began to understand the problems a single mother must face. There would never be enough money to survive, so divorcing partners will always end up arguing. I had to hire an attorney to fight for what I needed, and filed an application to return to my teaching job. However, due to severe cuts in the New York City budget, the Board of Education moved me to layoff status. This meant that I would have no source of income of my own, and I would be solely dependent on Drew's child support payments. When I realized I could not afford to buy my children food, I applied for and entered into the food stamp program for needy families.

On some days, loneliness overwhelmed me. Having devoted my life to Drew, I had abandoned my friendships. For years after graduating from St. John's, I had kept in contact with Megan. But when Drew refused to leave the house or participate in social engagements with other couples, I was reluctant to explain my situation to anyone. It became easier to remain alone and never return phone calls.

What would I do now? Could I begin a new life? Where would I start? Thoughts raced inside my head. In desperation, I reached out into the community and found the support group for divorced and separated Catholics at a nearly Catholic Church. Looking for a place to socialize my daughters with other children of divorced parents, I also became involved with the activities and events of Parents Without Partners.

The support group met once a week on a Monday evening under the guidance of a priest. The people attending arranged their chairs in a circle facing each other, which made verbal communication a powerful, interactive force. Listening to their stories, for the first time in my life I realized that sharing painful experiences and opening up one's mind and heart to others without fear was a source of healing that I had never known. After sitting in silence for the first two sessions, I began to speak at last. And with the sound of my voice, I entered a new place, a place without fear.

From that moment forward, I changed. No matter where I went or whom I met, I was no longer afraid. I spoke openly and honestly about my anguish, my disappointments, and my dread of the future. And as I reached out to others, I experienced their amazingly warm and receptive responses. With my newfound skill, the path to new friendships and relationships opened before me.

Each weekday Allison attended the half-day pre-school program at the YMCA. At noon, all the mothers waited outside for the dismissal of their children. I rarely talked with any of them, but sometimes acknowledged them with a friendly smile or nod of my head. One day as we waited, Alicia, another mother, observed me and decided to initiate a conversation. Having overcome my shyness at last, I eagerly responded. Within a few minutes, the class ended and the children walked outside.

"This is my son Jacob," said Alicia.

"And this is my older daughter, Allison." Rebecca just clung to me while we spoke. Together we all walked to our cars.

"Is your daughter enjoying the pre-school class?"

"Yes, very much. It gives her a chance to meet and play with other children besides her sister."

"I feel the same way about Jacob. He's an only child, and he's really enjoying the friendships he's been making here. The only problem for me is that I just interviewed for a full time teaching job in a private school. I'm waiting to hear from them. If I get the job, I'll have to find a child care center that provides all day care. I just have to work as soon as I can. My husband and I got separated a few months ago, and luckily we've been able to live with my father who's helping me. I don't know what else to do."

"Alicia, you're not going to believe this. Right now I'm in the same predicament as you. My husband left me three months ago, and now I'm trying to get my teaching job back."

We talked excitedly as we shared our anguish, and then exchanged phone numbers. I had no idea she would become not only a devoted friend, but also one of the most influential people in my life.

## October, 1977

Initially, I had no interest in dating or getting involved with another man. But a few days after my episode on the sandy beach with my car, that man Peter began to call, trying to convince me to join him for a drink. I continually rejected his offer, but finally one day feeling desperate, I agreed. Drew had already picked up the girls for the weekend, and I preferred not to face the time alone.

We spent some time together in a local restaurant, and then I decided to end the evening. He didn't really want to say goodnight, so I foolishly invited him back to my house for some coffee.

This turned out to be my first introduction to the perils of being a single, inexperienced woman in the world. I should have known that it was poor judgment to invite a man into my house when I knew nothing about him. So rather than drink my coffee, Peter began to sexually assault me, and I had to punch and kick with all my strength to fight him off and regain control. Fortunately, I succeeded and Peter left. Triumph for me again. Long ago with Uncle Scott, I had learned how to avoid being a victim of dangerous predators – ever!

Shortly after this incident, I met a man at Parents Without Partners. He appeared to be a gentleman, and we had much in common. He also worked in the New York City school system, and recently his wife of fifteen years had filed for divorce. Although Andy was seventeen years older than me, the age span seemed unimportant as I viewed him as a possible friend. When Andy asked if I would be interested in dating him, I said yes.

I asked myself why did I even want to date? Was it just my hormones working? Did I crave sex and the feelings of being caressed and loved again? Could I ever remarry and introduce a stepfather into my daughters' lives? What path should I follow, and how would I get there? I just didn't know.

## January, 1978

By January, I had been dating Andy for three months and considered introducing him to my daughters. But I knew that I had a long road of recovery ahead in dealing with my divorce. I didn't want my girls to became attached to him, and then have him disappear from their lives as Drew had done. Finally the day came when my daughters met Andy. I introduced him as my new friend, and they accepted him instantly. Now at ages two and four, they thrived on anyone's attention. They played hide and seek with him, showed him their favorite toys, and asked him to read them a story. After he left, they asked when he would come back again.

Despite this step forward with Andy, feelings of guilt and loss remained within me. This had not been my plan. My daughters did not have a real family life with their mother and father. I had introduced them to another man. And now they spent every other weekend in Drew's new apartment, with him and Cosmina, the woman who had been influential in destroying my marriage. I feared their futures, and the emotional impact of this situation in the years ahead. Already the girls expressed their feelings over our visitation arrangements. Weekends with Drew usually began with tears and crying. "No, Mommy, no. Please, please don't make me go there."

Their words resounded in my ears long after they left. They could not easily adjust to two different lives, two different homes, and two sets of caretakers. Also, I found it difficult to release my children into the hands of a father who had mental health issues. After visiting one weekend, Rebecca complained that she hated to take a bath at Daddy's house.

"Mommy, Daddy filled the tub with very hot water that burned me, but he said it had to be that way to kill all the germs. Then Daddy said we had to get all the germs out of my ears, so he made me turn my head sideways while he poured alcohol into both of them."

Upset with his paranoid behavior toward the girls, I called Drew and boldly confronted him.

"You may think it's ok to clean the girls' ears with alcohol, but I'm telling you that's dangerous and abusive. I have primary custody of them and I'm in charge of their well-being. If you ever do that to them again, I'll be in court to end your visitation rights forever."

I was proud of myself. I stood up to Drew because I had changed from being a cowering little girl. But despite my concerns, I wanted my daughters to know their father and have him in their lives. So I promised myself that I would speak only kindly about him and learn to bury my anger.

## January, 1979

The year 1978 had passed with changes and opportunities. Realizing I did not love Andy, I ended our relationship. Finally, the Board of Education rehired me when a second grade position became available. Now I had a job in a nearby neighborhood with an income of my own. Relief!

I also decided to move out of the house that I lived in next to Drew's family. I just could not remain in an environment that had become so unfriendly and unsympathetic to my plight. Besides, it would be an uncomfortable situation if any of my future dates arrived at my doorstep and were forced to greet my former in-laws.

I rented a one family house from another New York City teacher who had taken a one-year sabbatical leave of absence for the purpose of travel. He would be in Europe, and then return within the year to his place of residency. This meant that within that time, I hopefully would have my divorce papers signed and be ready to purchase a condo of my own.

Although I thankfully had a full-time job, there never seemed to be enough income. Expenses for the girls had increased. I had to pay for a full-day kindergarten for Allison in a private school, because at that time the city schools only offered a half-day kindergarten program. Rebecca attended the YMCA half-day pre-school program, and I had to hire a babysitter to pick her up each day from the Y and care for her until my school day ended. The total cost of my children's day care amounted to one half of my take-home pay. This expense continued for several years until both girls reached school age. It was often a struggle to live on a budget that provided only for the necessities of life.

Yet, despite my woes over money, something inside me made me feel triumphant. Each morning my alarm would ring at 5:00 a.m., and my day would begin. I had an energy and vitality that I had never before experienced. After dropping off the girls at their programs, I arrived at my school early to prepare the day's lessons. Then I stood before my class and talked for six-and-a-half hours, usually working through my lunch hour grading papers and completing required paper work. When the bell rang to end the school day, I rushed to pick up the girls, and my life as a mother and homemaker would begin and continue until I could do no more, and collapsed with exhaustion.

For the first time ever, I realized that maybe I could succeed on my own. Possibly, I could provide for my children without a husband, and I could enjoy my rewarding career. I had learned to interact with my peers in the support group, and my phone often rang with calls from my new acquaintances. As the days passed with growing tranquility, I came to understand that money and dependence on other people were not the keys to happiness. My happiness would have to come from within myself. It no longer depended on my father's approval or Drew's mood. I was poor, but in many ways I was growing rich in the wisdom of life, learning to accept and value the simple things with which we are blessed.

## January, 1980

Allison continually missed having her father in her daily life, and often spoke of him. I remember vividly the day she played with her stuffed animals in the toy room. She looked up at me without warning and said, "Mommy, is Daddy ever coming home?" I couldn't believe that she still had a dream that someday we would all be together again. At this point, Drew and I had been separated for more than two years. As I searched for the words to help her accept reality, somber thoughts intruded into my mind, and I remembered that she would never have the family life that I had planned for her.

After hearing Allison's question, I began to consider why Drew had been unavailable to visit the girls for the last eight weeks. I had recently learned that he and Cosmina had broken up, so I wondered if he was too absorbed with his own personal problems or interests to spend time with them.

Hearing the update about Drew and his significant other had a deep impact on my mind and emotions. One part of me felt sympathy for him and the choices he had made, while the other part of me experienced a satisfaction that perhaps she had not been better than me after all. A few days later, I received a startling phone call from Drew. The girls were sleeping, and I picked up the phone in my bedroom. Before I could speak, Drew began crying and sobbing on the other end of the line. When he composed himself I heard, "Please forgive me, I made a terrible mistake. I know now that I still love you. Will you take me back?"

I couldn't respond at first. I thought perhaps I had just had some kind of delusional experience. For a brief second, images of marital bliss flashed before my eyes. But no, I had decided long ago that I could never go back, and I would face whatever the future held without him. I had already accepted my situation and was prepared to move forward. I finally found the words.

"No, Drew, I'm sorry too, but it just can't happen. Please let's just go through with the divorce as quickly as possible to put this all behind us. I believe our attorneys have our legal documents ready. Will you make an appointment and sign them?"

A quiet moment while he processed my request.

"Ok, if you won't reconcile with me, then I'm going to marry Ariana."

That ended our conversation, but I didn't understand. Who is Ariana? I suddenly realized it didn't matter. Drew and his women were no longer my problem. My happiness would never again depend on him.

***

# Chapter 10

## *Empowerment*

**May, 1980**

WE FINALIZED THE divorce and I chose to resume my maiden name, Cavelli. Drew did rush into a marriage with Ariana, someone he had recently met and known for a very short time. Not only that, but within a few months I learned that Ariana had become pregnant and carried their child. I found this difficult to accept at first, but after Chloe came into the world I realized that my daughters would have a new half-sister in their lives, someone who would bring them affection and friendship. I held no anger inside me, and hoped that Drew may at last find the contentment and peace that he never had.

During this period my own goals and ambitions dominated my time. In the divorce agreement, I did have a lump sum settlement of $10,000. With this I purchased a spacious three story condominium in a desirable neighborhood with an easy commute to my school. We would move into it at the beginning of July, and I would have the whole summer to unpack and organize before September. Success. For the first time in my life I would have a home of my own.

With these active days of teaching, raising children, and moving, I had little time or interest in dating or meeting any eligible men. However, I did meet a group of other single New York City teachers who invited me to join them in attending a single's group which met on Friday nights at a Unitarian Church in New Jersey. Although traveling to New Jersey would be a commute, I decided that socializing for an evening would be worth the undertaking.

When we arrived at the church, the event began with a one hour support group during which singles shared and discussed their problems and issues. At the end of the session, everyone relocated into the larger room to talk, interact, and have snacks and drinks. Within a short time, a handsome, attractive young man approached me. Our conversation began when he warmly extended his hand.

"Hello, my name is Ray Brooks. It's very nice to meet you. Have you ever been involved in this Unitarian Church before?"

"No, I haven't. I'm actually Catholic, but some of my single friends suggested I come here tonight to enjoy the experience. I'm Hope Cavelli. Ray, what do you do for a living?"

"I'm an attorney. I used to work for a large law firm, but I recently opened my own law practice in the field of real estate law. I've owned my own home in Millburn, here in New Jersey, for the last eight years. How about you?"

"I live on Staten Island, I'm a teacher, and I have two daughters who are four and six years old."

"I also have two children. But I've been going through a very difficult time. When my wife Sarah and I separated, she left me for another man and took the children with her. In court, the judge awarded me custody of my children, Danny, age eleven, and Ashley, age three. One day when Sarah picked up the children for a visit, she kidnapped them. I haven't seen them in two months, and no one can locate them. Today they're among New Jersey's missing children."

"That's so sad, Ray. I wish you luck, and I hope you can find them soon."

"I'd like to see you again, Hope. Would you give me your phone number so we can plan a date?"

Thinking about his story, I didn't know what to believe. I knew that I did not want to live with any more trauma or mistakes. I definitely did not need another man with problems. So when Ray asked me for my phone number, I gave it to him but with reservation, not knowing if I ever really wished to see him again.

Little did I know at that moment Ray was destined to be the love of my life.

## Summer of 1980

At the end of June, a crisis arose in the New York City school system. The mayor was at odds with the teachers' union, and announced that next September there would be severe budget cuts in teaching positions and personnel. The principal of my school called me and three of my co-workers into her office to discuss how this situation would impact us. The possibility existed that we four teachers, lowest on the seniority list, would face layoff status at the beginning of the next school year. She advised us that job openings in the field of special education would definitely be available. If we had never taken any special education credits during our college years, we should consider taking the required six credits during the summer to secure our employment.

Although I never believed that I would lose my job, my parents helped out and watched the girls while I returned to Richmond College two days a week and completed the required coursework. At the end of August, I received the dreaded phone call from my principal.

"Good morning Hope, this is Mrs. Edwards calling. I'm sorry to inform you, but the layoffs have been implemented, and the city budget has been cut. I won't have a position for you when school opens."

My mind raced. Another setback? How could this be happening to me? How could life be so unfair? I had just settled into my new home and had a mortgage to pay. The only income I would have was Drew's meager child support check of $280 a month. What will I do?

"Mrs. Edwards, I did earn the six credits required for working with children with disabilities. Can you advise me on how I can apply for a job working in this area? Is there someone I can contact to make an appointment for an interview?"

"I know there will be hiring halls scheduled for different school districts. Keep in touch with the main Board of Education office, and they will give you the information that you need. Good luck."

With a few phone calls, I gathered the information I needed. Yes, there would be hiring halls scheduled, but only for districts in Brooklyn. Although repulsed by the idea of a daily commute over the Verrazano Narrows Bridge from Staten Island to Brooklyn and paying the toll, I saw this as a better alternative than nothing. Next, I headed to the mall to shop for an impressive new interview suit that would surely present me as the most desired professional.

I entered the hiring hall carrying my resume and feeling confident. There were numerous tables set up in a large auditorium, each of them labeled with a sign indicating which school district it represented. I selected the school districts I preferred to work in, and stood in lines, one after another, waiting for my turn to be interviewed. I presented myself to five different school districts that day, but despite my experience, I was repeatedly shunned and promptly dismissed in the process. I could not understand why. Then a woman who worked in one of the districts approached me. She had been observing me from across the room and seemed aware of my frustration.

"Hi there. Do you have a moment to speak with me? I see that you seem intent on securing a job here today, and I would like to share some information with you."

"Sure," I replied. She summoned me to walk with her to a quiet corner of the room.

"I don't want you to be disappointed, but when you leave here today, my prediction is that you won't have a job. All of these districts that are hiring today are in black neighborhoods. Truthfully, the people interviewing you prefer black teachers over white, because they feel that the black teachers could better relate to their school populations. As a white person, I suggest that you go home today, but don't be discouraged. Put your time and energy into finding a job that is more appropriate for you."

I stared at her. Then I looked around the auditorium and studied all the people. Maybe she was right. Maybe I had just wasted my time.

For the first time in my life, I realized what it was like to be discriminated against because of my color. Some people reading this may not believe that this really happened to me. But it did. I made my way slowly to the nearest phone booth to contact my parents and share my disappointment. I hesitantly lifted the receiver and dialed their number. When my father answered my words stumbled past my lips. Through my uncontrollable tears I blurted out, "Dad, I did not get a job."

## October of 1980

After composing myself, I redirected my energy to finding resources that could get me through this difficult time. I reapplied for food stamps, and took a temporary office job during the month of September. Thankfully, my parents helped me out with paying some of the bills.

I continued to interview for teaching jobs. Finally during the middle of October, a pregnant teacher of special needs children took a leave of absence, and I replaced her. Although pleased with the location of my new school in a nearby neighborhood of Staten Island, most of these children were bused in from the ghetto. I feared working with them, feeling that I lacked any previous expertise. All of my new students had been labeled NIEH, meaning neurologically impaired, emotionally handicapped. My new principal asked me to observe the class and participate in its daily activities before the existing teacher left, in order to prepare me for assuming her role.

The class consisted of fifteen fifth and sixth graders led by the teacher, with a strong, young male aide to assist. In the first lesson of the day, reading, the teacher stood in front of the room with the students gathered near her. On the board she had a list of new vocabulary words. She pointed to the first one.

"Who would like to read this word and tell us the meaning?"

None of the students looked at the blackboard or even cared. She could not get their attention, and I listened while they talked and called out across the room incessantly.

"Hey, Arnold, whachu doin' after school today?"

"I'm meetin' Jamal at the park, he be my new friend."

"Teacher, we don't want to do no work today. Can't we go to the schoolyard to play basketball?"

"Yeah, yeah," responded several of the others, and they began to clap their hands in unison.

While absorbing the turmoil, I noticed one boy boldly facing another at a desk directly across from him. He looked into his classmate's face and screamed, "Motherfucker!" The boy who had been verbally attacked jumped out of his seat, picked up his desk and hurled it across the room, aiming at the instigator. Quickly, the aide stepped forward and intervened. When the forty minute reading period ended, no work had been accomplished and the students had learned nothing. Similar behaviors occurred throughout the day. Some of the students, having been left back due to failing grades, approached their teen years and were bigger and stronger than me. I doubted I could be successful at this job.

The following Monday I took over the class. I decided to make a chart and set up the classroom rules which would enable us all to survive.

Remain in Your Seat
No Calling Out
No Bad Language
Raise Your Hand to Speak
Complete Your Work
Show Respect to Classmates
Show Respect to Teachers

Great idea, but they needed a lot more than a chart to get them interested in learning or behaving. After I survived the first week, I began to realize the source of the problem. These children did not come from ordinary families. As I learned about their backgrounds, I began to understand why success in school meant nothing to them.

The class was a mixture of white and black students. Eight of the fifteen children existed in the foster care system, and had moved from place to place, even during their earliest years. They had never been loved or valued. Most of their parents were either drug addicts or prisoners in the criminal justice system.

Witnessing the suffering these children endured opened my eyes to a kind of life that I could never have imagined. Jamal had been thrown from a window by his raging father at age three, resulting in permanent brain damage. Emily had loved her foster mother deeply, but recently the foster mother had become ill and passed away. Shanice had immigrated from Africa, and told stories of how she had been disciplined by her mother with live, biting ants thrown into her underwear.

Steven's story touched my heart most of all. This boy, an interracial child with blond hair and gorgeous blue eyes, had been in the foster care system since birth, but his mother chose not to give him up for adoption at that time. Now ten years old, he often would recount stories in class about the visits he had with his natural mother and the places she had taken him.

"Mrs. Cavelli, did you know that last year my mom took me to Disney World?"

"No I didn't know that, Steven. But you sure are a lucky boy to have had that opportunity. What is your favorite memory of the trip?"

"We went to the Magic Kingdom. I saw all the Disney characters like Mickey Mouse and Donald Duck. They looked real. Most of all I liked the rides."

Another day Steven talked about the next upcoming visit with his mother.

"Guess where my mom is going to take me during winter break this year."

"I have no idea. Where?"

"We're going to Florida! I'm going to see alligators and go swimming in the middle of the winter. I can't wait."

One day while Steven related one of his stories, another teacher overheard our conversation. She had known Steven for several years, and she quietly approached me, whispering into my ear.

"I'm so sorry to tell you this, Hope, but Steven hasn't seen his real mother since the day he was born. All of the stories he's telling you are imaginary dreams that never happened. He's been fixated on her for years, always thinking about her and craving her love. I just heard that she recently signed papers to make him available for adoption."

Within the next few weeks, the theme of Steven's stories changed drastically.

"Mrs. Cavelli, I have some news. I'm going to have a new Mommy and Daddy. A lot of Mommies and Daddies have been coming to meet me, but I don't know where I'm going to live yet. When I get to my new home, I'm going to have one of those cute little dogs for a pet. I can't wait."

Steven interviewed with many prospective adoptive parents that year. But because of his age and his emotional issues, no one chose him. My heart grieved with unrelenting sadness as thoughts of that boy stayed with me and intruded into my sleep. I felt that as his teacher, I had no control over his life or destiny. Although I wanted to improve the lives of my students, I sometimes had to accept my inability to make that happen.

Every one of my students had a story, and every one of them had been a victim. As I grew in understanding, my attitude toward them transformed from fear to compassion. Could there be any hope for their futures? What would happen to them in their adult years?

## November, 1980

On the first day of November, a special education supervisor, Mrs. Miller, knocked on my classroom door and asked me to meet with her during my next free period. She explained that since I had no prior experience working with children with behavioral disorders, she had been assigned to help me set up a behavior modification system in my classroom. She explained that once we implemented the plan, my classroom situation of unruly students would hopefully improve. Thrilled with the idea, I could not wait to have my first learning session. Mrs. Miller was very clear with her instructions.

"Begin by making classroom charts for all seven periods of the day for each student. At the end of each period, record on the chart how many points each child earned for that period based on their behavior and completion of the assignments. At the end of the day if the child earned a total of 20 points, he will receive a reward."

"Can you give me some ideas on what rewards might motivate these youngsters to work for something?" I asked.

"It depends on each child and what he or she likes. Start with trial and error. Sometimes free play at the end of day is successful. Or a game period with hands-on activities that they enjoy. If the weather is nice, they sometimes might earn an extra gym period, or be chosen as the child to go on errands for the teacher. Try it. Implement the plan. I'll return one day next week to see if things are improving."

By the end of the first few days, things began to settle down. I tried all of her suggestions for rewards, and most of them worked. Amazingly, I found that all of these children would do anything to receive a candy or cookie at the end of the day, or even a small hands-on toy out of my newly created prize box. A token of their success that they could taste, eat or hold in their hands meant the most to them. Mrs. Miller enabled me to succeed at my new job. Within a month, anyone walking by my classroom observed the transformation. Soon all of my fifteen students remained seated in their chairs, doing work, and for the most part, following the rules and earning their points.

I can't say that every day was always perfect. Sometimes Tawanda had a meltdown, and she would run to the coat closet and hide. Sometimes harsh words between students would result in physical altercations or chair throwing incidents. Other times students arrived at school distraught with their home situations, unable to function or even care about their points.

Despite the obstacles, with each passing day I became more empowered about what I could do for these children. I maintained a calm voice, and learned to respond to their actions with patience and fortitude. I learned a lot through this new experience about these children with special needs in our society. My confidence soared as

I rose above my fears and faced the challenges that I had not been prepared for.

## January, 1981

This time, I would allow nothing to stop me. I could manage my job and pay the mortgage on my condo. My daughters would have a home to live in, and seeing them grow and thrive would be the essence of my being. I had done it at last. I had completed a another traumatic phase of my life, and at the end of it I saw myself as the person I had always wanted to be, the person I thought I never could be. And now I realized that no one could ever again take away my newfound sense of self by their words or thoughts, or actions. It was a gift of a new life, as if I had been born again.

# Chapter 11

## *Forgiveness*

**February, 1981**

THE DAY BEGAN early on a Wednesday morning, and the wintry snow had already fallen and blanketed the ground. I listened to the radio broadcast and heard the prediction for a total accumulation of two to three inches. No school closures, both the public and private schools would remain open. I dressed and prepared for my day, ready to wake up the girls. Unexpectedly, my phone rang at 6:45 a.m. It was my father calling with an important message.

"Listen to me very carefully, Hope. It's already slippery out there, and it's going to be too dangerous to drive anywhere." His voice increased in volume as he continued. "Keep the girls home from school today, and don't even consider driving to your job. Promise me that you'll take a personal day and stay home."

It took me a moment to contemplate my response. Here I am in my thirties, I thought, and he's still trying to control my life. But then it was as if a miracle happened. For the first time ever, I heard his words, but felt no anger. On this memorable morning, they were only words, and I suddenly realized that the power he held over me through all the years had only been in my mind. Now being a person of strength, I had the freedom to choose my plan of the day, and whether or not we would all go to school. While I still held the receiver to my ear, I became even more enlightened. I realized that all the demands and rules that my father had imposed upon me had been founded in his love and concern for my well-being. Although he wasn't perfect and sometimes made mistakes, he had given me the best that he could in a way that I had not understood.

From that moment forward, I admired my father despite what he said or did. For the first time, I understood the meaning of forgiveness. I am thankful that I had this opportunity for personal growth because it enabled me to enjoy and appreciate him through all of his remaining days on this earth.

With a smile on my face, I walked through the snow with my girls. We drove away and headed for school.

*** 

# Chapter 12

## *Moving Forward*

**April, 1981**

As spring approached, the girls began adjusting to the divorce, and I had continued to date Ray. Although I had been hesitant to trust him and had doubts about why his wife had abducted his children, in time my faith in him flourished. I decided to introduce him to my girls, who were now five and seven years old. On the day they met, Ray became delighted. While I watched them play together, it seemed as if Ray had become a child again himself. We all went down to the play room that I had set up in the basement. We turned on the record player, and Ray and the girls began to dance wildly to the lively music, spinning around in circles together and giggling with glee. This was a time to be treasured, a time for laughter and happiness that I thought I would never see again. In that brief moment, I pictured us as a family, and I wondered if that dream would ever become a reality.

The next day, Ray approached me with great emotion. He told me how much spending time with my children had meant to him. He described the longing for his own children and how his new relationship with my girls had filled his emptiness. In response to this I felt a warmth radiate throughout my body, and as I threw my arms around Ray, I realized I was falling in love. Meeting Ray had added richness to my life. Never before had I known a man with such gentleness of temperament and kindness of heart.

My relationship with Ray continued to thrive as we supported each other through the adjustments that had to be made during these most challenging days. On weekends when I had the girls, Ray would stay in my condo and sleep downstairs on the living room couch. We wanted to send the message that only married couples should sleep in the same bed. During our time together we planned many family oriented activities such as trips to the zoo and amusement parks, and visits with my parents and sister.

On alternate weekends when the girls had visitation with Drew and Ariana, I usually drove to Ray's house in Millburn and spent Saturdays and Sundays in a new environment, suburbia. Here I was surrounded by massive trees and forests, farms, hooting owls, and wild deer roaming the nearby wooded land. I enjoyed the quiet time away from my busy life, and the opportunity for romance and personal interests.

After Drew and Ariana married, they moved and started a new life together in a small town on the Jersey shore. Allison and Rebecca immediately bonded with their new baby sister, Chloe. Little Chloe loved them deeply in return, and when the girls arrived at their dad's new home, Chloe would be waiting for them by her front door, excitedly jumping up and down.

Ariana seemed to be an accepting stepparent, and on one occasion she brought the girls to a photography studio for some professional pictures of just her and the girls. This made Allison and Rebecca feel important and accepted, and they were excited to be part of Dad's new family.


**May, 1981**


It had been more than one year since Ray had any contact with his children. At this point, his daughter Ashley was four years old, and his son Danny twelve. Ray often expressed concern about why his son had never used the phone to call him and let him know where he lived or that he was safe.

At the beginning of May, Ray finally received the long awaited call from an attorney.

"Mr. Brooks, I represent your wife, Sarah. She is anxious to settle the legal issues between you and draw up a new agreement. She is asking for child support and temporary custody of the children, while waiting for a judge to make the final decision on who would now be the permanent custodial parent. If you accept these temporary arrangements, she will allow you visitation with the children."

Thrilled with the anticipation of seeing Ashley and Danny, Ray would have agreed to anything.

"Oh yes, I'd agree to that. How soon can I visit my children?"

"If you come into my office to sign the papers, you can plan on next Saturday."

The arrangements were finalized. In a few days, Ray would pick up his son and daughter and spend the day with them. While preparing for their reconciliation, he expressed both relief and concern about the welfare of his children after their long separation. "What had their mother told them? Do they think that I abandoned them and never loved them or tried to find them?"

Soon he would know the answers to all of his questions.

At last the long anticipated moment arrived. After the initial emotional greeting and hugs, things settled down and the children began to speak openly of the events in their lives during the past twelve months. Things had not been easy for them. Danny seemed to carry the pain and confusion of his situation more than his sister, who as such a young child, did not really understand what had happened to her family.

While Ashley happily jumped onto Ray's lap and hugged him, Danny shared his narrative of the fears and distress that he had suffered. After Sarah had taken the children, she feared that she would be found and Ray would again be granted custody. So when she moved to another town of New Jersey and registered Danny in the local public school, she changed his last name so that he could not be identified. And each day of his life in this new town, this young boy had to keep his real identity a secret, and he had to pretend that he was someone he wasn't.

Finally Ray confronted Danny.

"Danny, why didn't you ever call me during all these months?"

Danny responded with great anguish in his voice.

"Dad, if I ever called you or told anyone my real name, my mom might get arrested and go to jail for taking us. And if that ever happened to her, it would have been all my fault. I always thought of you and wanted to call, but I just couldn't do it."

Ray pondered what Danny had said. Then he reached out and embraced his son.

"Danny, I love you, and I'm so sorry. Know that I am here for you now and always. Never be afraid to pick up that phone again."

## August, 1981

Ray continued to visit with his children regularly over the next few months, and by the end of August we made a plan to have all of us meet for the first time. We planned a relaxing afternoon at Ray's house, just having our three girls play in the backyard with some toys, and Danny practicing his baseball skills with his new bat and ball. The girls immediately bonded and created imagination games with their Barbie dolls and wooden dollhouse. By the end of the day they had made plans for all the fun things they planned to do together during their next visit.

Ashley easily accepted me as well. She talked and laughed as I chased her around the yard. I enjoyed this day of wonder as I perceived this child as another little person who might be in my life in the years to come.

I tried with great effort to relate to Danny that day, but failed at making any progress. I asked him questions, hoping to draw him out of the shell he seemed to have built around himself.

"Danny, what grade are you in now?"

"What's your favorite subject?"ß

"Do you play on any sports teams in your school or town?"

"I'm going to cook a homemade Italian dinner tonight. Do you like Italian food?" He answered all my attempts with one word responses. He seemed distant and sad, and I realized how upsetting it must have been for him to be in the family home he had grown up in, with another woman and her two strange daughters.

I gazed at Danny in awe as he practiced his baseball skills with Ray. He was undoubtedly the most beautiful boy I had ever seen. His fair skin, his handsome facial features, and his expressive blue eyes made him an extremely good looking young man. I hoped that at some point, at some other time or place, the barriers between us would dissolve, and we could become friends.

**December, 1981**

Our lives continued on a positive path. Allison and Rebecca continued seeing their dad, their stepmom, and Chloe regularly. Ray had re-established his relationships with his children, and began working on legal matters to resolve his divorce. And I remained steadfast in succeeding at my teaching career and achieving my personal goals.

Still seeking closure for many of the things I had faced in my marriage to Drew, I considered applying to the Catholic Church for an annulment. Although neither Ray nor I had ever discussed marriage at this point, I felt that this would be important to me for two reasons. First, being granted an annulment would help to release me from any inner guilt I still carried about Drew. Secondly, if I ever remarried, I would want to take my vows before the altar of God, with His blessings, to be an example for my children. After discussing this with Ray, he became enthralled with the idea of a Church annulment as a final step forward in ending his relationship with Sarah also. So we both reached out to our local parishes, and began hours of phone calls and paperwork to resolve another of life's situations.

## January 1, 1982

It had been many years since I had visited Aunt Ava, and I missed her deeply. Although she had continued to host family gatherings, it had been too painful for me to attend and deal with the presence of Uncle Scott. As January 1st approached, I received the annual invitation to Aunt Ava's New Year's Day celebration. I kept thinking about it over and over again. I would love to go, I thought. It had been so long since I had seen not only Aunt Ava, but all of my cousins and other aunts and uncles as well. I guess being a single mother and having a full time job, I failed to make the time in my busy schedule to maintain contact with all those people who had been part of my childhood.

Being the newly empowered person that I was, I felt confident that I could actually attend the gathering. I contemplated my fear of facing Uncle Scott, and my desire to be with cousins and other members of my extended family. I told myself *that man will never dominate my life again and rob me of the things* I *hold important.*

The day came, and I attended with my parents, my children, and Ray. Upon entering the house, a room filled with people and loud, boisterous voices greeted me. But despite the talking, laughing, and noisy guests, the only object my eyes could see was my uncle. He stood across the room, beer in hand. He was slender, with a mustache which had whitened significantly since I had last seen him. Upon seeing my family, he approached us and in the usual Italian fashion, grabbed each of us with a tight, welcoming hug. His words sounded phony and cold.

"Hope, how nice to see you again. Ray, it's very nice to meet you."

My arms froze at my sides without response when he embraced me. I thought for a moment my body had become paralyzed. But gathering all my determination, I managed to look away and turn my energy to enjoying the people I loved. I was proud of myself. I could remain in the same room with him, and not allow him to ruin my visit.

My daughters had a great time meeting many of their relatives and playing with their young cousins. I watched them carefully throughout the afternoon, ensuring that they would never be alone anywhere with my uncle. And of course, Aunt Ava gave me the time, love and attention that I had longed for. This was a day for me to remember, another time when I triumphed over obstacles and fears, and took control of my destiny.

## March, 1982

In so many ways, this was the happiest time of my life. It seemed as if I now lived all of my hopes and dreams. I loved my Staten Island condo, and treasured our days with Ray. Usually we only spent time with him on Saturdays and Sundays, since we lived in different states and both had busy careers. But weekends with our children together became special, as with each new visit we bonded more and more, and began to grow into a family of our own. Our three girls continued to thrive and enjoy each other's company. I can still visualize the day that Ray drove to pick up his children from their mother while I waited for him with my girls at his home. When Ray pulled into the driveway, my daughters screeched with joy as Ashley exited the car. They greeted each other with hugs, jumping up and down with anticipation of the good times ahead.

"Hi," yelled Ashley. "Look what I brought for us to do today! It's a new jump rope with red handles on it, and I could show you how I learned to jump."

"Cool," said Allison. "I love jumping rope. I brought some arts and crafts supplies for us to make finger puppets."

"Girls, I have a better idea," Rebecca interjected. "It's cold out here, so let's go upstairs and just practice jumping on the beds." And off they ran to begin their adventurous day. My relationship with my parents flourished. They had supported me through my divorce, and helped out babysitting. When I needed to complete required teacher workshops, they watched the girls every Tuesday. They provided dinner, completed school assignments, then brought them home, ready for bed. The girls created their own names for their grandparents, who became known to them as "Grammy" and "Granpy."

While babysitting, my parents often made a trip to the toy store. While Rebecca remained fascinated with Barbie dolls, Allison always chose to contribute to her growing collection of stuffed animals which she displayed in her room. When showing off her collection to anyone, Allison described them as presents from Granpy, her most favorite grandfather in the whole wide world. Also during these days, my sister and I became closer than we had ever been. Tracey, now also divorced, never had any children of her own. She treasured her nieces and loved cooking. We often spent afternoons together as she prepared some of her freshly cooked, creative meals.

And then there was Alicia, whom I had met at the YMCA. My first true understanding of friendship. A joy and inspiration in my single life. We talked endlessly and supported each other through every new challenge. Alicia had recently become a New York City teacher, so now our lives paralleled each other in even more ways than before. We endlessly shared stories about our students, parents, principals, and teaching strategies.

But most important of all, our topic of concern always turned to our children. One evening during a quiet moment alone, we talked about the long term effect that our divorces might have on them.

"Alicia, how is Jacob handling his separation from his father? Has your ex been visiting more regularly? Do you see any progress in your son's acceptance of the situation?"

"I'm upset over things right now. Jacob holds a lot of anger towards his father and sometimes acts out with temper tantrums. His father doesn't visit much, but Jacob asks for him often. I also have an upcoming court date about child support. My ex wants to go to medical school and avoid paying me any child support at all until he becomes a doctor. Do you believe that? I'm so glad I made the decision to remain in my parents' home, so I don't have to worry about paying a monthly rent. How are your daughters doing? Anything new with you, Hope?"

"No, not really. Things seem stabilized for me at the moment, but I sometimes think I'm ready to move on. Deep within me lives that dream of building a family again, and I know that I love Ray. But what's the success rate of remarriage with children involved? Ray and I have four children between us. Could we triumph over all we've been through?"

We talked intently and honestly into the night. Together we analyzed every circumstance and sought solutions. I was no longer alone. Inspired by my new appreciation of friendship and family, I continued on my path to growth.

# Chapter 13

## A Sudden Loss

**April 23, 1982**

It was 7:00 p.m. on a Friday evening. I had just arrived in New Jersey to spend the weekend with Ray. Upon my arrival, my sister called unexpectedly with terrible news. She spoke softly, almost inaudibly.

"Hope?"

"Oh, hi Tracey."

"Listen, something just happened. I…I'm on the way over to be with Mom."

"Why? What's the matter? Is Mom ok?"

She hesitated, and an alarm went off in my head. This was not going to be good news.

"It's not Mom, it's Dad."

My sister proceeded to tell me the story.

"Dad had been in the bedroom talking and laughing on the phone, with Mom nearby in the kitchen. She heard his voice, filled with life and enthusiasm, as he made plans for an upcoming gala event at St. John's University. When Mom realized he had become quiet for a period of time, she went into the bedroom to check on him. She found him motionless, lying on the floor, not breathing. She dialed 911 and with a neighbor's help attempted to revive him. When the ambulance arrived, she called me and told me of the situation."

My heart began to beat rapidly. I could hardly breathe. But I knew what I had to do. I gave Ray a quick update and began traveling over the Goethals Bridge, back to Staten Island. All the while, I wondered if Dad would die and I would never have a chance to tell him how much I loved him.

The paramedics revived my father and carried him away by ambulance. But within minutes, he left this earth and disappeared from our lives forever. When I arrived in Staten Island, I hesitantly walked up the steps to my parents' house, gripping my chest in fear.

"Sis, he didn't make it," Tracey informed me.

No, no, it couldn't be really happening. I walked into the living room which began to darken around me, and I wondered why faces and people seemed to disappear from sight. My sister's words faded more and more into oblivion. Finally, I lost my balance as dizziness overwhelmed me, and I collapsed, motionless, onto a chair. I slept over my mom's house that night, not wanting to leave her. As the sun rose the next morning, I walked outside to the front porch and sipped a cup of coffee. I gazed into the brightening sky and thought that here is the first day without my father. What would life be like without him? I feared for my mother, who would now be alone and had never learned to drive a car. How could I tell my daughters that there would never be another Tuesday after school adventure with Granpy? And if I ever married Ray, my father would not be there to walk me down the aisle, to give the wedding toast, or to bestow his blessings.

Surrounded by many of my father's possessions, I continued to think about the kind of person that he had been and the endless sacrifices he had made for me and my brother and sister. He had instilled in us the value of learning and working toward our goals. He had worked hard and diligently to send all three of us to college, and give us the opportunity for better lives. He walked with us to Sunday Mass, and taught us the difference between right and wrong. Being the model that he was, he impacted our lives and his teachings would remain within us forever. I thanked God that I was able to appreciate him during his final days.

It would be a while before I could accept my loss and let him go. But then peace overcame me, as I became aware that I had kept the promise that I had made to myself in childhood. I had kept the secret and never shared what had happened with Uncle Scott or what I had endured. I had done it. I had given him the best gift that I could. He left this earth cherishing his life, his brothers, and people he believed in.

A few weeks after Dad's passing, I heard the song, "Dance With My Father Again" play on the radio. The words and message of this song deeply impacted me, as I continued to deal with the reality of it all. I knew he was in heaven, and would hear me speak.

"Dad, each day of my life will be a dance with you beside me. Having you there will give me courage and strength."

✳✳✳

# Chapter 14

## *An Unexpected Disclosure*

**September 1982**

RAY RECEIVED AN invitation to his college reunion and excitedly made plans to attend. He asked me to join him, and looked forward to reuniting with people from his past who had known him as a young, promising student. Before the reunion, Ray contacted his old friends Bobby and Beth to ask if they would attend. Bobby and Beth had met in college and married. They had been close friends with both Ray and his wife Sarah.

I enjoyed the reunion immensely and had conversations with bright, interesting men and women. Many of them shared funny stories about the crazy, unforgettable things that went on in college, especially in the wild fraternity house. The highlight of my evening was dancing with Ray, who had mastered the art of swinging me around the dance floor as an accomplished leader and dance partner. By the end of the night I felt relaxed, happy, and glad that I had connected with so many people from a different chapter of Ray's life.

During the drive home, I noticed Ray's quiet mood. He didn't speak or say a word, and I thought that perhaps he felt ill or had too much to drink. I questioned him and asked if something had upset him, but he didn't answer. Silence reigned in the car for what seemed forever.

Finally, Ray stuttered as he attempted to explain. During the evening his friend Bobby had taken him aside and made a revelation.

"Ray, I hope this won't upset you too much, but at the time you graduated from law school, Sarah confided in me and Beth that she had become deeply involved in an extramarital affair. I never told you, because I didn't know what to do. Although I thought you should know, I didn't want to be the one to break up your marriage. Now that you're separated from her, I feel more comfortable telling you about it."

Ray continued to express his feelings.

"I never knew. We had problems in our marriage, but I never suspected that. Could I have been such a fool as to never realize she was cheating on me? I'm appalled at this news. Maybe it's possible that Ashley is not my child, my natural daughter. What should I do?"

I paused while I contemplated my response.

"I don't know the answer, Ray. Any decision you make would be yours alone. But what difference does it make now? No matter what, she's been your daughter since birth, and you've been her father. You love each other. Can you forget what you've heard tonight and just go on?"

"I don't know. I need more time. I'll think about it."

**November, 1982**

As the girls got older, school performance became an important aspect of their lives. With the first report cards of the school year, they both showed achievement above grade level. Allison in particular maintained a straight A average and excelled in every reading or math assessment. Rebecca seemed to be less intent and more social, surrounded by many friends. I was proud of both of them. But one day an inexplicable incident involving Rebecca occurred at school. Now in second grade, she announced to her teacher and classmates that her Daddy had been killed in a car accident. At the end of the school day, Rebecca's teacher reached out to our family and contacted Nanny, Drew's mother, to offer her condolences and inquire about the impact of this tragedy on Rebecca and her sister.

With the teacher's call, Nanny came to believe that she had lost her son but had never been notified. She hung up and dialed my number in a state of panic.

"What happened? Where's Drew? Is it true?"

"What are you talking about?"

"The accident that Rebecca told her teacher about. My son was killed?" she sobbed.

"Nanny, calm down. That didn't happen. Give me a little while to deal with this. I need to talk to Rebecca."

I sat Rebecca down next to me on her bed and cuddled her. She hugged me back. I asked her why she had made up the story at school about Daddy. She shrugged her shoulders and never answered me. She wouldn't talk about it. The event plagued me for weeks. Why would a child fabricate such a myth? What thoughts and emotions caused her to do this? It would take me years before I understood that she saw Drew's absence as a great loss and emptiness in her life. In her delicate mind, her father had disappeared from her life, as if he had died.

***

# Chapter 15

## A New Phase

**January, 1983**

AFTER MY FATHER died, loneliness and depression began to overshadow my mother's relish for life. The arrival of wintry snowstorms only isolated her even more from her social network of family and friends. One day when I visited, she advised me of her decision to move to Dallas, Texas, where my brother Steven and his family had now lived for seven years. The climate would be warmer there and my brother, financially successful, had offered her a house to live in.

I felt so abandoned. This news was another unforeseen loss. My father had left me through death, and now Grammy would be thousands of miles away and miss seeing my children grow up.

By the beginning of the new year, Ray became legally divorced, and we both had been awarded our Church annulments. Sometimes I thought, since we are both free now, maybe we should consider marrying and building that family. But my first marriage experience had been so disastrous, I set aside that idea and wondered if I could ever make that lifelong commitment again.

Getting the Church annulment had been a draining experience, like a trial in court. I had to be analyzed and interviewed by priests, and I had to bring in family members as witnesses to what had occurred in my marriage to Drew. Finally, I was granted the annulment based on the fact that Drew had been unfaithful within just a few months after our wedding. In the eyes of the Church, this meant that Drew entered the marriage without the maturity or knowledge and ability to keep such a permanent commitment. Therefore, our marriage was declared null and void. If I ever wished to marry again in the Catholic Church, I would be able to do so.

## February, 1983

Ray became haunted by his thoughts about Ashley. Whenever he saw her, he examined her hands, her feet, her hair, and her features. He wanted some evidence that she had a resemblance to him or any other member of his biological family. But during each visit, he became more and more convinced that she was not really his. The day came when Ray decided he needed to know the truth and advised me of his plan.

"I can't live like this any longer. I've contacted an attorney who will obtain a court order for an HLA paternity test. In about two weeks the results will become available. I'll still be her father and love her anyway. I just need to know. Can you understand that?"

"I'm scared, Ray. I'm afraid of the unknown."

After an intense fourteen days filled with apprehension, the blood test results became available, and Ray experienced his worst nightmare. Ashley was not his child. Upon receiving the news, he drove to Staten Island to tell me in person. I never saw a man cry before as Ray did. Through his tears he sobbed, "Why, why God, did this happen to me?"

## March, 1983

As Ray had pledged, he remained devoted to Ashley. We continued to have alternate weekends with Danny and Ashley, and time spent with our four children. Trusting that Ray had resolved and accepted the issue of paternity, my attention turned to another challenging experience with a new emotionally disturbed student in my class. I thought I had my classroom under control with my continued use of the behavior modification plan. Then one day the principal knocked on my classroom door to introduce a new student, Monica, who would be enrolled in my class as of that day. Monica was a graceful, beautiful eleven year old who seemed quiet and reserved at first, but I knew that any new student assigned to my class was there for a reason. I mentally prepared myself for another challenge ahead.

Within the first half hour of her arrival, I stood near Monica's newly assigned desk and noticed the scars of cut marks on both of her wrists. I looked in disbelief and thought that it could not be possible that this lovely, promising child had attempted suicide. What could have occurred in her short life to make her want to end it? Before the school day ended, I made time to review Monica's records with the psychologist on the school study team. My suspicions proved to be correct. After being a victim of physical abuse, she had cut her wrists in an attempt to end her suffering. Having no caring family, she also had recently been placed in the foster care system.

By the second day in my classroom, Monica began to release her anger and anxieties. I sent her to the blackboard to complete a long division example. She stood with the chalk in her hand, not knowing where to begin. I tried to help her by asking,

"Monica, what is 81 divided by 9?"

Thwarted by the problem, she turned away from the board and screamed,

"Who the hell cares?"

Following this outburst, she kicked her desk repeatedly, then ran out of the classroom and down the hallway in a panic. The simplest situations seemed impossible for her to bear.

These behaviors continued for weeks. I spent days trying to educate the other students whose classroom environment become invaded by her outbursts, screaming, and distractions. My frustrations mounted as I made frequent calls to the principal's office asking for help, after all my efforts to work successfully with Monica had failed.

One day while she raged, I thought I would try one final approach. I threw my arms around her and spoke in a quiet, calming voice.

"Monica, you can do this. You can handle this situation without running out of your seat and losing control. Do you know how much I care about you? I want you to do well in my class and succeed. You are a special girl with great potential. Do you want to try coming back to your seat now? I know you can do it."

I had hoped that maybe if she believed my words, she could trust me and change. But when she stood steadfast in her refusal to sit down, I came to understand that after eleven years of life without knowing love, it would take a lot more than what I could give her to make that happen. Each night sadness plagued me as I tried to block the day's events and rest. Monica had been placed in my care, but I could not help her. Sometimes I asked myself if I should give up trying. Was it really worth all this effort? Could I continue much longer at this job?

I left school that day with feelings of failure, plagued by the daunting task of trying to save my tormented students. But something inside me told me that this is where I was meant to be, and I should never give up.

**April, 1983**

The weekend approaching would be a quiet two days with the children visiting Drew. Ray wanted to take me out for dinner so we could discuss important matters. I didn't feel prepared for any serious conversation about our future, but I looked forward to a relaxing meal. Shortly after we arrived at the restaurant, the conversation began.

"Hope, I have never loved anyone as I love you. I want to spend the rest of my life with you. But I've been thinking about how much I fear another legal entanglement with a woman after what I had been subjected to with Sarah. Are you willing to move into my house in New Jersey with your children, and live as a family without getting married?"

Shocked, I had not expected this. I had already decided that if Ray refused to marry me, I would end our relationship. Speaking emphatically, I knew I had to make my message strong and clear.

"I've already thought about that, and my answer is no. My girls have been through enough already. I'm not going to teach them by example that it's all right to just live with a man. Do you remember who I am? An Italian girl from Brooklyn with the old fashioned ideas. I want to have a family with you as my husband and our children together. I could have it no other way."

I feared facing him and gazing into his eyes. He responded without hesitation as he passionately grabbed my hand and asked the question, "Then will you marry me?"

I didn't have to answer. My instant giggle and jubilant smile foretold our future.

## May 1983

Marrying Ray meant months of work ahead, planning our ceremony and deciding where to live. Most importantly, the girls would need help in adjusting to a new home, a new school and new relationships. We arranged a formal ceremony at St. Joseph's Catholic Church in Millburn. We wanted it to be an event of meaning and significance, supported by our family and friends. We selected a date and booked a reservation at a nearby banquet hall. My sister Tracey agreed to be my maid of honor, and the best man would be Ray's brother, Andrew.

Near the end of May, I met with my mother, my brother Steven, and Ray's mother, Christina, to make wedding plans.

"I'll design and sew the dresses for the three girls. Just tell me the color material you would like them to wear," offered Christina.

"I'll take you shopping to buy your wedding gown," volunteered my mom.

"Thank you so much." I turned to Steven. "You're the only one I'd want to take Dad's place. Will you hold my hand and walk me down the aisle?"

"Of course I will, Sis. It will be my honor."

Plans made, I had no doubt. Ray and I were soul mates, meant to live the rest of our lives together. I believed in him as I had no other, and this time I knew that my passage through time with this man would be blessed and cherished.

## July 29, 1983

Tomorrow I would marry Ray. The preparations seemed endless. We had made the decision that I would move into Ray's house in New Jersey where he had lived with Sarah and his children, so we used all our time and energy reorganizing our possessions and consolidating our furniture. In the midst of all this, we had all four children staying with us for a full two weeks before the wedding. Life was full of action and activity!

On the afternoon before the wedding, Rebecca approached me with watery eyes and red, flushed cheeks. She gazed at me sadly.

"Mommy, I don't feel good." I touched her burning forehead, evidence of her raging fever. I rushed to the medicine cabinet with shaking hands to find the oral thermometer. She just couldn't be sick, I told myself. But within minutes the mercury in the thermometer rose to 103 degrees F, and I knew that the situation was serious. Just hours before my marriage, Rebecca had become ill. Fear gripped me as I thought of my wedding day, ruined.

I looked at the clock. I still had time to get Rebecca to the pediatrician and the pharmacy for medicine. I grabbed my purse and called out to Ray.

"We have an emergency. Rebecca is sick and I'm taking her to the doctor."

I grabbed my child, and waved goodbye to Ray as he stood bewildered in the driveway. Then I drove at top speed to Dr. Wheeler's office.

After a brief stay in the waiting room, Dr. Wheeler examined Rebecca. He swabbed her throat and announced,

"There's no doubt she has a bacterial throat infection. I'm giving you a prescription for an antibiotic, and she should respond well to this medication."

By 5:00 p.m. we left the doctor's office and headed for the pharmacy. By 5:30 I had Rebecca wrapped in warm blankets and tucked her into bed. Overwhelmed, I collapsed beside her in the bedroom chair, with no sleep or appetite for the remainder of the night.

Rebecca fell asleep instantly but I never slept at all. I stayed awake, administering the antibiotic every four hours and the fever reducing aspirin in between. The night seemed endless as I focused on my child with concern, and the vision of my wedding day vanished from my thoughts.

## July 30, 1983

The morning sun rose brightening the sky. As I sat in that chair, my eyes remained focused on the clock on the nearby night stand. It was 6:00 a.m., and in a few hours I would marry Ray despite all obstacles. We all needed time to shower, get dressed, and proceed on with the girls to our early appointments at the beauty salon. I wanted everyone to be beautiful! Then suddenly I remembered why I was there, sitting in Rebecca's room. I jumped up to feel her forehead with my hand, not knowing what to expect. She felt cool, and her color had returned to normal. After feeling my touch, Rebecca opened her eyes and smiled. "I'm all better, Mommy! Let's get up now and get ready for the party!" A miracle had happened. Rebecca happily grabbed my hand and laughed as we skipped down the hallway together to wake up Allison, Ashley, Danny and Ray.

The photographer arrived at the house early that afternoon to take pictures before the Church ceremony. My sister and the girls wore light pink dresses, accentuated with bouquets of dark pink flowers, and rings of matching flowers in their hair. I dressed in a simple white gown and wide brimmed, elegant hat. When Ray entered the room dressed in his formal black tuxedo, I realized he was the most handsome man I had ever laid eyes on.

The last person to be ready for our day was Danny. He joined us for the photographs, but could not conceal his sadness. He bore no smile, no evidence of joy. His eyes remained downcast, as if he could not accept what was to come. I promised myself that somehow in the years ahead, I would convince him that I loved him as a valued addition to my life.

At last, we drove to the Church and my anticipated moment arrived. I fondly squeezed my brother's arm as he led me to the altar. Walking with him side by side, my thoughts turned to my father, the only thing missing from my wedding. In my mind I spoke to him,

*Dad, I love you, and I wish you were here.*

Suddenly his inner spirit touched my heart, and I heard him whisper in my ear,

*Daughter, I am here with you today and share your happiness. Know that I bestow my blessings upon you and your flourishing family, and I will be with you always.*

# Chapter 16

## *Remarriage*

**September, 1983**

Remarriage meant endless adjustments. Now I lived in the state of New Jersey and continued working in New York, so I had a commute of two hours a day added to my schedule. Being a new wife, mother, teacher and homemaker, I also had to adjust to my new surname, as I became known to the world as Mrs. Hope Brooks.

I enrolled my daughters in the local Catholic school, where the small, nurturing environment played a role in their transition. Life with Ray exceeded all my expectations. His calming temperament brought stability to our daily living. The girls thrived on his attention and sense of humor. He possessed a gift to connect with children in a way I never before witnessed. Allison, the more reserved of the two girls, followed him everywhere, and insisted on sitting next to him at dinner, at the playground, or simply watching an evening show on TV.

Within days after moving, Allison and Rebecca became friends with two neighborhood girls. They often played together on weekends or after school. Within a short time, my daughters began to feel comfortable and accepted in their new home town. Ray became active in the Knights of Columbus which often held social gatherings and holiday functions. This enabled us to meet new people, and within a few months we initiated a social life with other couples who would be involved in our lives for years to come. He also developed an interest in local politics and decided to attend some meetings of our county Republican Party. One night after a Republican meeting, Ray returned home ecstatic. He rushed into our bedroom to wake me up.

"Hope, something incredible happened to me tonight at the meeting. There will soon be an upcoming election in Millburn for new members of our Township Council, and the Republicans asked if I would be willing to run as a candidate for this public office. What do you think? Should I do it? Would such a commitment take too much time out of our lives together? Will you support me in this?"

We talked for a long time and I had many questions. "Does being a candidate mean launching an active campaign for the council seat? Would it be like a presidential election involving our entire family? I don't know, Ray. It might be exciting, but it also might be stressful."

We both sat quietly for a few moments while we each became lost in our own thoughts. Finally, I spoke.

"Ok, Ray, this is what I think. I'm going to let you make the decision to run or not to run for the council seat. Whatever you decide, I will support you in your choice."

"Yes!" he yelled.

So he launched the campaign. Being part of the American system of government in action turned out to be an amazing experience for all of us. As a candidate, Ray worked hard to become well-known in the community. He gave speeches and talks and campaigned door-to-door. He described the goals and changes he would stand for and fight for. He became acquainted with many well-known people who devoted their lives to the political system, and began to believe that if he won, he would be successful in improving the quality of life of the residents of our community.

On weekends when we had all four of the children together, we made campaigning for Ray a joint undertaking. Sometimes we would all stand by the entrance to Shop Rite with our hand-made signs, and the children would hand out flyers to shoppers as they exited the store. Danny, now fourteen years old, took this event more seriously than the younger children. With each flyer he handed out, he would enthusiastically shout, "Vote for my Dad." Through this shared endeavor, Ray and Danny began to reunite and make up for the lost time of the last four chaotic years.

## November, 1983

Ray won the November election. We rejoiced together and soon Ray assumed his new role as someone of importance in our small town. As anticipated, accepting the seat on the Council demanded hours of work.

One evening Ray arrived home and announced that he had to rush off to a meeting at the Town Hall.

"But Ray, the girls are in a play at school tonight, remember? You're not going to miss it, are you?"

"Please don't be mad at me. I have to be there."

"Aren't the children important too?"

Ray missed the performance. The loss of his presence at home and treasured time with the girls became an unwelcome adjustment. But I continued to admire him for his energy and dedication to what he believed in.

## April, 1984

I looked forward to the first Easter with my new family. I now had four children, a dedicated husband, a network of friends, and a place in society. I had found and achieved all of the things that I wanted but thought I would never have. At this time and place, I believed I had arrived. Nothing but peace and tranquility lay ahead.

Ashley and Danny came to spend the Easter holiday with us, and we had a beautiful weather forecast for the weekend. The morning began with the girls dressing in their Easter outfits and bonnets for Church. Danny looked handsome as ever in his dark blue suit jacket.

When they were ready, Ray lined up all the children in front of the living room fireplace to take their pictures. They laughed and smiled while he recorded the day on film to be remembered for decades.

After the 10:30 a.m. mass, the children changed into their play clothes and headed outdoors. They all had a different plan of action.

"I'm getting my bike out of the garage and heading to the trail by the stream," said Danny.

"I want to climb up the tree with the white flowers in the front yard," said Allison. "Does anyone want to come with me?"

"I do," said Ashley.

"Me too," laughed Rebecca.

Suddenly they all raced to the blossoming dogwood tree. They boldly reached for the branch low enough to grab onto, and pulled themselves three quarters of the way up the tree, almost to the top. When each of them reached their highest goal, they looked down on us, waved their hands for our attention, and called out our names repeatedly.

"Hi Mom!"

"Hi Dad!"

This day ended with my holiday dinner being served, and Ray continuing with his picture taking expedition. Pictures of our Easter dinner, the Easter egg hunt in the yard, and everyone devouring the chocolate bunnies. I felt growing feelings of trust and affection among us all. As I tucked the girls into bed that night, I asked them, "Did you have a nice day?"

"Awesome, Mom," said Allison.

"I feel like we have a bigger family now with Ray and his kids," responded Rebecca.

I did not know that within a short time the next crisis would emerge, and I had thus far traveled only a short distance on my journey of life.

**May, 1984**

Unexpectedly, Ray received a phone call from Sarah that altered our lives. I stood nearby listening to their conversation, not wanting to believe what I heard.

"Ray, I called to advise you of some decisions that I've made regarding Ashley. I've been very upset over the court order for paternity testing. Now that you know the truth, I want to tell you that I've been seeing a psychologist to help me decide what to do. I want to do what's best for Ashley. Someday soon we'll have to tell her that you aren't her real father. I plan to marry my boyfriend Rob, and he has agreed to adopt her. This will be best for her, because she will grow up in an intact family with me as her mother and Rob as her father. When you come to pick up Danny next weekend, be prepared, because Ashley will no longer be coming with you."

"What? Sarah, how could you do such a thing? She's known me her whole life as her father. She'll be torn apart. How could you do this to us?"

"There's no discussing it any more, Ray. You no longer have any legal right or power to demand visitation or decide her future. That's just the way it is."

"But…"

The conversation ended when Sarah hung up. After composing himself, he turned to me.

"Hope, I just wanted to know the truth, but did not foresee the consequences. Why did I even order those blood tests? Now it's too late. We may never see Ashley again."

Hearing these words brought me heartbreak and regret.

"Ray, I don't know the law involved in this. Maybe you really do have the right to see her, based on the fact that she has had a relationship with you since birth. Maybe you should hire an attorney to represent you again and bring this new situation to court. This is unfair to all of us. How will we ever explain this to the children?"

The situation impacted each of our children in different ways. Ashley, of course, suffered the most. The first time that Ray picked up Danny for his weekend visit, he heard Ashley in the distance, crying.

"Mommy, please let me go with them. Please."

But her cries were ignored. She remained behind, no longer a part of our family, never again to spend time with the man she had known as Dad, and never again to play with the two little girls who had become her stepsisters.

After this, when we visited Danny, he seemed visibly upset. As a protective older brother, he loved his little sister. Seeing her situation and the abandonment that she endured aroused anger in him toward both of his parents. Although old enough to realize that his mother had been unfaithful, he questioned why his father needed to know the truth. One day he confronted Ray.

"Dad, why did you do this? Our lives will never be the same."

"I'm sorry, son. I love you and it grieves me to see you hurt. I hope someday you could forgive me for making that mistake, and thinking only of myself."

Rebecca handled the trauma of having Ashley ripped from her life by dreading her separation from me, fearing that maybe someday she might lose me too. I began receiving frequent phone calls from her teacher, advising me that Rebecca had stomach aches and had to be picked up from school. I began to fear that being pulled out of my classroom for her imaginary illnesses might affect my job.

Allison, now in the fifth grade, repeatedly asked for explanations.

"Mom, I just don't understand. You told us that Ashley would be our new sister, and now that's not true anymore. Why can't she come over and be with us? What happened?"

"Allison, sometimes we don't have control over other people, or what they think and do. Right now, Ashley's mother is the parent who makes all the decisions. We'll talk more about it when you get a little older. I understand your disappointment, because I feel the same way. I will think about her always, and hope that someday she will realize how much she's missed."

Allison looked away, obviously not able to accept my explanation. She couldn't make sense of it all. Truthfully, neither could I.

* * *

# Chapter 17

## *A Blended Family*

**June, 1984**

AT TIMES SADNESS blanketed my days. I had tried so hard to build this new family, and again what I had built was destroyed. But as the months passed I slowly began the process of acceptance. Looking through my desk drawer one day, I found a copy of Mother Theresa's Anyway Prayer that I had saved. It was a prayer of encouragement, and just what I needed to help me see the light at the end of the dark tunnel. Three of the paragraphs in the prayer enabled me to go on and appreciate what I had:

*What you spend years building,*
*Someone could destroy overnight:*
*Build anyway.*

*The good you do today,*
*People will often forget tomorrow.*
*Do good anyway.*

*Give the world the best that you have,*
*And it may never be enough.*
*Give the world the best you have anyway.*


Eventually I reached another plateau of my personal growth. I became strong again and relied on what I had learned from my past. I concentrated on what I had, and not what I had lost. I could do it, I knew I could. I could support Ray in this upheaval, and Ashley would remain forever in our hearts and thoughts. If she ever needed us, the door to reconnect would remain open forever.


## July, 1984


Another traumatic call from Sarah, with a quivering voice.

"Ray, I'm calling to talk to you about our son. Danny's been having a really tough time during the past few months acting out at home. His behavior at times has been totally out of control, to the point where I feel I can no longer parent him. I think maybe he needs you now and would do better living with you, rather than me. Are you willing to resume custody of him?"

Ray responded instantly.

"Yes, I will. When do you want me to come and get him?"

I wasn't prepared for this. It had happened so suddenly, and now I faced many new concerns. The weekends I had spent with Danny had been pleasurable because during the time we spent together, I had tried to be his friend, not his disciplinarian. But now our relationship would be different. With this change in custody, I would become a person who, along with Ray, would be responsible for his conduct, his grades, his choice of friends, and his family life. While a part of me yearned to welcome this young man into my home, another part of me gripped with hesitation.


## August, 1984


We rearranged the house in preparation for Danny's arrival. We converted the basement into a fourth bedroom where Danny could enjoy his own space. A few days after his arrival, I tried developing a warm relationship with him by asking him leading questions. But again, as in the past, he answered each time with only one word responses.

"Danny, is there anything else you would like to decorate your new room?"

"No."

"Did you enjoy your first day at your new school?"

"Yes."

"Do you have a favorite subject or teacher that you enjoy?"

"No."

Despite my efforts, he remained detached and unable to share his feelings. I tried to imagine the thoughts in his mind. He had recently learned that his sister had a different father. His mother chose to relinquish custody. He just returned to the house where he had spent his early years with his parents and sister. But now his two new stepsisters lived in it, along with the woman who had recently married his dad. I knew we would all need counseling and advice.

At the end of the first week as a blended family, an incident occurred. Allison and Rebecca found an old pinball machine that had belonged to Danny stuffed away in a closet. They took out the game and started to play. When Danny came into the room and saw the girls using it he became angry and upset. He ran up the stairs, looking for Ray and shouting,

"Dad, they can't have my things - this house is mine! Don't you remember that I lived here long before they did?"

I realized the long road ahead would not be easy.

## September, 1984

September arrived, time for school to resume. I looked forward to having the girls settled back into their routines, and Danny attending the local Catholic high school. I planned on resuming my job as a special education teacher. But when I arrived at my school to begin the new year, the principal called me into his office to advise me of a change in my assignment.

"Welcome back, Hope. I wanted to speak to you about a new program that has been initiated, and I've decided that you will be the teacher implementing it. The title of this position is Crisis Intervention Teacher. Your role will be to deal with any out-of-control students from the three existing classes for the emotionally disturbed. This might involve removing them from class, intervening in fights, using skills to calm them down, or providing a quiet tutoring environment separated from other children. I have confidence in you, and I know you could do this. If you have any questions or need assistance, please come to me at any time."

It took me a few minutes to process this. Adjustments at home, and now a dramatic change at work. I wondered if I could really face dealing with children constantly in crisis. Would this have a devastating impact on me both at work and in my personal life? While happy to still be employed, I knew that I would not have chosen this assignment.

"Ok, I'll do it. What classroom should I move my teaching supplies into?"

"Room 203, across from the students you will be working with. Good luck."

With so many changes at once, I sought the resources to survive. With Ray's position on the Town Council demanding so much of his time late into evening hours, he was rarely available when his son and our new blended family needed him. He considered resigning, but decided that with perseverance he could still be the father and husband he wanted to be, and succeed in his other ambitions as well.

After the first month of school, we all began to adjust. Danny did well in academics and soon I recognized him as a brilliant young man, with potential for great success. He possessed an uncanny love of nature which led him to boating, fishing, and exploring the wilderness trails of New Jersey. Ray often joined him in these activities, and with the time spent together, their relationship flourished.

Rebecca, now a fourth grader, joined the elementary school orchestra and chose to play the clarinet, the same instrument I had played in high school. When she arrived home from her first practice session with her teacher, she proudly showed me her clarinet.

"Mommy, look at what I learned to do."

She opened the clarinet case and took out four separate parts of the instrument. Next to it she laid a mouthpiece and reed.

"See, this is how you do it. First you put the four pieces together, then you put the reed on the mouthpiece. And last, you put the mouthpiece on the top. Now watch how I could play."

While Rebecca demonstrated her newfound skill, I sat in awe. Then suddenly I had an unforeseen reaction.

"Wait a minute, Rebecca. There's something I want to do."

I ran upstairs and climbed the ladder to the attic, searching for the forgotten clarinet that I had saved from long ago. Rebecca and I now had a new interest to share, as we created music and practiced duets together for hours after school. As the tones of the clarinets synchronized, it seemed that our two spirits bonded into one. Months later, our efforts would culminate in an amazing mother and daughter duet on the stage at the annual Spring Concert in Rebecca's school.

Allison, now a sixth grader, began to grow in independence. She loved her teachers, became fascinated with reading, and excelled in drawing and art. Her zest for life had been restored. She now willingly accepted Danny as a part of our family. I often observed her staring at him with admiration and wonder, craving his attention and approval. Seeing the children's positive experiences, I became excited about the potential success of our two families becoming one after all. At dinner one evening, I came up with an idea, and made an announcement.

"I just figured out what we have become. We have a new identity, a reincarnation of the comedy TV series, The Brady Bunch. Although the parents had six children between them in the show and we only have three, we have become united, just as they did. What do you all think of my idea?"

Everyone laughed.

Allison said, "Yes, Mom, we're the Brady Bunch."

## November, 1984

While our family life improved, my job as Crisis Intervention Teacher had become exasperating. Dealing with children in crisis every day for six-and-a-half hours now seemed more than I could bear. Again, I stayed awake many nights reliving some incident that had occurred that day in my classroom. Sometimes thoughts of some innocent child's horrific living conditions permeated my mind. Other times I relived my fears of flying desks, calls to the police for help with students who exited the building and could not be found, and episodes of violence that placed both me and other individuals in danger.

I knew my career reached its turning point the day my co-worker, Barbara Peters, summoned me into her classroom for help. Mrs. Peters had tried to begin her third grade math lesson, but Joseph, another one of the foster children in our program, interrupted her efforts. He had isolated himself underneath the teacher's desk crying, and refused to come out. With some coaxing, I convinced him that if he came out from under the desk we could spend some quiet time alone together in my room across the hall.

Joseph eventually agreed, and we stopped by the fountain in the hallway for a sip of cool water. I carried his math assignment with me, hoping that he would complete his work in my therapeutic room, an environment free from noise, apprehension and overactive classmates. Alone with Joseph at last, I began my interaction by asking what had upset him. Not expecting an immediate response, I was shocked to hear his candid reply. Joseph gazed directly into my eyes.

"Mrs. Brooks, God was good to me today. Every day when I ride the bus to school, the bus driver passes the apartment where my Mommy lives. This morning I looked into her window and saw my Mommy for the first time in a very, very long time. Then when I got to school I kept thinking about how much I missed her, and I started to cry and couldn't do my work. After that I hid under the desk and Mrs. Peters got mad at me."

Shock. Disbelief. Within seconds, my stomach cramped with nausea and the room whirled around me. Gathering my strength, I looked at Joseph and saw the heartache in his expression. Suddenly the math assignment seemed unimportant. Just getting Joseph through the day would take precedence, so we talked for a while.

"Joseph, thank you for sharing your story with me. Talking about your feelings is a very grown up thing to do. Instead of doing work right now, would you like some paper and crayons to draw a picture that describes what happened to you on the school bus today?" Joseph nodded his head. He seemed calmer and began to cooperate.

Although I had managed to help Joseph through this critical situation, I left for home that day thinking about him, and so many of the other students that I could never reach. Their rage and frustration. Their lives without love. My lack of power to improve their situations. My life felt out of balance as I became drained of my needed energy. Doesn't society have any other resources to help these struggling young people? How much longer could I keep this job?

## July, 1985

It had now been a year since we had become our version of "The Brady Bunch". At times, Ray and I would observe Danny or the girls and warning signs would indicate difficult times in the days ahead. But we refused to acknowledge our fears and chose to believe that our problems were no different than those of any other family. It would be a while before we could see that denial is not a healthy path to resolutions.

We decided that we wanted to experience some memorable, exciting excursions with the children, so we planned a trip to Disneyland in California to have some fun and do some sightseeing. After an exhilarating two days at Disneyland, we proceeded on to Hollywood to take the historic tour through Universal Studios. We boarded a tram and began to ride through the sets of many well-known movies. We rode through sound stages, and observed photo shoots currently in progress on the lot. It was truly an occasion of warmth and togetherness.

On Rebecca's ninth birthday, we had a swim party at the YMCA, attended by classmates, cousins, and her half-sister Chloe. After the party, Chloe came home with us and began dancing and singing songs using our new handheld vocal microphone. Allison followed by making an oral presentation of a speech she had been rehearsing for a school play. With poise and grace, she read to us the Finest Hour Speech delivered by Winston Churchill to the House of Commons on June 18, 1940. Each day brought memories to cherish forever. The girls participated in the Brownies and stage performances at school. They became members of the school choir and sang at Sunday Mass, filling the Church with the richness of song and the voices of innocence.

Danny's world began to become impacted by music, but differently. He became an avid fan of the Grateful Dead, and another American rock band, Kiss. Soon Danny and two of his friends made a plan. They wrote a song with lyrics. With Danny as the lead singer, all three practiced their guitars to synchronize their beats and coordinate their movements. Within a month they were ready, and together headed down the New Jersey shore to compete in the popular Battle of the Bands.

During this year, Ray and the girls presented me with my most treasured birthday gift. A billboard at the mall invited shoppers to create a video of choice using available recording devices and instruments for special effects. They agreed on making a video for me and chose to perform to the song *Walk Like an Egyptian*. The girls strummed guitars and danced, while their images were transformed and enhanced with the use of computer generated imagery. Ray joined them by swinging his arms and gyrating his hips, attempting to re-enact the character of Egyptian art and the hilarious movements of Steve Martin in his famous Saturday Night comedy sketch called King Tut.

Today, years later, I cherish the memory of that moment, recorded forever with love.

✳✳✳

# Chapter 18

## *The Pain Within*

**September, 1985**

THE NEXT SCHOOL year began with exciting news. I received confirmation from the Board of Education that my application to return to teaching in the regular classroom had been processed and confirmed. I would return to teaching second grade, my favorite grade level, in a more relaxing, rewarding atmosphere.

Focused on my job, I did not yet understand that as our children grew older, the confusion they carried over their parents' divorces would begin to overshadow their thoughts, actions, and human relationships. Hiding their emotions, each of them struggled with their inner pain and sought relief in different ways. Before the road to healing could begin, their feelings of fear, anger, loneliness and abandonment needed to be addressed. For them, finding that road was destined to be a long and arduous task.

Danny was the first whose behavior symbolized a cry for help. He had become popular with his peers. After school hours, they loved to hang out at our house with Danny in his spacious basement bedroom.

They did not openly socialize with me or Ray, but I accepted this as part of the teenage rejection of adults and supervision. They were more than welcome in our home. One night after the visitors left, Ray went down to Danny's room for some father and son time together. Ray immediately became suspicious when the odor of alcohol prevailed, and Danny seemed bleary-eyed and tired.

"Son, what's going on here? Have you and your friends been drinking in our home? Are you high? You're not old enough to legally drink. To bring alcohol into our home and party with your friends is an insult to me, and puts me in a questionable place with the law. Tell me the truth. What's going on?"

"Dad I swear - we didn't do anything! I haven't been drinking. It's the truth!"

Not easily convinced, Ray raised his voice, and soon their conversation escalated into an argument. Acting on his suspicions, Ray searched the basement but failed to find the proof that the boys had been drinking. But for us, a parental alert had been issued. Without a doubt, serious issues loomed.

Living with Danny became more challenging as the weeks progressed. We endured sleepless nights when he stayed out until 2:00 or 3:00 a.m., and we had no idea where he had been. Ray would pace by the door, glaring at the clock, waiting for his son's safe arrival home. We confronted Danny and set a curfew of 11:00 p.m., but our words went unheeded as our concerns skyrocketed

"Ray, we are powerless," I said. "Our lives are turned upside down by Danny's actions. We need help and we don't know what to do. We need counseling, not only for him but for us as well. We must learn how to set limits and handle the situation. Should I make some phone calls to find someone who could help us?"

Ray agreed, and we anxiously looked forward to our first session with the counselor. But the session apparently had not been scheduled soon enough. Before our meeting took place, another disturbing phone call came that impacted us. Alcohol had been found in Danny's locker at school. The principal called Ray to advise him of this serious infraction of the Catholic school rules. As a consequence, Danny would be expelled.

"I feel bad for my son. I guess it's time for more adjustments. He's going to have to transfer into the public school system. What else could we do?"

"Nothing. We should begin counseling as we planned, and hope that this begins to address all of Danny's growing needs."

"It looks like we have a long road ahead."

## April, 1986

A new week began. I stood before my second grade class on a Monday morning, ready to begin a hands-on science experiment with my students. Within minutes, my world came crashing down on me again. An announcement came over the loud speaker system into my classroom. A voice spoke, "Mrs. Brooks, please report to the office for a phone call. Your daughter Rebecca's teacher, Mrs. Keenan, is calling with an emergency."

A co-worker agreed to supervise my class while I ran to the office. I picked up the receiver and could not believe the words. "I'm sorry to tell you this, but your daughter Rebecca is missing from school. The students were outside in the schoolyard after the lunch period ended. When they lined up to return to class, Rebecca and her classmate, Barbara, couldn't be found anywhere. We've notified the police. How quickly can you get here?"

"Mrs. Keenan, could you please check the bathroom to see if Rebecca is in the stall with some kind of problem? She's had a lot of stomach issues lately, and I'm sure that's where she is. I'd appreciate it if you would do this before I leave my school and drive back to New Jersey."

"No, you don't understand, Mrs. Brooks. We have searched everywhere. Rebecca is missing."

My heart thumped in my chest as I grabbed my purse and headed out the door. In my car, I hesitated before driving. I stopped to ponder if this was really happening, or was it just a dream. I had always obeyed the speed limits, but not today. I pressed down on the accelerator and drove at 110 miles per hour. I didn't care. I had to find my baby. Where could she be? Had she been kidnapped? Did she run away somewhere with Barbara? Would I ever see her again? The agonizing thoughts continued non-stop. I drove straight through stop signs and red lights, barely even noticing them. Finally, I could see Rebecca's school in the distance, with police cars and flashing lights lined up before the entrance.

I pulled up behind them and exited the car. An officer approached me and questioned my identity. He then led me to the back seat of a nearby police car. There sat Rebecca, crying and disheveled, her head buried in her lap. Bloody scratches, dirt and bruises covered her legs. I asked her what had happened, but she continued to sit quietly, refusing to answer.

The police officer summoned me to approach him.

"I just want you to know what happened, Mrs. Brooks. Rebecca and Barbara ran off together into the wooded area behind the school, after the lunch hour. A patrolling officer found them about a mile off the road, hiding from sight in a small, abandoned cabin."

"Thank you for letting me know," I responded.

I returned to the police car and cradled Rebecca in my arms, then I brought her home, where Ray anxiously waited for us. I filled the bath tub with warm, soothing water and placed her in it to wash away the dirt and heal her wounds. Feeling calmer at home, and believing that I would love her no matter what she had done, my daughter opened her heart to me at last.

"Mommy, you don't know what happened last weekend when Allison and I visited Daddy and Ariana and Chloe. Daddy and Ariana argued and yelled at each other. Ariana told Daddy that she didn't want me and Allison coming to visit them. We're just too much trouble. So she grabbed Chloe's arm and pulled her away into their car and they left. Chloe cried because she loves me and Allison and wanted to play with us, but Ariana wouldn't let her stay. Mommy, I don't want to go there anymore. Could I please, please always stay home with you and Ray? I really, really, don't ever want to visit them again. You and Ray are my real family and this is where I belong."

Another one of my children in anguish. Many questions came into my mind. How can I have control over anything that happens at Drew's house? Should I confront him about this incident? I couldn't change things when I was married to him, so how could I change things now? Should I allow my daughters to continue visiting their father in that environment? Should I involve Allison in this and ask her how she feels? I needed time and a lot more advice.

When the children went to bed, I collapsed on the living room recliner, alone in my thoughts. *This just isn't fair,* my spirit raged. *I've worked so hard at so many things, are there no rewards? Why must I see my child suffer like this?* Tears streamed down my cheeks, while I cried myself to sleep. I began to think about my mother with sadness, and spoke to her across the miles to Dallas.

*Mom, why did you abandon me and move so far away? I need you now, but you are not here to walk with me through the trials of my life.*

While I slept, my dreams took me back to the memories of those tree-lined streets of Brooklyn, my childhood, and the way that families were meant to be.

## May 10, 1986

Spring had arrived. I drove to work feeling confident and elated, with my mood soaring. The trees had blossomed and the birds had returned from their winter getaways. With the sun casting its rays on my mind, I enjoyed the return of life, and somehow managed to become accepting of my continuing home situation. I looked forward to the approaching summer with time to relax and enjoy days with Ray and the children, free from the stresses of homework, school and the issues of our former spouses.

I usually spent the hour of my morning commute listening to the radio news broadcast. That morning I heard a moving story about a family from Staten Island. A fire had erupted during the pre-dawn hours in the home of a family with seven young children. The family had been trapped inside their burning building, but the father had been able to extend a rope from the second floor of the building down to the ground. He located six of his children and helped them climb down the rope. Despite his heroic efforts, the seventh child could not be located. The boy perished along with the home that they lived in. How sad, I thought. I wondered if that family lived anywhere close to my school.

Once at school, my supervisor, Mr. Magliano, stood in the hallway awaiting my arrival. When he saw me, he lifted his arm and motioned me into his office. "Sit down, Hope," he said, with a serious intonation to his voice. I thought for sure he had received some kind of parental complaint against me.

"I don't know if you heard the news this morning, but one of your students, James Parker, died in a fire today that destroyed his home. I wanted you to be the first to know. Perhaps at some point you could address this tragedy with your class."

Dazed for the moment, I displayed no reaction. I pictured James in my mind, a beautiful, quiet, respectful little boy, loved and admired by all who knew him. I thought about his family and his twin brother, a student in my co-worker's class. How could this have happened? Although the bell rang for class to begin, I could not rise from the chair.

Mr. Magliano asked me if I would like some water or coffee. I shook my head and eventually walked slowly down the hallway to my classroom. I sat at my desk and waited for the students to enter the room.

The children came in smiling and happy. None of them knew about their classmate's tragedy. We began the day with our usual schedule of salute to the flag, morning work, and checking homework. I hadn't thought it through yet - I did not have a plan about telling them. The morning proceeded on with one subject after another and the hours passed. As they did their work and interacted, it seemed as if their presence became only shadows in the spacious room. My eyes fixated on James' empty desk, and I realized that I would never see that little boy again.

I decided that the best plan would be to address the issue during the ending period of the day. At 2:00 p.m. I instructed the children to move their chairs and form a round circle in the center of the room, facing each other. I asked them to extend their arms and join together by holding hands, because I had some very serious news to tell them. Reading my expression, the children looked at me, motionless and silent. I proceeded to inform them about the fire, and what had happened to James. Some of them sobbed, some of them cried, and others sat quietly. Then the little hands that had formed the circle of love gripped each other more tightly. I led the children in prayer for James and his family, and then a miracle happened. The voices of the children around the circle cried out, and each of them prayed aloud with voices of innocence, for James to rest in heaven and his family to recover.

The little hands gripped tighter and tighter, and they held on to each other for what seemed forever. A period of silence reigned throughout the room, as we all became lost in our thoughts. Then one of the girls raised her hand and asked, "Mrs. Brooks, may I please have something of James' to remember him by?"

"Yes, you may," I replied. And within minutes, each of the children extended a hand for an eraser, a pencil, a sticker, or a paper that had belonged to James. The children hugged each other goodbye as they exited the room with their treasures in hand.

As I drove home that afternoon, my mind questioned why this had happened. I understood it now. Maybe that's what being a teacher is really all about. Simply helping others through the difficult times is our destiny, not focusing on math or reading scores. Thankfully, I had survived a very difficult day in my professional life, a day that will remain with me always.

*** * ***

# Chapter 19

## *The Continuing Legal Battles*

**November, 1986**

OUR FAMILY LIFE settled down once again. Danny made friends in his new co-educational high school and had many attractive girls chasing him with their persistent phone calls. He enjoyed his newfound popularity as his ego soared. Ray lost interest in working nonstop for the Township Council and launched his new role as a weekend windsurfer. He met some other adventurers from our neighborhood who also loved the sport. If he woke up on a Saturday or Sunday morning and the forecast predicted wind, he went out the door and headed down the shore.

The goal we set for our children was stability. Most importantly, we wanted them to have safe and regular visits with their non-custodial parents. Danny needed to continue counseling and address the feelings that had led him to find solace in alcohol. Also, we had recently learned that Allison and Rebecca would be facing a major new adjustment. Drew and Ariana had filed for divorce. Drew would now be living alone and the girls expressed fear that with Ariana and Chloe moving away, they may never see their little sister again.

As the school year progressed, I realized that it had been ten years since Drew and I had separated. Allison, now an eighth grader, would graduate from elementary school in June. In a few months I had to decide if she would attend public or Catholic high school. Also, we had no legal agreement in place for the expenses of college which loomed ahead in the not too distant future. I contacted Drew to ask if he would share the tuition cost of private high school or pay an increase in child support. He responded angrily and refused to discuss it.

Although I felt compassion for his situation with two failed marriages and three children to support, I only wanted to provide my children with the best possible opportunities. If he would not cooperate now, I had no alternative. I would take him to court and let a judge decide.

Then Ray had an idea. "Why should we pay someone else to represent you in court when I'm an attorney? I could represent you myself, and that would save us thousands of dollars in attorney's fees. I'll contact Drew and try to work out a settlement." That sounded like a great idea and I agreed with the plan. But little did I know that in the interest of my children, it was one of the worst decisions that I would ever make.

Drew would never agree to anything. He hired his own attorney and our case headed to court. Finally my day before the judge arrived. Before entering the court room, I stood in the hallway, traumatized. I had been unable to eat or drink anything that morning. Conflicting emotions tore me apart. Shortly I would be appearing against the man I had once loved, but today he was my enemy. When I returned and entered the court room, I saw Drew standing inside with his attorney, waiting for the court process to begin. His six foot eight commanding presence reminded me of the power he had over me in the past, and I firmly grasped Ray's hand for courage and support.

Drew's attorney, Mr. Swazey, began by addressing the judge.

"Your Honor, I object to Mr. Brooks representing his wife. It is not a proper procedure to allow a husband to represent his spouse. I ask that he be removed from the case."

The judge responded without hesitation.

"I have represented my own wife in legal matters that have arisen over the years. I will allow Mr. Brooks to maintain his role as the attorney representing Hope Brooks."

The issue of increased child support arose. Mr. Swazey began by objecting to any increase in Drew's child support payments.

"My client cannot afford to pay any more money in child support because he currently pays $1,000 per month for the support of the child from his second marriage. To ask him to pay any more for his first two children would be an injustice."

The judge responded angrily.

"Why would you think that the value of his third child is greater than the value of his first two children? If your client currently pays $1,000 per month for one child, he should pay the same for his other children. He is hereby ordered to pay the requested increase."

The third issue addressed tuition for private high school and college.

"Your Honor, why should my client be forced to pay tuition for private Catholic schools when the girls could attend the highly rated public school system in their town?"

The judge responded by addressing Drew directly.

"Sir, did you attend Catholic high school when you grew up?"

"Yes."

"Then I believe that your children have the right to the same kind of advantage in education as you did. You will therefore be responsible for 60% of all their tuition incurred for both Catholic high school and the college years ahead."

Thus ended my session in court. I left with a great feeling of relief and satisfaction, seeing myself as a great mom who had achieved something wonderful for her children. But it didn't take long before reality struck.

The girls spent the next weekend after the court appearance with Drew. He arrived at our doorstep and had no greeting for his daughters as they exited the house, and drove away together. On Sunday afternoon the girls returned home. Rebecca came in and waved hello, while Allison ran to her room, avoiding all eye contact and closing the door behind her. I sensed something serious, so I followed her into the room and sat down next to her on the bed.

"How was your weekend?"

"Terrible."

"What happened, Allison, why?"

"It's all your fault and Ray's fault. Dad told us all about it. He told us how Ray went to court with you to take away Dad's money. Now you and Ray get most of the money he earns, and this makes my father poor. He can't take care of himself or the place that he lives in. Dad showed us the giant crack in the kitchen floor, but he can't afford to replace the tile. He showed us the kitchen cabinet that's falling off the wall, but he can't hire anyone to fix it. Why did you do this? Now my dad hates you both, but especially Ray. Everyone is fighting, and my life is ruined!"

Allison threw herself on the bed and buried her head under the pillow. I guessed there would be no explaining or talking to her that night.

Ray had a plan of action.

"Allison is a bright young lady. Let's make a chart that shows all the expenses we pay for her and her sister. If she realizes how much things cost, she may understand why we went to court and how the child support laws work."

So the following evening we sat down with Allison in the living room and hung up our chart. Ray presented the information as she sat quietly and listened for the duration. When he concluded, it became obvious that the plan had been doomed to failure. Allison had been brainwashed by her dad that Ray and I were the evil ones, and she closed her mind to any new ideas. Without saying a word, she rose from the couch and went back into her room, rejecting us. I could do nothing to relieve the sadness of my child. Now it was Allison who had been shattered by the two parents that she loved.

"Ray, our idea didn't work at all. I guess we can't control her thoughts or what she chooses to believe."

"We tried. I predict that with time, she will grow in wisdom, but that can only come from within herself."

## December 1986

The holiday season approached once again. Displays of Christmas trees and Hanukkah menorahs illuminated the streets of our town. It was meant to be the time of year for love and happy family gatherings, a time for gift giving and sharing treasured moments. Joyous music and songs could be heard everywhere. As I walked through the mall listening to the gentle lyrics of the song *Home for the Holidays,* my thoughts turned to Allison. Her spirit remained torn and she struggled with so many feelings. I only hoped that in time she would overcome her latest trauma and understand why I took her dad to court. Although I realized this would be a difficult holiday, I remained determined that nothing would stop me from enjoying Christmas with Ray and the children that I cherished.

As I continued walking my thoughts moved to Drew. Would he continue to upset our daughter and involve her in our differences over finances? Didn't he realize that his words and behavior damaged not only our child but her family life as well? I feared my future dealings with him.

The next day, I had the answers to all of my questions. Drew called to make arrangements for his next visit with the girls. When Ray answered the phone, the words, "Fuck you, Ray Brooks!" greeted him. Why did Drew never want to take responsibility for the children he brought into the world? His rage would continue and impact our lives for the next fifteen years.

***

# Chapter 20

## *A New Perspective*

**March, 1987**

A QUIET MOMENT alone, sitting on my front porch, reflecting on the events that had led me to this day. I had survived my marriage to Drew and the years as a single parent. Ray and I had supported each other through our divorces, Church annulments, the loss of Ashley, and the impact of these events on our other three children. Our four years of marriage had certainly been disconcerting, but they brought with them an amazing awareness. For the first time ever, I experienced love and fidelity. I had married a man who gave his time and energy to me and my children with patience, hope, and a sense of humor that could not be surpassed. Looking ahead to our promising future, my passion for him blossomed. I believed that together, our souls blending into one, we could endure anything.

My teaching job continued to be enjoyable. Still working with second graders, I had mastered the curriculum and presented each day's lessons with little or no preparation. I now worked with a group of teachers whom I considered friends more than co-workers. Each day we arrived at work early, brewed the morning coffee, and shared stories about our marriages, families, and worries.

Danny remained our biggest concern. He would graduate from high school in only three months, and we looked forward to the day when he would receive his diploma. Despite his potential, good grades were not his priority. He often appeared groggy, with increased apathy toward the things that had previously engaged him. He had no plans for college, and we just hoped that he would pass all the required subjects. We persevered in family counseling, but changed therapists three times. We never trusted that any of them addressed the underlying problems correctly.

Then came the morning when Danny refused to get out of bed or go to school. Ray tried to wake up his son and get him into the shower. But this morning, nothing worked.

"Danny, please wake up now. If you don't get up now, you're going to be late for your first class."

No response. No movement. Ray raised his voice and tried again.

"Danny, please wake up! You're getting me very upset. Do you want to miss school?"

No response. I walked into the bedroom to ask Ray if I could help. Then we both heard the sound of snoring coming from Danny's bed, and realized that there was no hope of awakening him.

"Is he unconscious, Ray?"

"I'm not sure, but I smell alcohol again. He must have gone to bed intoxicated after hanging out with his friends last night. I think we should let him sleep it off and deal with this later."

I agreed. The girls left for school, and Ray and I for work. It would be another worrisome commute thinking about Danny. If he couldn't function as a student in school, how would he ever be able to keep a job? He had lived with us for almost three years, yet still never revealed his thoughts or feelings. I wondered what went through his mind. Did he miss living with his mother and Ashley? Had he never really accepted me and the girls as another family? Did he just choose to be popular with his peers who chose partying, alcohol and drugs? I remembered how the support groups I attended after Drew left me had led me to healing. There had to be a better way for Danny.

Danny slept until the early hours of afternoon. When Ray came home from work that evening, he confronted him about the day he had chosen to spend in bed.

"Danny, do you want to tell us the reason for your refusal to get up today? Do you want to discuss your drinking?"

"No, I don't."

"It's starting to disrupt your life. Do you think you have an addiction to alcohol?"

"I don't want to talk about it. Leave me alone, Dad."

"Have you turned to drugs?"

"Stop harassing me, Dad."

"This is getting serious. I want you to consider going into a rehab. I can't do anything more to help you. Now it's time for you to choose to help yourself."

The next morning came, and the next, and the next. Danny chose to drop out of school, and we could do nothing to change his mind. The high school graduation we had envisioned would never happen. With this final loss of ambition, Danny remained home with no goal, no dream, and no future.

We both felt frustrated and inadequate as parents. The climax came for us on the night when I looked into our driveway at 10:00 p.m. and noticed that my car was missing. Fear gripped me. Stay calm, I told myself. It must have been stolen. I tried to maintain my composure. Failing at this attempt, I frantically ran upstairs, calling out to Ray.

"Ray, where's my car? Help me, I need you!"

Ray heard the panic in my voice and rushed to meet me at the top of the staircase.

"Are you sure it's gone?"

"Yes, what should we do?"

"Ok, we'll call the police. But first let's check on the children to ensure that an intruder hasn't entered our home." The girls were safely asleep in their rooms, but we couldn't find Danny. We looked everywhere, including the attic and the garage, but he had left the house and disappeared.

I reached for the phone to call about my missing car, but before I dialed 911, we heard the sirens of a police car pulling into our driveway. Quickly running outside, we observed a police officer helping Danny out of the rear seat of his vehicle.

"Are you the parents of this young man?"

"Yes we are," we both replied.

"He's gotten himself into a lot of trouble tonight. We found your son's friend driving a Chevrolet Chevette in circles around the grounds of the local elementary school, with your son as a passenger. The driver caused damage both to the car and to the school's playground. We checked the license plate and realized that Hope Brooks, at this address, is the owner. Please take charge of your son, and come down to the police station tomorrow to advise us if you will be bringing theft charges against either or both of the two boys. The Chevette is locked and still on the school grounds. Here are your keys. Good luck."

We thanked the officer and he drove away. My anger flared as I confronted Danny.

"You took my car? You found my keys and let your friend drive away with it? Why? Why? Why do you keep hurting the people who love and care about you?" I lost control as I lunged at Danny. Ray intervened and managed to prevent a physical altercation by grabbing my shoulders and holding me in place. Then I heard him scream uncontrollably, at a level I had never heard before.

"I've had enough, Danny. This is the end of it! You'll never again bring harm or disrespect to anyone in this family. Never. Get to your room. We'll deal with your consequences in the morning. Do you have anything to say for yourself?"

Danny held his head down with remorse. Exhausted, we all went to bed and knew what tomorrow would bring.


**April, 1987**


Not able to help Danny, Ray and I had to help ourselves. We gave up our counselor and decided to try a program called Tough Love.

Through this program, we hoped to gain insight and skills that would help us deal with our out of control teenager. We nervously entered the room of our first Tough Love meeting, led by a moderator. The audience was filled with other parents who had similar problems with their teenagers. Everyone there focused their eyes intensely on the speaker.

"Welcome to all the new members. We know you're here tonight because you seek help in dealing with your home situations. Briefly, the theme of our program educates parents on how to change their behaviors, in order to effect positive change in their teenagers. If you are permissive and understanding with your out of control youth, most likely you are simply allowing him to continue his unacceptable behavior. Here we encourage you to set boundaries and limits for your children, and to live by them. Tough Love thrives on families helping families, using this new perspective to address what is intolerable."

After Ray and I attended several meetings, the parent group devised a plan of action for us.

"Advise your son that he either must attend school full time or begin a full-time job. Give him a time period of one month. If he's not doing either of these things within thirty days, instruct him to pack his belongings and move out of your home. The best thing he can learn through this approach is the meaning of responsibility. Words cannot teach him that, only consequences."

After the meeting, we got into the car, each of us wondering if we could actually implement such a plan.

"Danny has been through so much. We know he needs more help and direction. But would throwing him out of our home into the street with no job and no money really be something we could do?"

"I can't commit to this right now, Ray. In a way it sounds so cruel, but everything else we've tried has failed. Maybe it's really the right thing to do."

Within a few days, we made the decision to implement the plan. But circumstances at home became more difficult than ever. The stress mounted each day as we monitored Danny's progress toward his chosen goal. Would he choose completing high school or finding a job? Or would he do nothing?

Day five came with no action taken. On day ten we overheard Danny making phone calls to inquire about jobs. Our spirits rose. On day fifteen, Ray and I left for work with Danny still in bed. Being a parent had been my life's dream, and being a stepparent had been my plan to extend my family. But this job turned out to be more difficult than I ever imagined. Ray and I needed help to survive the thirty days. Tough Love recommended another program for us. The program, Families Anonymous, further extended our entrance into the new world of thought, ideas, and ways of living. Like Alcoholics Anonymous, it was based on a twelve-step program. Hearing Step 1 of the program read aloud at our first meeting immediately brought me some insight. It reminded me that we are powerless over other people's lives, and have no control over their decision to remain addicted to alcohol and drugs.

When the meeting ended, one of the regular attendees handed me a card with the words Serenity Prayer written on it. I read the prayer, and its message touched me so deeply that I hung it on my kitchen wall and recited it often throughout my day.

*God, grant me the serenity to accept the things*
*I cannot change, the courage to change the things that*
*I can, and the wisdom to know the difference.*

I knew that our plan for Danny would be the only path of hope.


## May 1, 1987

Day number twenty-nine arrived. Nothing had changed, and Ray knew what he must do. He looked at me, revealing his heartache.

"I don't want to do this, but there's no turning back."

"We must have faith that things will work out for him."

He knocked on the door of Danny's room, hand shaking, to begin the final conversation with his son.

"Danny, I know we talked about this over and over again, so I know there's nothing else to say. I want you to understand this is a very difficult thing for me to do, but you know that tomorrow morning you must pack all of your belongings and move on. You have my love and my blessings, but from this moment forward the rest of your life is up to you."

Danny nodded his head in response, eyes downcast. He said nothing, and quietly closed his door.

***

# Chapter 21

## *Joys and Sorrows*

**Fall of 1987**

IT HAD BEEN five months since the dramatic moment when Danny left. He kept regular contact with us during this time, and the updates sounded encouraging. He had moved to a town on the Jersey shore and rented an apartment. He got a job in a restaurant as a dishwasher, then upgraded to a cook. He worked many hours, long into the evening. It appeared that Danny had taken his first steps toward independence and responsibility. We took pride in his progress, and even more so when we learned that he had arranged for an AA sponsor, and had chosen to actively participate in his local AA program.

Ray breathed a sigh of relief. "Danny's tumultuous teen years seem to have passed. Hopefully things will be easier now."

"Our new household with only two children living home does seem more tranquil and promising."

"I hope it lasts!" said Ray happily, but with a slight sound of doubtfulness in his voice.

Having won my court battle against Drew, Allison started high school in a secluded, Catholic academy for girls. Located on a scenic campus, the academy held a high rating in preparing students for college, promising them success in being accepted into the college of their choice upon graduation. Academically, Allison thrived. She admired her teachers and loved learning, especially in the freshman class science laboratory. In the science lab, Allison had been given the assignment of incubating chicken eggs with artificial heat, monitoring them as they developed, and seeing them through to hatching. One day the teacher invited all the families into the lab to view the progress of their children's projects. We observed six eggs growing in Allison's incubator, and we wondered how many of them would survive. At the end of twenty-one days, only one of them hatched. Ray, Rebecca, and I made another visit to the lab to meet the baby chick. He was the cutest thing ever! Allison named him Clyde, and we all fell in love with him. What an exciting experience this had been, witnessing the creation of new and unusual life. We held a discussion about Clyde's fate. Where would he live? Should we find a farm in New Jersey where we could bring him? Ray and I had ideas, but Allison would not listen. She was adamant and determined to put her own plan into action.

"Please, please let me bring Clyde home. I promise I'll take care of him. He won't be any trouble. He could live in the garage and roam around outside in our yard. Please, please, I'm begging you!"

She managed to convince us. We carried the chick home and placed him in a cardboard box in the garage. Since our house and yard faced an area of land designated as a nature preserve, we often observed deer, wild turkeys, and raccoons wandering through our property. With this in mind, we feared leaving Clyde outside alone to become prey to wild animals. To address this, we implemented a plan and took turns watching him. Surprisingly, he never strayed or even left the yard. Of course, the afternoon came when no one remembered we had let Clyde out of the garage.

"Mom, did somebody let Clyde outside after school today?" Rebecca asked.

"Now that you mention it Rebecca, I don't really remember. It's been such a hectic day, I think we completely forgot about him. Let's go check on him now."

All three of us walked together down through the basement door into the garage and yard. Roaming through the grass, Allison found the evidence of disaster. A cluster of chicken feathers, blowing across the lawn. She grabbed the feathers, holding them tightly in her hands.

"I don't believe this," she cried, her eyes searching in all directions. "Where is he?"

"He's gone," yelled Rebecca. "I bet it was that big raccoon that carried him away and ate him for dinner!"

A moment of silence, then tears. We never saw Clyde again.

## Winter of 1988

During the first few months of seventh grade, Rebecca continued with her clarinet lessons. But her focus on the clarinet diminished as the music teacher in her school captured her interest with song. The teacher organized a choir, and introduced her singers to the Church parishioners for the first time at Sunday Mass.

Attending the Mass, I learned something about my daughter Rebecca. She had been chosen by the teacher to sing a solo on the altar, and the audience sat hypnotized as the sound of her voice echoed through the aisles. She had been endowed with a talent that she chose to surprise us with that day. Sometimes if I close my eyes, I can relive that moment, and hear the words of the song *Wind Beneath My Wings*, echoing in my ears, as if it were yesterday. My soul rejoiced with jubilation and pride.

At last, thankfully, a respite from stress and a time to treasure.

## Spring of 1988

The year had progressed, mostly without incident, but by spring I became aware of approaching issues with both of the girls. Although Allison loved her teachers in high school, she felt socially rejected by the other girls in the freshman class. Each day she experienced sadness and depression, and finally asked if she could transfer to another school. Shocked, I just didn't get it.

"Allison, I don't understand. Your grades at the Academy are good and you've learned so much. If you want more of a social life, why don't you just participate in some after school activities that the school offers?"

"No, that wouldn't help me, and I don't want to be around those girls more than I have to. They don't like me and sometimes they call me names, like prude or weird. I just don't fit in, Mom. I hate it there!"

What disturbing news to hear that after paying such high tuition, my daughter had to endure being harassed and verbally bullied. What is the world coming to? Is there nowhere that a young person in this society could be safe? Although I made no decisions to transfer her to another school at that time, I realized I had to deal with this before sophomore year began.

While putting aside my worries about Allison, Rebecca suddenly demanded all of my attention with a series of incidents. First came the day when I picked her up from her friend Karen's house. I rang the doorbell and Rebecca answered. I took one look at her. Almost unrecognizable, she stood behind the door with her long, straight nose bent sideways, and I knew instantly that it had been broken.

"Rebecca, what happened? Why didn't you call me?"

"Sorry, mom. Didn't want to worry you, but Karen accidentally bumped into me while we played at the park down the block. I put some ice on it for a while and it stopped bleeding."

"Where's Karen's mother? Did she know you got hurt?"

"She's upstairs in the shower, but Karen and I thought we could handle it on our own. Mom, are you mad at me?"

"No I'm not mad, but get in the car. We're going to the emergency room."

Nasal surgery followed, with days of school absences. After her recovery, Rebecca seemed changed. She had no energy or appetite. She slept a lot, and lost interest in everything. Her grades fell, and getting her to complete homework assignments became an endless battle. Finally, we received a bad report from her teacher at the end of the marking period. Rebecca had become inattentive and distracted, and the teacher was concerned. Although Rebecca had no fever, I began to suspect an illness. We consulted the pediatrician who ordered blood work. Our suspicions were correct. Rebecca had contracted Legionnaire's disease, and the doctor admitted her for another hospital stay.

We quickly learned about Legionnaires' disease, a severe form of pneumonia accompanied by lung inflammation, caused by the infection of a bacterium known as legionella. Untreated, it could be fatal. Rebecca had become so ill she could no longer eat. The doctor immediately placed her on intravenous antibiotics. Ray and I would visit and sit by her bedside day after day. As the weeks passed and she became weaker and thinner, we realized she battled for her life. *She just has to get better,* I thought. Nothing else mattered to me. How could I ever face life without my beautiful child? Having no other resources to help me, I prayed.

*God, I ask for your kindness and mercy. May Rebecca survive, and I promise to be grateful for your gift of her life all my remaining days on this earth.*

After two weeks and a loss of twenty pounds, Rebecca at last opened her eyes.

"Hi guys, how long have I been here?"

I said nothing but ran to her, and we hugged and caressed each other. I wanted to hope, but feared disappointment. Then Ray patiently handled the situation.

"Hi, Rebecca, how are you feeling? Do you think you could sit up now and talk to us?"

She nodded.

Ray lifted her onto the pillow and raised the hospital bed.

"We've been worried about you. You've been sleeping for a long time and haven't been eating. Would you like me to ask the nurse to bring you some lunch?"

She nodded again. My spirits rose.

The nurse arrived with a luscious bowl of chicken soup and placed it on the bed tray within Rebecca's reach. Afraid that she lacked the strength to lift the spoon, I began feeding her while Ray caught her attention with entertaining stories of funny things that had happened to him when he was a boy. By the end of the day Rebecca began talking, and two days later she returned home. Together Ray and I had triumphed over our latest dilemma. Our daughter survived, and with endless gratitude, we were thankful for her recovery.

# Chapter 22

## *Rebellion*

**Fall of 1988**

THE GIRLS CONTINUED to have regular visits with their father. After Drew and I had settled our legal agreement, we rarely talked. When he picked up the girls, he remained parked in front of our house without coming to the door. A new problem arose as the girls began to protest giving up every other weekend with their friends to spend it with Drew. As teenagers, fun with their peers became more important to them than time spent with what they considered a boring, older man.

If given a choice, I would block many events of their teenage years from my mind, and deny that they had ever occurred. They were a time of turmoil, rebellion, and dangerous choices. After freshman year, Allison transferred from the Catholic high school for girls into a co-educational private school with less emphasis on academics. Here, for the first time, she bonded with other girls and enjoyed an active social life. Rebecca, now an eighth grader, also became popular in her social environment, and suddenly it seemed that our home had transformed from a quiet residence into a haven for teens. The biggest new problem confronting us was their attitude of arrogance. The girls seemed to think they knew everything, while Ray and I knew nothing. Endless arguments intruded into our daily routine.

It all started with confrontations over late night phone calls. Ray and I would fall asleep and advise the girls to shut off all lights by 10:00 p.m. with no more talking to friends. If we woke up at midnight or later, we always found one of them defying our rules, whispering in secret conversations. Then the next morning began like a nightmare, with the young people too tired to wake up for school.

Weeks passed and we had no control. What do parents do when their children adamantly disobey them? Ray had an idea. He made a trip to the electronics store and came back with some wiring, a lock and a key. He hooked up the wiring onto the phone line that entered the house through the laundry room. Then he managed to connect the lock and key onto the wiring, giving us the ability to disconnect all the phones in the house at night. We took the key and hid it in my jewelry box under a pile of some costume jewelry. We believed they would never find it there.

Our success continued for a few weeks, until we finally became aware that the girls had outsmarted us. They had vigorously searched the house while Ray and I were at work, made copies of the key, and then placed the original back into the jewelry box. With their new-found power, they renewed their late night conversations, continuing to implement their plans of deception.

Ray finally figured out what they had done. Being suspicious, he ventured downstairs one night at midnight and found Allison on the phone. A confrontation ensued.

"Allison, how dare you be so disrespectful and break the rules of this house. Get off that phone, and give me back the key! You're in big trouble, and you and your sister will have consequences for this."

Allison slammed down the receiver.

"I don't care! I'm tired of being told what to do. And guess what. I don't have to listen to you because you're not my *real* father."

Ray had expected an argument, but not words that penetrated him to the core. He came to me, upset. "Why did she say that? Does this mean that the family we have tried so hard to build is not a family at all? All our efforts have been for nothing?"

Ray's heartbreak became mine as well. I sought some logical explanation. "I don't know why she reacted as she did. But I do know one thing. We should remain positive, and not let some words recited in anger keep us from following that dream."

## Fall of 1989

Time passed quickly. Rebecca, now a high school freshman, preferred attending our town's public school rather than any of nearby private schools. Hesitant at first, not happy with the idea of having two children in two schools with different schedules, we finally agreed. It continued to be Ray's role to wake up the girls and drive them to school. Although we had regained control over the late night phone calls, that didn't seem to always help the morning situations. In her freshman year, Rebecca often refused to get out of bed, and now we relived with her a scenario similar to what we had faced with Danny. I tried to analyze the source of the problem. Didn't she care at all about school? Did her body really need twelve to fourteen hours of sleep just because she experienced hormonal changes? Was she just being oppositional? I had no answers to any of my questions.

## April, 1990

Now each school day began with arguments between Rebecca and Ray. First it was Allison who had rejected him, and now Rebecca had become the problem. Ray felt endless frustration. When the girls were young, they had thrived on his attention. But now they both either ignored him or treated him with disdain. Some days he couldn't face being home with them.

"I must have done something wrong. I'm not important to the girls anymore. I need to get away. Do you mind if I spend next weekend windsurfing again with the group that I met? I really need to do something enjoyable for myself that will relieve my stress."

"You deserve a break. I think we do nothing but work too hard anyway. It's fine with me."

Before the weekend, Ray bought a new surfboard, along with a wetsuit to deal with the cold ocean temperatures of April. When he arrived at the beach on Saturday, he interacted with the other surfers and thrived on developing friendships. Surfing on the waves with the wind and water became a therapeutic exercise for him, and he returned from the day's adventure with a smile and a story of how he had fearlessly conquered the ocean currents.

Later that night, I began thinking about the unacceptable behaviors of my daughters towards Ray. Maybe, I thought, Ray shouldn't be in the position of being their disciplinarian. As their natural parent, perhaps I should be the one in charge of teaching them responsibilities and getting them to school on time. So I made an appointment with my principal to discuss changing my work schedule. The principal agreed. He arranged for me to begin my school day later. I would make up the time by staying past dismissal, counting and monitoring students as they boarded the school buses after the last period of the day. Now I could be home every morning with my daughters, and Ray could be relieved.

With the start of the new plan, the first week went well with both girls. During the second week, Allison's school closed for Spring break, so I only needed to get Rebecca to class. Mornings with her continued to go well. On Thursday of that week, she ran right from the bed and into the shower, seeming to be in high spirits. She jumped out of the car, book bag in hand, and waved goodbye, throwing me a kiss. I watched her enter the main entrance of the school building and drove off for my day.

I could not believe what happened next, as another nightmare unfolded. Again, I heard the voice of the school secretary on the loud speaker in my classroom, advising me that I had an important call from Rebecca's high school. She would send someone to watch my class while I took the call. My thoughts returned to the year 1986 when I had received the frightening call from Rebecca's elementary school advising me that she had disappeared and could not be found.

"Good morning, Mrs. Jones. This is Rebecca's mom speaking."

"I'm sorry to bother you at work, but I'm calling to inquire about the reason for Rebecca's absences this week. You know it's the school rule that when a student is ill we need to be notified. Usually the parent comes in to pick up any missed class and homework assignments."

"What are you talking about? My daughter hasn't missed any school this week. Isn't she there right now?"

"No, she's not in today which is the reason for this call. And she hasn't been here any day this week. This is her fourth day of nonattendance. Are you telling me that you are unaware of her absences and she is truant?"

"Mrs. Jones, I need some time to investigate and find my daughter. I will call you back when I have further information."

I notified the office that I had to leave immediately. I jumped in the car and began my journey home, pledging to stay within the speed limit this time. But my right foot kept pressing down hard on the gas pedal despite my determination not to speed and break the law. And all the while I kept asking myself where could she be? How will I find her?

Things turned out to be easier than I thought. I decided that first I would return home and check out the house. I walked through the front door and there was Rebecca, hanging out with Allison and Allison's best friend, Amanda. The questioning began.

"What are you doing here, Rebecca? Why aren't you in school? Mrs. Jones has advised me that you've been playing hooky all week. How could you have deceived me like this? I saw you enter the main entrance of school this morning, and you purposely tricked me, walking out the rear door as I drove away. Now you're in big trouble at school, as well as with me. And Allison, you and Amanda have been part of this? How could you all be so dishonest?"

I turned and faced Amanda. "Get out of my house, right now!" I raged.

She quietly ran out the front door and Rebecca mumbled, "Sorry, Mom. It's just that they had Spring break this week and I'm not off until next week. We just wanted to hang out, that's all."

"I don't want to hear your excuses. I'll call your school now and make an appointment with the principal tomorrow morning to discuss the consequences for this."

The next morning Rebecca and I waited quietly in the school office for the principal. He entered, accompanied by the school guidance counselor, and sat across from us. He confronted Rebecca, and asked her to explain the reason for her four day absence.

Rebecca responded by reaching into her purse and pulling out a small piece of paper.

"Mr. Rogers, this is my doctor's note which explains why I stayed home. You see, I wasn't feeling well at the beginning of the week. When I told my mom about it, she just ignored me and told me that I had to go to school no matter how I felt. So instead of obeying her, I made my own decision and went to the doctor. I thought that was the right thing to do. Please don't punish me for this. I didn't mean to do anything wrong, I just felt too sick to come in."

What? Could this be true? Rebecca must have gone to our family doctor on Monday, paid the $5.00 co-pay fee, and acted out the part of a sick teenager well enough to convince him of an illness. I sat there in total denial that this could really be happening.

The principal and the guidance counselor excused themselves for a few minutes and stepped into an adjacent room to discuss Rebecca's defense. Mr. Rogers returned to announce their shocking decision.

"Rebecca, do you feel well enough now to return to your classes today?"

"Yes, I do."

Mr. Rogers looked at the clock on the wall. "Second period is just beginning, so why don't you report to class now and ask your teachers to help you catch up on missed assignments."

"Ok. Thank you, Mr. Rogers," said Rebecca. She picked up her book bag and nodded goodbye to me.

When I left the school I noticed that both the principal and the guidance counselor looked at me suspiciously. Apparently they viewed me as some kind of abusive mother. Amazingly, my teenager had out-smarted me again.

## May 7, 1990

Each day I witnessed the transformation of my daughters from children into adults. Soon their interest in the opposite sex became the next source of conflict that Ray and I had to deal with. Every time the phone rang, it was a boy. I trusted that we lived in a town with good quality families, but I had already learned that you never know what teenagers might try next. A parent must be vigilant at all times, and be prepared for the unexpected. This turned out to be another day I would never forget.

Now with Allison in her junior year, some of her classmates had reached the legal age for driving permits and licenses. I began to worry that someday she would have poor judgment and jump into a car with some wild, inexperienced driver, without my knowing about it.

The evening began with another argument. A boy named Jason from Allison's school called and invited her to come out with him and his friend. It was Wednesday, a school night. I would not allow her to hang out late into the night with some boys that I had never met. But Allison wouldn't stop harassing me about it.

"Mom, please let me go. Please. Jason and Bobby are really nice guys. Why don't you trust me? I'm not a baby anymore, so stop treating me like one."

The incessant begging continued. Finally, I couldn't control myself and raised my voice.

"The decision is not yours to make, Allison. It's already eight o'clock and getting dark. It all sounds like trouble to me. What do they plan on doing with you? I already told you, I don't want you driving around in cars with these kids."

"I hate you! I can't wait until I'm old enough to go to college and move out."

She proceeded to her room and slammed the door. Tired from the confrontation, we all fell asleep early that night. At midnight the phone rang. I almost didn't answer, but forced myself out of bed, wondering who would be calling our home at this ungodly hour.

"Hello," said an unfamiliar voice. "I'm looking to speak with someone named Allison."

"I'm Allison's mother. May I ask who you are?"

"I apologize for calling at this hour. My name is Father Malloy, and I'm calling from St. Barnabas Hospital. I'm here with a young man who sustained serious injuries in a car accident tonight. He is barely able to speak, but has asked me to contact Allison so he could talk to her.

"Oh my God! Is it Jason who was in the accident?"

"Yes."

"Please hold on, Father. Give me a moment and I'll wake up Allison."

When I tapped on her shoulder and explained the situation, Allison jumped out of bed and ran to the phone. I stood by, listening to the conversation.

"Jason, what's going on? What happened? Are you going to be ok?" she asked.

Jason told her about the accident. After a brief pause, Allison began to scream.

"No, no, no. Don't tell me that! It couldn't be true. Bobby died? Oh, no."

Unable to bear the news, Allison handed me the phone and collapsed on the floor, sobbing uncontrollably. I wanted more information, so I put the receiver to my ear, and heard the voice of Father Malloy.

He hesitantly revealed that the boys had been drinking and Bobby had been the drunk driver. They had been speeding down a hill without wearing seatbelts, and their car crashed head on into a tree. Bobby lost his life instantly, and Jason faced a long road of recovery ahead. Father Malloy requested prayers for both the boys and their agonizing families. Allison and I stayed up together all night, talking.

"Mom, should we wake up Ray and Rebecca and tell them the news?"

"I'd rather not, Allison. If we do, they'll be up all night too. Let's just deal with it in the morning."

"Did this really happen, Mom? I'll never see Bobby again? Everyone at school will find out about it. The hardest part will be facing tomorrow."

## June, 1990

The loss of a young life had lasting effects. Thank God I had not allowed Allison to go out with those boys that night. I probably saved her life. But after the incident, she changed. Her interests faded, and she cared about nothing. She spent time at home alone in her room, lying on her bed or sleeping. She stopped eating, and I feared she had become anorexic. I had never seen her like this before. Her sorrow followed her to school, where she became distracted and unable to function in class. I reached out to the school guidance counselor for help. The administration implemented a plan to help all the students deal with the loss of Bobby, and grief counselors worked tirelessly in therapy sessions, at different intervals throughout the day. Ray and I both became concerned that Allison needed more help than the school could provide.

"Hope, let's find a psychologist trained in this field, and get her some private counseling."

"It might help, but I'm not sure. We can't expect an overnight recovery. We need to be patient, because the healing process for everyone needs time."

Allison's friend Amanda also suffered during the aftermath. Amanda had a crush on Bobby, and had asked him to be her date for the Junior Prom. The girls had already begun making plans for the prom. Now that fantasy of teenage happiness would never materialize, and the dream was shattered and gone.

Jason, who survived, had difficulty facing each day with the guilt he carried, realizing that his irresponsible choices had contributed to Bobby's death. After his release from the hospital, Allison visited him at his home. He cried and told her that he could not face returning to school, with everyone knowing the harm that he had caused. Shortly after the visit, Jason's parents hospitalized him for depression and threats of suicide. It would take him years before he could forgive himself for the mistakes of his youth.

Ray, continuing to carry feelings of rejection from the girls, felt helpless once again. He, like Allison, now remained aloof from family life and the people around him. Windsurfing on weekends became his obsession. Every Saturday or Sunday morning he woke up, then left the house until darkness set in. I no longer had my soul mate. I felt abandoned and alone again, as I had been in my past. And soon I realized that our trials were tearing us apart, and our marriage headed for trouble. Things had to change. We needed a plan to help us solve our problems, but I didn't know where to begin.

***

# Chapter 23

## *A Look into the Past*

**July, 1990**

As the years passed and I continued to be occupied with my children and family, I decided that I would avoid all further contact with Uncle Scott. Although I had been successful in facing him at that family gathering several years ago, seeing him and being drawn back into those memories didn't seem worth the pain. I needed to move on, and not allow what had happened to haunt me forever. With a little effort, I realized I could maintain personal relationships with my cousins and other family members, without ever having to interact with him again. But one day I learned that Aunt Ava was in distress. Uncle Scott had become critically ill, and she had assumed the burden of caring for him at home. I knew I had to visit her, and at least be there for that one time to show her that I cared.

When I walked into the house, Uncle Scott sat in the front porch in his wheelchair. Aunt Ava explained to me that due to years of smoking cigarettes, he had a blockage in one of his legs, and the doctors had decided that the only way to give him a chance at life was to amputate his right leg. So there he was, in an agitated mood, while I stared at his missing limb. An oxygen tank had been set up next to him, but that didn't stop him from smoking cigarette after cigarette during my visit. I knew that Uncle Scott would not be long on this earth.

Seeing him like this, I experienced a great feeling of relief. I would no longer be afraid of him, and I knew that man would never harm me or anyone else again. As I witnessed his suffering, I wondered if this was God's way of punishing him for his sins. A part of me felt compassion, but another part of me could not help but rejoice in his agony. When I returned home, I knew it was time for me to think and pray. I had to process many emotions. Today I had found strength to visit him. Had my childhood wounds healed? Not completely, but I had made progress. Could I ever forgive him? I did not yet know the answer. I looked up to the heavens and asked God why this had happened to me. Then I told myself, remain idealistic, God has a reason for everything.

# Chapter 24

## *Seeking Solutions*

**August 15, 1990**

IT WAS A quiet summer morning. I woke up at 6:00 a.m. and just
wanted to enjoy sipping my refreshing cup of coffee, sitting alone
in the back yard. On this day I yearned for my own space with no
one around me, to think, to analyze, to plan where my life and
family were headed. Both of my daughters had been giving us difficult times, and it frustrated me. Why did they both act so angry
when Ray and I did nothing but love them and plan for their futures? The clock ticked silently as I sat there, immobilized, lost in
my thoughts.

Time for a second cup of coffee. My thoughts continued, as I
slowly became enlightened. Yes, part of their behavior reflected typical
actions for teenagers seeking their own identities. But the other part
still carried the effects of their parents' divorces. Drew had walked out
on us thirteen years ago and they hadn't fully recovered yet. Weekends
with their father continued to be stressful, as they left their safe, secure
environment, back and forth with visits. And when Drew spent time

with the girls, he continued to express his endless anger over money and our unforgettable court battle.

My mind reflected back to Danny. He had been forced to move out of our house almost three years ago, and I missed him. He called recently, with some good news, and seemed happy. Ray and I both picked up the receivers for a three way conversation.

"Hi Dad and Hope. How are you guys doing? I haven't seen you in a while."

Ray replied, "We're fine, son, just dealing with life as usual. And you?"

"I'm doing great. I just got a promotion at my job, and I've been doing my best to save enough money to buy my first car. I think maybe this weekend I'll visit some automobile dealers to price the models I'm interested in. I can't wait. Freedom at last!"

We all laughed. We didn't see Danny often because he lived more than an hour away and worked weekends, so finding time to visit became difficult. Somehow things would never be the same as when we all lived together. And then there was Ashley. I had not seen her for six years. I wondered if she remembered me, or if she would ever know how much she had touched my life. I prayed for her each day, hoping that she would somehow find strength to survive the injustice that she had endured.

I continued to drink my coffee, as a nearby chirping robin briefly caught my attention. I asked myself where I would go from here. I needed a plan to get me through these tough times. I would start by making a phone call to resume my counseling sessions. I would commit to safeguarding my daughters from bad decisions or influences by monitoring their whereabouts, despite their tantrums and quests for freedom. And last, I would reach out to Ray, and together we would find the way to resolve the issues that now isolated us from each other. None of these things would be easy, but I knew what I had to do.

Suddenly I had another idea. I had worked enough years at my job to qualify for a sabbatical leave of absence, for the purpose of returning to college for additional credits. If I did that, I needed to take only nine credits each semester, and I would be home more hours with my girls to give them the attention they needed. In September Allison would begin senior year of high school, and we needed time to visit college campuses. The next day I made a quick trip to the Board of Education office, where they approved my application. My new plan had been launched.

## September, 1990

Another school year began, and this time I had become one of the students. I wondered if I could still open my mind to learning and new ideas. After the first two weeks of classes at Rutgers University, Ray questioned me about my new experience.

"Now that you've attended your courses for a while, how do you feel about your decision to do this? Do you like your professors? Does it feel strange not being the teacher in charge?"

"Ray, I'm so excited I did this. Every moment in class, I feel stimulated and alive, like I'm being carried away to a new place, to a whole other world of knowledge. I'm being absorbed into it, becoming part of a new universe. For so many years I worked with those special education students, and now I'm studying the scientific basis for the neurologically impaired child and the emotionally disturbed child. I can finally understand the factors that contribute to their disabilities. Next semester I'll be studying the effects of drug use and abuse on the brain, and taking my first course learning how to use a computer. And the best thing about it is that it's helping me focus on myself, something positive rather than worrying about the children every minute."

"I'm glad to hear you say that, Hope. Now maybe you can understand why I go windsurfing so much. It allows me to stop thinking about my problems."

"I do understand. But I don't plan on making my return to school a full-time commitment, like you've done with your trips down the shore. I'm asking you now to please make more time for the both of us and the girls. If we want this marriage to survive, we have to put some hard work into it. Do you understand?"

"I think I do. I'll try again to deal with Allison and Rebecca and improve our relationships. I promise. I'll try."

**November, 1990**

Step One of the plan proved to be the easiest. I resumed my counseling sessions and enjoyed talking to my therapist, who always had lots of sympathy for my situation and often made me feel like some kind of heroine. Step Two, my pledge to protect my daughters from foolish actions and decisions, turned out to be the next series of battles and confrontations. Their craving for independence continued to rule our everyday lives. I had to always be on guard, ready to jump into action at any given moment, and to stand up for what I believed in.

Rebecca started to develop interest in an older boy named Tyler. One afternoon Tyler drove his car into our driveway and rang the doorbell.

"Hello, Mrs. Brooks. Is Rebecca ready?"

"Ready for what?"

"Ready for our date. We have plans to go out for the evening. Didn't she tell you?"

"No, she didn't. But do you know what, Tyler? Rebecca is only fifteen years old and she doesn't have my permission to go out with you tonight. She has chores to do at home and school work to catch up with. I suggest you leave now and call her later."

Before he had a chance to respond, Rebecca arrived at the door, attractively dressed with her makeup applied. She had apparently overheard my conversation with Tyler, and intended to change my mind.

"Mom, why can't I go out tonight? You're just being so overprotective. I can take care of myself. Nothing bad is going to happen to me. I won't even stay out late."

Then she looked at Tyler and said, "Let's go. It's fine." She walked down the driveway, opened the door on the passenger side of Tyler's car, and sat down, ready to ignore me and leave for her evening out. I quickly ran down and stood behind Tyler's car, proudly blocking his exit onto the street. Now the only way for him to leave my driveway would be to run me over on the way out.

Rebecca realized I meant business at last, so she stepped out of the car and began walking back toward the house. Success, I thought. I did it! I won! My child had listened to me and the fight came to an end. I triumphantly began following Rebecca back to the house, walking around the front of Tyler's car as I headed for the steps. Then I heard a loud noise. Tyler had started the motor of his car, but instead of backing out of the driveway, he put the car into drive, stepped on the gas pedal, and moved forward, heading straight for me. I stepped aside into the grass, but he continued to follow me. I ran faster, circling the tree in my front yard, then realized he was only inches away.

I screamed, "Tyler, what are you doing? Are you trying to kill me? Have you lost your mind?"

He continued to chase me with his vehicle, but with the tree as my source of protection, he finally gave up, drove across our front yard into the street, and sped away down the block. Rebecca and I stared at each other in disbelief. As soon as he sped away, my daughter ran to me, hugged me in her arms and whispered, "Mom, are you all right?"

Dazed at first, I answered, "I think I am, but I'm frightened. This isn't over. What if he comes back? I'm not sure, but I think a crime has been committed against me. I'm going to the police station to discuss what happened here."

As I drove to the station, my fear changed to rage. How could he have done such a thing? No, he won't come back, I promised myself. Time to implement Step Two: Anyone who acted like this would suffer the consequences of his actions, and he would never, ever be welcomed into our home again, or have contact with my daughter. I arrived at the police station and described the incident to the officer on duty. He listened intently.

"Officer, do you think I've been a victim of a crime?"

"Ma'am, with no doubt, you have been a victim of attempted vehicular homicide. Please come into the next room where I will assist you in completing the paperwork to file charges against your attacker."

With my hand shaking, I signed the complaint. I filed the charges and left the police station feeling, once again, empowered because of what I had achieved. When I arrived home, Rebecca stood by the door, waiting to greet me.

"Mom, did you really do it?"

"Yes, Rebecca, it's done."

"I just can't believe you were brave enough to do that. I've never seen you react to anything like that in my whole life. You've always been so calm in handling things, no matter what."

"Maybe I'm changed now."

That evening, I described the events of the day to Ray and Allison. Surprisingly, I noticed that now my daughters began to view me differently. Sometimes they actually feared me, because they never knew what act of aggression I might take next. Now I had power and control. I held tight to the pledge I made to myself to stay in charge of my teenagers as each future crisis emerged. The new me would be difficult for my daughters to accept.

Step Three: resolving the issues with Ray that isolated us from each other. No progress had been made, despite my efforts over the last three months. My frustrations mounted, and it seemed as if we lived two separate lives, but shared the same home. His love of windsurfing continued to be his respite and dominate his plans. One afternoon I followed him into the garage and observed him measuring the length of his surfing boards.

"Ray, what are you doing? Why do you need to know how long your surfing boards are?"

"You know I need to buy a new car. I've decided to buy a van that will be long enough to keep my boards inside it at all times, so I can be ready to drive away to the beach without having to pack up my car each time I go."

His words pierced my heart as I realized his windsurfing schedule continued to take precedence over me. I felt rejected and scorned. But a part of me was still madly in love with him, the man that I had married. The man who had built snowmen with my daughters, and made them laugh when he used a carrot for its nose. The man who had spent an afternoon with Allison, teaching her how to ride her bike without the training wheels. The man who had danced wildly around the living room with Rebecca, twirling her in circles until they collapsed on the floor, smiling radiantly.

No, I would not give up. I kept telling myself, we just need more time.

**January, 1991**

A new step forward for Allison. She just turned seventeen, and passed her New Jersey State driving test. Her grades at school continued to excel, so we allowed her to use the money she had saved from birthday presents, gifts, and a summer job, to purchase her first car. While we all enjoyed this exciting moment, Ray and I both had reservations about any new teenage driver being responsible on the road. We promised each other we would monitor her whereabouts and set limits.

Our family life calmed down after the incident with Tyler. I eventually dropped the charges after his parents begged me to give him a second chance, not wanting an arrest or conviction recorded on a police record. They gave their word that their son would never see or contact Rebecca again. With their promise, I looked forward to closure and moving on.

The next weekend, Danny called to say he would like to visit and spend the day with us on Saturday. Both girls looked forward to this, but Allison especially seemed anxious to see him. The day arrived, and after a warm and pleasant lunch together, the young people decided to pursue their own interests. Rebecca answered a phone call from a friend, and Allison and Danny went downstairs into the den to talk. With Allison's growing maturity, she and Danny seemed to have much in common. We heard them engrossed in conversation, and after a while we decided to join them.

"Hey, Dad," Danny said. "Allison just had an idea and invited me to go out with her and her friends tonight. I'd really like to do that if you and Hope don't mind. She said she has some really cool girlfriends that I'd enjoy hanging out with. Did you have any other plans for us?" Ray looked at me, waiting for my approval. I nodded my head.

"Ok, son. But Allison has a curfew and she has to be home by 11:00 p.m."

"No problem. I can't stay out too late anyway because I still work on weekends and I have to be at work early tomorrow."

"You have some time before you go out, so I'd like you to do me a favor. I just bought this expensive new camera, and I want to take some pictures of the two of you together."

"Sure," they both agreed.

Ray arranged the lighting for the photograph, and posed his subjects. Everyone enjoyed the event, and eventually Rebecca had her turn. Later that afternoon, Danny and Allison left for the evening. Unexpectedly, during the next few hours, I began to feel uneasy about their being together. Although Danny seemed to be doing well, I wondered if he still had issues with alcohol. Did he still attend AA meetings regularly? Allison was still underage for drinking. Would he offer alcohol to her or her friends? I just wasn't ready to trust anyone. I had to bring up the subject with Ray before I could put my fears aside.

"Ray, do you think Danny is still drinking?"

"I'll never know all the answers in life, but he's kept his job and appears happy and successful. Why don't you just enjoy the moment?"

Yes, enjoy the moment. At last, one of my fondest wishes materialized as my daughter and stepson stepped out in friendship. A few days later, Ray came home with the photographs he had taken. As he watched, I hung up a picture of Danny and Allison on the living room wall, to remind me of the progress we had made in uniting our children. Maybe, just maybe I thought, that dream of a family would finally come true. As he continued to observe me, Ray commented,

"Hope, I know exactly what you're thinking. Seeing our children together like that seems like a long awaited miracle."

The picture remained there for months, and I stared at it obsessively. I took a deep breath. Something inside me told me to stay strong, and prepare myself. Somehow I sensed that the difficult times had not come to an end.

* * *

# Chapter 25

## *The College Controversy*

**February 1, 1991**

ALLISON HAD SUBMITTED several college applications at the beginning of senior year. We discussed her opportunities for admission, and her major field of study. We hoped for her acceptance into a college of good standing, not too far from where we lived. On her list of most desired universities were New York University in Manhattan, and Boston University, in the heart of Boston.

Each day after work and school, we all raced to examine the mail, looking for some news on the update of her applications. Finally two large, thick envelopes appeared in the mailbox, one from NYU, and the other from Boston University. Since I was the first to find them, I craved to tear them apart and look inside. But Allison hadn't arrived home yet, and I wanted her to experience the thrill of opening them herself. I carried them to the kitchen table and stared at them for what seemed hours.

Finally, Allison arrived. She walked directly into the kitchen, and her eyes settled on the envelopes.

"Oh my God, I heard from both of them the same day," she exclaimed.

"Open them, Allison. Hurry!"

She paused, then grabbed the first envelope from NYU, frantically tearing open the seal.

"They've accepted me, Mom! I can't believe it. Now let's see what Boston U has to say."

She reached out for the second envelope. When she realized she had another acceptance, Allison began jumping up and down, squealing with delight. We laughed and hugged, cherishing her long awaited success.

"Wow mom, I did it! I did it! I can't wait to tell Rebecca and Ray. And I'll call Danny and Dad. I'll be seeing Dad this weekend, but I'd like to call him now. He'll be so proud. Oh, don't forget, we have to plan a date for the campus tours."

"Don't worry, I would never forget. I just want to take a moment to tell you how honored I am to be your mother. Your efforts in achieving your college goals have been superb. You are my shining star."

Allison excitedly carried her envelopes into the dining room, and carefully organized the enclosed papers on the table. Then she called Drew. I did not listen to their conversation, but apparently Allison did not get the response from him that she had anticipated. She ended the phone call with a sullen expression, and I immediately questioned her.

"Allison, what's the matter? Why do you suddenly seem sad?"

"I don't exactly know what the problem is, Mom, but Dad didn't seem so happy about my news. He said he would talk to me about it on the weekend."

I didn't have to wait until the weekend, because an hour later Drew called me to have a heart to heart. He quickly communicated his disapproval of the college plans and began speaking to me with the usual furious tone to his voice.

"So, Hope, I'm supposed to pay 60% of the college tuition, and room and board, and you think that I would agree to send her to either of those very expensive private colleges that you encouraged her to apply to? No, I won't do it. I won't agree to it, and I don't care if she's disappointed. I'm going to take charge of what college she attends, and hopefully it's not too late to apply. She's only going to a state university somewhere, where the tuition and cost of everything is a lot less than NYU or Boston U. Tomorrow I'll do some research, and I'll have some information for Allison by the weekend."

I felt so crushed, like a cockroach being stepped on. I had waited so long for this day. This was meant to be one of the happiest days ever, but now, in an instant, the thrill had been destroyed. What about my daughter? How could she handle the upcoming weekend, dealing with him? Another mother and father controversy about to unfold. How could he do this to her? How could he so cold heartedly shatter her dreams and act like he didn't care at all? I kept trying to analyze the situation, trying to figure out why this had happened.

Perhaps it had been my fault. The best idea would have been for both parents to develop a college plan with Allison and come to an agreement. But I had not been able to converse with Drew in years, and I had feared even trying. I should have made the effort, but now the window of opportunity has passed. How can I help Allison through this next crisis? I didn't know where to begin.

## February 5, 1991

Sunday evening, and Ray and I sat in the living room, anxiously awaiting for the girls to return home from the weekend with their dad. Worried about Allison, we had not enjoyed our quiet weekend together at all. I thought I heard some footsteps, so I hurried to look out the front window to see if they were home. No, it wasn't them. A few minutes later I heard voices in the driveway. I ran to the front window again. Still not them. After some time, Drew's car finally appeared.

Rebecca walked into the foyer first, and waved hello. When Allison came in behind her, things seemed to be exactly what we had expected. She appeared angry and upset. And in her usual pattern of dealing with frustrations, she walked directly to her room and closed the door behind her. Of course, I couldn't wait to speak to her, so I gave her a moment to recoup, and knocked on the door.

"Allison, may I come in?"

"If you really want to."

"How did it go? What happened?"

"He won't let me go to any of the colleges I want to, Mom. I'm so mad I feel like breaking everything in this room, like this book, and this lamp."

Allison picked up one object after another in her room, and threw them at the wall with the greatest force that she could muster. First the book, then the lamp, then the jewelry box, and next the pencil sharpener. Finally, she grabbed a pile of papers from her desk and tossed them into the air, and they came floating down on our heads and all around us.

"Allison, do you think you can calm down, or should I leave the room and come back later?"

She sat silently for a short time, and took a few deep breaths.

"No, it's all right, Mom. He wants me to go to the North Carolina State University in Raleigh, and apply for a scholarship there too. If I get the scholarship, you and Dad will only have to pay the in-state tuition rate, and then he would be happy. We already filled out the application form on the weekend."

"Are you going to be alright with that? Are you willing to go to North Carolina? It's pretty far away. It's probably at least a twelve hour drive by car, or maybe we would have to fly there."

"I don't care, Mom. Whatever. You two have been fighting over everything my whole life. I should have known that going to college wouldn't be different. I can't wait until I grow up and can make my own decisions. I'm so tired of being in the middle of all your arguments. You and Dad are my parents and you're supposed to love and respect me, but instead you always find a reason to fill my life with turmoil. I'm done talking about it. I'm going to call Danny now. I never had a chance to tell him about the acceptance letters on Friday. Now I really have a story for him."

I felt numb. I knew I needed someone to talk to, but still doubted if Ray would be there for me. We managed to stay married through it all, but I had been unhappy for so long. I still hadn't made much progress in achieving my Step Three goal. There was just a coldness that kept us isolated from each other. Now another stressful situation we must get through. I walked downstairs and returned to the living room, searching for my husband. Yes, my husband. That's what I needed him to be right now. Suddenly he appeared before me, and for the first time in a long time, compassion highlighted his eyes.

"Hope, how did it go? How is she?"

"She's devastated, and it's all my fault. I did this to her."

"No, it'll all work out. She'll get through it. Take one step at a time. One day at a time. This will pass, as everything does. We'll figure it out together."

Then he put his arms around me and held me tight, and I felt that once again I had him by my side, to walk with me and guide me through the endless chaos.

***

# Chapter 26

## *Drew's Announcement*

**April, 1991**

IN APRIL OF senior year, Allison received notice from the North Carolina State University. Good news. She had earned the in-state tuition scholarship and accepted the offer. In a few months she would be gone, living independently in a dorm, beginning an exciting new phase. Ray's prediction proved correct. She had overcome her disappointments and looked forward to living in a different culture in the southern part of our country, where winter never came and children never saw snow. At times she tried to replicate a southern accent, claiming that my Brooklyn speech patterns were totally unacceptable. She prepared herself to move forward to a new step in her young life.

Allison and Danny had continued a warm connection over the past few months. They socialized often with a group of friends. She even drove down the Garden State Parkway for the first time, to visit him. Rebecca seemed to thrive in her life as a high school sophomore. Popular in school, she had so far passed all her subjects this year, although still with little effort. The constant fighting over those phone calls, homework assignments, and boys never ended. I was glad I had taken the time to take my sabbatical and be home more for my daughters. It really helped, and that's exactly what they needed.

Another window of serenity to briefly enjoy, because within a short time, the next upheaval would unfold. It began after another weekend visit with Drew. Rebecca ran into the house to tell us about it.

"Mom, Ray, guess what. My dad is getting married again."

"What, are you serious?" I asked.

Ray responded. "Getting married? Who is he going to marry? Did you ever meet the woman?"

"Her name is Brenda, and no, Allison and I never met her. But I don't want him to get married again. I don't want another stepmother. I already had one, Ariana, and my memories of her and Chloe living with my father are terrible. I'll never forget all the arguing and yelling, and how I always felt that Ariana hated me. I really don't want to go through that again. And guess when he's getting married. Next month. They're having this formal wedding at this really fancy catering hall. I'm dreading it, and I don't want to go."

Wow. A third marriage, I thought. I hope he knows what he's doing, but it sounds like he hasn't known this person for very long and he's rushing into it. Of course I realized what this meant for my daughters. Another change in their lives. Feelings of apprehension and uneasiness. A new situation to accept, and a new relationship to develop.

Rebecca left the room and Ray and I faced each other.

"What do you think, Ray? Is this going to be another disaster?"

"This marriage doesn't look so promising to me. I think we need to schedule a session with the family counselor to help them adjust to this change and openly voice their emotions and opinions. They're going to need help, for sure."

**May 18, 1991**

Today Drew would marry again. He had contacted me to ask if I would help him plan the day's schedule by driving the girls to the reception hall by one o'clock, and I agreed. At that time there would be an exchange of marriage vows, followed by a cocktail hour, dinner, music, and dancing. Although still not thrilled with the idea of their father's new marriage, the girls eventually became excited about going to a party. They had finally met Brenda two weeks before the wedding day, and she had been attentive and kind. But mostly they looked forward to spending time with their little sister Chloe, whom they rarely visited. Chloe had just celebrated her tenth birthday.

I still felt a little strange knowing that in a few hours I would be driving them to Drew's third wedding. This wouldn't be an easy day for me, but the best I could do would be to wish Drew luck, and hope that this marriage would work for him.

The phone rang and I answered it. A meek little voice spoke to me, mostly in a whisper, and I did not recognize the caller.

"Hello, is this Hope?"

"Yes. Who is this?"

"It's Chloe."

"Chloe? Oh, hi Chloe. How are you? Are you excited about going to the wedding?"

Chloe burst into tears. She began sobbing, trying to speak in between her sobs.

"Chloe, what's the matter?"

"My mom's not here. She went away for the weekend, and I've been staying at my friend's house. Today my dad is getting married, and I have no way to get there. No one will drive me. And I want to see my sisters so bad and be with them. I miss them so much. Please, please, Hope, could you help me?"

"What exactly would you like me to do?"

"Can you pick me up and drive me to the wedding? There's just no one else I can ask. Please, I'm begging you."

"Where does your friend live?"

"In my town, just a few blocks from my house."

The trip would take three hours of driving, and I could get Chloe to the reception hall just in time. But did I really want to do this? Should I drive three hours to make Drew happy on his wedding day?

As his first wife, should I accept the responsibility of driving the child of his second wife to the marriage of his third? The whole idea just seemed crazy. But then I realized that none of this was about Drew. Only the children mattered. If I didn't do this for Chloe, she would remember forever that I had abandoned her when she needed me. And my daughters would be devastated without her presence.

"Ok, Chloe. If there's no traffic, I should arrive at your friend's house at 11:30. Can you please be ready to leave the moment I arrive?"

"Thank you so much, Hope. I'll be ready, I promise."

Now I had to quickly find Ray and explain the turn of events. I ran upstairs as he exited the shower.

"Ray, I need you to help me by driving the girls to the wedding. Is there any problem with that?"

"No, I can do that, but what's the matter? What happened? Why do you seem so nervous and upset?"

I briefly explained my conversation with Chloe and the decision that I had committed to. I had anticipated Ray's reaction, and hoped that he would give me his support. His eyes revealed a look of shock and concern, as if being hit by a bombshell.

"Hope, are you sure you want to do this? Can you handle getting so involved?"

"Yes, Ray, but I have to leave right now. Right now."

I began the drive in a trance, with my mind alternating between dreams and reality. The trip went quickly with no traffic, and surprisingly, I pulled up to the house exactly at the estimated time. Chloe stood by the front door, anxiously looking up and down the street, hoping to recognize my dark red Nissan. Upon seeing my car, she quickly ran and entered the passenger side, reaching over to give me a hug.

"Thank you, Hope. I appreciate this so much."

Surprisingly, the drive to the reception hall proved to be a pleasant experience. Chloe and I finally relaxed, now that the day's problem had been solved. We talked and became better acquainted.

"Chloe, you've grown since I last saw you. What grade are you in now?"

"I'm in fourth grade. And you? Are you still teaching those little kids? I remember you always had lots of reading books and workbooks around your house."

"Yes, I am. Sometimes those little guys are a lot of work. But I enjoy what I do and it's worth it."

Chloe smiled. The ninety minutes passed quickly, and sooner than expected, we drove up to the entrance. Allison and Rebecca had just arrived, and they stood together right before us, ready to enter the building. Chloe's expression turned into sheer joy, as she ran up to them, calling out their names, one after another. I sat quietly in my car and watched. Relief at last. I had no doubt, the children would remember this day.

As I sat there, my thoughts returned to the day twenty-four years ago when I had married Drew. I closed my eyes and saw myself as the beautiful bride in the elegant white dress, surrounded by my parents and family. I was so young, so innocent, so trusting, so unprepared.

✳✳✳

# Chapter 27

## *The Unthinkable*

**June 1, 1991**

My sabbatical leave would end in one month. In two weeks I would take my final exams, so now I needed to set aside all other issues and study.

Studying continued to be my salvation. Using my mind never failed to distract me from every concern. Absorbed in my books, I never noticed if Ray paid any attention to me, never harassed the girls about cleaning their rooms, and never worried about keeping up with the mail or paying the bills on time. None of those things seemed to be important at all. And with me making no demands on anyone in the household, home life remained quiet and serene.

**June 21, 1991**

School ended at last. Rebecca had passed all her subjects with decent grades, and Allison ended her high school career ranking high in her class. We had much to be thankful for and a lot to celebrate. I suddenly had an idea that I presented to Ray.

"Ray, why don't we have an outdoor graduation party for Allison and invite all the people important to her? That would include Allison's aunts and uncles, cousins, friends from school, Danny, and her father and Brenda. And I would be delighted because this would also be a great opportunity for me to spend some time with Aunt Ava."

Mentioning her name, I took a moment to reflect back on my Aunt Ava, the woman who had continued to remain my idol from my childhood through the many decades of my life. So many years had passed, and now she would be with me to celebrate my daughter's graduation.

"That's a great idea. Let's plan a catered party in our backyard. It's been a long time since we've had a memorable family gathering at our home."

## June 30, 1991

We rented a large tent wide enough for forty people in case of inclement weather or a day too sunny. On the morning of the party, a team of men came over to set up the tent, and at noon the caterers arrived with trays of delicious Italian delicacies, pastas, cannolis and desserts. The weather forecast predicted a partly sunny day with temperatures in the mid to upper 70's. Perfect. I could not have asked for more, and believed this day was destined to be the fulfillment of every mother's dream. My heart leaped with passion. Successful children, gorgeous weather, friends and family to share it with. A truly perfect moment.

Our home abounded with life and activity. The guests arrived and platters of food were served, with everyone in good spirits. Ray connected speakers to the outside deck of the house, so the teenagers' music played loudly throughout the event, and Allison's friends danced impulsively in the grass. I had reservations about inviting Drew and his new wife to the gathering, but I wanted Allison to remember this event with both of her parents present. When they didn't arrive on time, I became concerned that maybe they had decided not to come, and Allison would be disappointed. They finally arrived at 2:00 p.m., and now Brenda and I would meet for the first time. I took a deep breath.

Brenda appeared to be shy and nervous as I approached them.

"Hello, Brenda. It's so nice to meet you. Welcome to our home."

I extended my arm and we shook hands, acknowledging our acceptance of each other. Then I turned to Drew. Greeting him would be more difficult, since for so long I had only known him as an angry, combative man. But I managed to face him and used a respectful, gracious tone.

"Hi, Drew. Thank you so much for coming."

"Thank you for inviting us. I'm so proud of our daughters."

Short but sweet. I don't think I could have handled any more than that.

A few hours later, I walked through the den to go outside, carrying a supply of paper dishes and Styrofoam cups for dessert and coffee. My usual path would have been the rear door of the kitchen to the yard, but for some inexplicable reason that day, I chose the alternate route. As I passed through the room, I noticed that the teenagers had decided to come inside. They engaged each other in conversation, enjoying each other's company. Then suddenly I noticed something out of the corner of my eye. Sitting in a chair, almost out of sight, sat Danny, with Allison on his lap, and they stared into each other's eyes, enraptured. When they heard my footsteps, they quickly stood up, hoping that I had not had time to observe them. I almost lost my balance, but I managed to hold on to all the plates and cups in my hands, and exited through the sliding glass doors back into the yard. Aunt Ava offered her help and distracted me from what I had seen.

"Hope, let me take those things from you. You have too much to carry. Sit down for a while and enjoy your guests, and I'll set up the table. Is there anything else we need to bring out from the kitchen?"

"No, I think we have everything we need. Thank you so much for helping me."

I really did need to sit down. My house was full of people, and I had just seen my daughter and stepson acting in a very inappropriate manner. What it all meant, I just didn't know. I didn't have time to process any of it right then. But my stomach began to feel queasy and nauseous. Suddenly, I wanted the party to end.

## July 1, 1991

The next morning we all woke up, exhausted from the excitement of the day before. I needed time to think before I would confront Allison about her behavior with Danny, or bring it to Ray's attention. We all sat together at the breakfast table and started to talk. I had a question for Allison.

"Allison, now that you're done with school, when exactly will you start your summer job at the car wash?"

"Actually, Mom, I wanted to talk to you about that. I know I agreed to take that job, but there's really something else I would rather do this summer. My friend Claire's parents own a house down the shore, and Claire has a summer job in a restaurant on the boardwalk as a waitress. She said she could get me a job there too, and I could spend the summer on the beach having fun. Her parents said it would be fine with them if you'd allow me to do that. After all, I am an adult now that I graduated from high school and own a car. Can I do it?"

"I'm sorry Allison, but that's just not going to happen. You're still only seventeen and I know all about the wild parties that go on all summer at the Jersey shore. Besides, this is the last summer you'll be spending with us, and in eight weeks it's off to North Carolina!"

"I knew you'd say that. You just want to always believe that I'm your little baby."

Allison spoke with a mischievous look about her, and I became suspicious about her response. Somehow I felt she wanted to distract me from the subject, and keep me from asking any more questions.

## July 2, 1991

I still had not discussed with anyone what I had witnessed in the den between Allison and Danny. When Ray woke up, I asked him to set aside time that evening after work to discuss an important matter with me. He agreed. I spent my morning running errands, and when I returned home, I noticed that Allison's car was not in the driveway. I had looked forward to having a serious mother-daughter discussion with her as soon as I got back. Now that would have to be postponed, and my anxiety level soared. I entered the house frustrated and angry. The situation escalated when I found the note from Allison on the kitchen table.

Dear Mom,

I know you aren't going to be happy with this, but I packed up my things and left for the shore. Please don't be angry, it's something I really wanted to do. And yes, I am old enough to make some decisions for myself. Don't worry, I can handle it. Besides, I'll be with Claire, and I'll call you every day. I promise.

Allison

My mind went crazy. Should I allow her to stay down the shore with a family I never met? Would this be a good experience for her, preparing her for the independence of college in September? Had she been honest about her plans, or did she have an ulterior motive for deception? Did she really drive away to be with Claire, or did she run away to be with…

I took a deep breath, then sat down. I would begin by calling Claire's parents to confirm Allison's story. I reached for the phone book, and searched for their last name in our town. I recognized their address, and hesitantly dialed their number. A young girl's voice answered.

"Hello."

"Hello, is this the Floyd residence?" I asked.

"Yes, who is this?"

Suddenly I recognized Claire's voice.

"Claire, this is Allison's mother calling."

Silence. No response.

"Claire, I need you to tell me the truth. Do you know where Allison is?"

Continued silence. Then finally, "No, I don't."

"Did you invite Allison to your family's shore house for the summer? I need the truth."

'We don't own a house at the shore, Mrs. Brooks."

"Ok, thanks for your honesty."

No more to be said. Now I knew. Most probably Claire had been part of Allison's plan, but when confronted by me, she just couldn't lie. Yes, Allison and Danny had fallen in love, and had run away together. Next, I had to update Ray. I then called Ray's office without giving details, and he agreed to come home.

"What's the emergency?"

"It's our children, Ray. I became suspicious yesterday at the party, when I noticed Allison and Danny seemed to be romantically involved. Allison's gone and she left me this note. I've also confirmed that Allison's not with Claire. She and Danny are together somewhere, I just know it. Ray, they're in love."

Ray read the note and looked at me, astonished.

"Is this for real, Hope? I'm so stunned I don't know what to say. I'll call my son to see what he says. We have to find her."

Ray called, and Danny answered.

"Danny, its Dad. I'm not going to make small talk. Allison left the house and we don't know where she is. Is she with you?"

A moment of hesitation.

"Yeah, Dad, she's here."

"Why? What are you two thinking? Stay home, because Hope and I will be coming over to talk to both of you as soon as we can get there."

As we drove together, my anger escalated. This is not going to happen. My seventeen-year-old daughter is not going to live with my twenty-one year old stepson. Allison is a minor, and cannot legally do this. It's against the law. Then I had a solution to the problem.

"Ray, I know what we must do. Rather than drive directly to Danny's house, take us to the local police station. I know they're breaking the law, and Allison as a minor does not have a right to disobey her parents and move out of our home. Please. Maybe we could just get an officer to come with us and explain to both our children that they cannot carry out their ludicrous plan. What do you think?"

"It's an idea that might work, as long as neither of them gets arrested."

"Then we'll do it?"

We drove into the first gas station in Danny's town to ask the location of the local police department, and within minutes we pulled into their parking lot. We approached the front desk and advised the officer on duty that we needed help with a problem. He led us into a small room where another officer greeted us, asking how he could be of service.

We explained the situation, and the officer quickly informed us that he knew the law pertaining to our situation. As he shrugged his shoulders, he stated,

"I realize your concern for your daughter, but we cannot assist you. You see, in the state of New Jersey, seventeen is the age of consent, and your daughter does indeed have the right to make her own decision in this matter. I'm sorry and I wish I could be of more help, but the law is clear."

Ray and I returned to the car and began the drive to Danny's house. We had no other options, we would confront them ourselves. We didn't speak during the ride, but when we arrived at Danny's door, Ray asked, "Are you ready?"

"No, I'm not ready. I would never be ready for this. But I have to do it anyway."

Ray held my hand and supported me as we walked down the pathway. We knocked on the door, and Danny opened it and invited us inside. Allison sat quietly on the living room couch, not acknowledging our presence. When Danny came in the room, he sat down next to her, and put his arm around her shoulder as if to protect her from us. My impulse was to scream but I knew that would get us nowhere. So I just stared at them for the moment and let Ray handle the situation. I knew it would be better to remain silent than to provoke them. Ray began the questioning.

"Do either of you want to explain why you're doing this? Why have you chosen to move in together when you know this decision hurts both of us? We're a family and that means we're supposed to respect each other, to honor each other. As your parents, we do not approve of this. It violates all the moral and religious beliefs that we've tried to instill in you since childhood. Allison, is there a chance you'll change your mind and come back home with us today?"

Allison just gazed at Danny, her eyes begging him to speak for her.

"No, Dad, she's not going home. We've discussed it over and over again. We don't want to be apart, and at the end of the summer, Allison will be moving to North Carolina to start college. This is the only time we have to be together. We love each other in a way that we've never loved anyone else in our whole lives. Please don't take that away from us."

I confronted Allison.

"Allison, be honest and tell me your plans. Will you still leave for college at the end of August, or is there a chance that you will forfeit your scholarship and remain here with Danny?"

"Mom, stop worrying. I wouldn't give up my opportunities. Yes, I'm going to college. But I'm also not coming home with you, because I want to be with Danny right now more than anything else in the world. Isn't what I want important, too?"

She began to cry, resting her head in her lap. There was nothing more that any of us could say. I looked at her and thought this is not my daughter. This young woman that sits before me is not my little girl, not the person I've known throughout all the days of her life. She's a stranger, but where's the real Allison? I miss her and I want her back. I wondered what the future held for them. Possibly their love will continue to flourish. Or maybe they will realize that this was never meant to be, and walk their separate ways. I had to leave it up to them, I told myself. It was their lives and their futures, not mine.

Ray and I left our children with no hugs, no words of love. We entered the car feeling weary and thwarted, as we began the journey home. Too tired to speak, we sat quietly for the duration, each of us consumed with apprehension about the sequence of events. Another tomorrow would come, and we would face another day.

# Chapter 28

## *Dreams Undone*

**July 3, 1991**

THREE DAYS SINCE the unfolding of events. I spoke to no one, not even Ray. I reverted to the child I had been after Uncle Scott molested me, again seeking refuge from my overwhelming world. When the phone rang, I wouldn't answer it. How could I share this shameful disaster with anyone? Outrage and fury filled my days. I had been hurt, insulted, violated. Violated by two people that I had loved deeply from my innermost being. But they didn't even seem to care. Ray and I had tried so hard to be good parents, but by their actions our children had chosen to dismiss the values and meaning of everything we had taught them.

Once again, my dream of our wonderful family came undone. I wondered how I could cope with this, how I could survive. This seemed to be the story of my life. I build and build and climb to the top of the mountain. I become strong and revel in my success. Then the mountain crumbles as I outstretch my hands to grab onto it. I fail, and plunge to the bottom, where I must begin the climb again. Finally, I opened my heart to Ray.

"Ray, how are you handling things?"

"This is so hard for me to accept, I haven't told anyone about it yet. Is Rebecca aware of what happened?"

"I don't know. The girls are close, but I doubt that Allison shared this secret with her sister. I'm just glad that Rebecca left for sleep away camp for the first two weeks of July. It gives us both some time to assimilate our situation. When I woke up today, I held a different perspective on things. The more I thought about it, the angrier I got with Danny. At age twenty-one, he obviously holds power over Allison. He is an adult, but she's not. She's just a kid who seeks love, and is being swept away by the first romantic interest of her life. She's a victim here, and the consequences of her running off with Danny will most likely disrupt her future in many ways."

"What are you saying, Hope? My son is the culprit, and Allison is innocent of all wrongdoing? She bears none of the blame?"

"Yes, that's the way I feel. I'm sure this was Danny's idea. To me Allison is just my child, my baby, who knows nothing about life. I want to protect her and save her from all harm. But I can't. It's another time in my life where I'm powerless, but I don't want it to be like this."

Losing control, the tears began to flow. I looked up at Ray, who unexpectedly seemed cold and removed, with no empathy for my distress.

"I can't take any more!" he yelled. "I'm upset with our children, and now I'm furious with you. My son has endured enough in his young life, and I don't need to hear words from you that describe him as some kind of an evil force. I refuse to be part of this conversation any longer."

Ray stormed out of the room and out of the house. I sat lifeless for a few minutes, then I knew what I had to do. I could not stay in this house another minute. Too much sadness. Too many disappointments. My marriage falling apart, as each of us defended our natural child in this turmoil. I went upstairs, packed a suitcase with everything

I would need, and drove away, heading for the nearest hotel and a place to be alone.

I settled into a cheap hotel in a nearby town, then reclined on a comfortable rocking chair in my room. Sleep would be impossible, but I needed time to think. Life. I'll never understand it. If you work hard at it, aren't you supposed to be rewarded with happiness? I always expect that but it never seems to happen that way. I closed my eyes and prayed for my strength to be restored once again. Then I remembered that I had brought my Families Anonymous book with me, the inspirational program that had gotten us through the difficult period with Danny's alcohol addiction. I opened the first page and my eyes focused on the Serenity Prayer. Yes, I needed to read it once again, at this moment.

> *God, grant me the serenity to accept the things*
> *I cannot change, the courage to change the things*
> *I can, and the wisdom to know the difference.*

I recited it endlessly, over and over again, until at last I let go of all my anger and fears. With serenity, I entered into a deep sleep. As I slept, my father appeared before me in my dream:

*My daughter, when growing up you rebelled against the way I loved you and tried to protect you. Yet today, in a way, you have turned into me.*

With the healing power of rest, I awoke the next morning with my spirit renewed. Like my father, I would love my children no matter what. They would write their own life stories, just like I wrote my own. And I would always be there for them when they needed me.

Maybe now I could call Ray.

***

# Chapter 29

## *One Year Later*

**June, 1992**

THE STREAM OF life passes so quickly. In the blink of an eye, another year is over. And what we do with the gift of time is up to us and the choices we make.

Ray and I had again survived the latest crisis of our marriage. Allison had kept her promise and left for college life in North Carolina after spending the summer of 1991 with Danny. A few months later, Danny followed her there and found a job, so they could be together. Now with only our youngest child, Rebecca, living at home, we actually found time to spend together. Growing in acceptance of our family situation, we greatly enjoyed this year. For each of us, it was a time to flourish, a time to mend and reconnect, a time to balance the things of importance. Redirecting my focus to my job as a New York City teacher, a new experience working with special needs children captured my attention.

A federal law known as the IDEA, the Individuals with Disabilities Education Act, had been passed. Under this law, the courts mandated the inclusion of children with disabilities into the general education classes, whenever possible. Implementing this law would ensure that every child would receive a free and appropriate public education in the least restrictive environment. For me and my co-workers, this meant that children with special needs would now be included in classes with regular students, and it would be our responsibility to provide services to meet their needs. The first student to be assigned to my second grade class under this law was Melanie.

Melanie arrived on the first day of school in a wheelchair, accompanied by a full time aide. Melanie had been born with a neurological condition which affected the muscles in her body. The weakness in her legs prevented her from walking. The weakness in her hands gave her limited ability to use pencils for writing or crayons for drawing. The role of the aide would be to work one-on-one with Melanie in academic assignments, and to escort her to daily sessions with the school's physical therapist. Aside from the movement issues, Melanie was a bright, interactive child. Having never worked before with physically disabled children, I found myself hesitant and nervous about what I could do for Melanie and what goals she could accomplish in my classroom.

After meeting Melanie on the first day of school, I assessed her needs. My classroom was arranged with five vertical rows of desks, with an aisle separating each of them. The students could walk down an aisle to the front of the room to write an answer on the blackboard, compute a math problem, or read aloud their written work. I wanted Melanie to be able to participate in these activities as well. I needed to reconfigure the desks so that the wheelchair could fit between the rows.

After studying the layout of the room, I managed to rearrange the desks leaving one aisle wider than all the others. But there was a second problem. How could Melanie navigate herself down the aisle with her arms too weak to push the wheels on her chair forward? I had another idea. I would assign a different child each week to be her helper and perform this task. This would be another way of having her successfully relate to her classmates. The children's reaction to this idea turned out to be something I never expected. On the second day of school, I chose a time when Melanie was out of the room in her therapy session to address this with the students.

"Boys and girls, you all know that your classmate Melanie is different from you. She's not able to physically do the simplest things that you can do, like walk up to the blackboard or use her hands to take out the pencils and books that she needs from her desk. She does have an aide to assist her with many things. But the most important thing that Melanie needs to succeed in our class is friends. She needs to know that you like her and accept her the way she is. So now I'm going to ask you to consider my plan. I would like you all to take turns each week, sitting next to Melanie and being her helper. Your jobs would be to push her wheelchair when I call her to the front, and help her get the things she needs to do her schoolwork."

I paused, giving them time to absorb my words. After a minute of silence, I continued.

"Who would like to be the first volunteer?"

Their response was amazing. I looked around the room, and almost every hand was raised. Some children jumped up and down in their seats, hoping to be the first one chosen. Others stood up as tall as they could, with arms outstretched, reaching for the ceiling and seeking my attention. I looked around the room and made my selection.

"Alex, you will be Melanie's helper beginning right now. Let's push your desk next to hers so you'll be ready when she returns to class."

"All right, Mrs. Brooks," said Alex with enthusiasm as he moved to the side of his desk and quickly slid it across the floor.

As the weeks and months of the school year passed, my plan continued with success. Melanie's expression, mostly serious at the beginning of the school year, now held a smile and a look of contentment. She felt like part of the real world. She had a life like other children, with things she could achieve. One morning as our class lined up for gym period, Melanie's helper of the week, Donna, walked up to me to share her brainstorm.

"Mrs. Brooks, instead of Melanie just watching us play soccer or basketball in the gym, why can't one of us play catch with her, using one of those small, light balls that are in the gym closet?"

"I'm not sure that she is capable of throwing a ball, but Donna, that's a wonderful idea."

I moved Melanie and Donna into a corner area of the large gymnasium, with the aide supervising the game. Donna began by throwing the ball to Melanie, and it landed in her lap. Then surprisingly, she found the strength to lift it and toss it back into the air. The ball continued from person to person, up and down, sideways, and bouncing. The rest of us witnessed their giggling and laughing, and I left school that day moved by the compassion of these children.

Melanie's school year continued in the least restrictive environment. During the spring parent teacher conferences, Melanie's parents shared some updates with me about their plan to improve her physical condition. They had found a specialized doctor located in Manhattan, and once a week had been driving Melanie into the City for innovative treatments and new medications that had become available. They hoped that in time, Melanie might one day be able to walk.

One morning, a few months later, Melanie began her school day in an especially good mood. At exactly 10:00 a.m., Melanie raised her hand to ask me a question.

"Mrs. Brooks, I can't wait any more to show you all something. I know we'll have show and tell after lunch, but can I show you right now?"

I didn't want to disrupt the morning schedule of math and language arts, but a part of me thought that this must be something especially important for this child.

"I'll give you a few minutes, Melanie, but then we have to finish our morning work."

"This won't take long," she replied. "But I need my helper to push me to the front of the room."

Once this was done, Melanie grinned and said, "Watch this."

She placed her two hands on the side of the wheelchair, and pushed down with all of her might. In a matter of seconds, she lifted herself out of the chair, and released her hands. There she stood proudly, planning her next move. So unprepared for this, we all watched in silence. Melanie took her first step with one foot, and her second step with the other. Standing for a few more seconds, she gracefully stepped back and returned to her chair. Surprised, shocked, everyone clapped and cheered. No one felt like doing any more morning work, including me. The children raised their hands, wanting to ask Melanie how she had triumphed over her affliction. The questions began.

"Melanie, how do you feel now that you can stand up and move your legs?"

"I feel strong, stronger than I ever have."

"What kind of doctor taught you to walk? Is he a magician?"

Melanie laughed. "Maybe he is."

"When did you first stand up?"

"About two weeks ago. I've been doing a lot of exercises to strengthen my muscles with my physical therapist."

"Someday will you throw your wheelchair away?"

"I'm not sure, but I'm planning on it."

"Will you ever be able to run?"

"Maybe by next year if I keep working at it."

Melanie became an example for me that day. At age seven, she had learned the value of perseverance and determination. What she worked for was one of the simplest pleasures of life, to walk. I vowed that I would be like her, never give up, and continue to pursue my dreams.

***

# Chapter 30

## *Two Years Later*

**June, 1993**

ANOTHER QUIET YEAR, filled with changes. This month Rebecca successfully completed high school and chose to attend California State University in Los Angeles. In two months she would follow in her sister's footsteps, leave home, and move into a college dorm. I wondered what it would be like to have an empty nest, with all the children grown and gone. Sometimes I visualized it as a delightful experience. Other times I imagined it as living in a silent home filled with three empty bedrooms, no longer feeling like a mother.

In North Carolina, Allison had completed her second year of study, while she and Danny continued their relationship. With 750 miles separating them from us, Ray and I were released from our attempts to monitor their lives. Instead, we watched them walk their own paths to independence from afar. During the two years they had been together, they both remained hesitant to speak to us. They rarely called or updated us with news about events in their lives. When thoughts of them came into my mind, I tried to block them by focusing on other things. On holidays we reunited, but these were difficult times. We smiled and used the words Merry Christmas and Happy New Year, but the words were cold, unfeeling utterances that lacked warmth from the heart.

At the end of June, Allison called with some startling news.

"Hi Mom, what's new?"

I recognized this as small talk and knew at once that some matter of importance was about to be announced. Not ready to confront her, I responded in the same casual manner.

"Nothing much, just life as usual in New Jersey. What's going on with you?"

"Mom..."

"Yes?"

"Danny and I broke up."

With the shock of this disclosure, I held my breath. What? It had taken me forever to accept this situation, and now it was over? So many thoughts raced through my brain, scrambled and disoriented.

"Is this for real, or did you two just disagree about something that you'll work out?"

"No Mom, it's over. Believe me."

"What happened?" I asked.

"Nothing really specific. We both finally realized that we really weren't meant for each other. We're too different, not sharing the same long term goals, not wanting the same things out of life. We'll always love and care about each other, but staying together and getting married would be a really big mistake. I know all this has been hard for you to understand, Mom, but are you now willing to accept the way Danny and I have resolved our relationship? Are you still angry with me for making the choices that I made? I know we've put you and Ray through a lot."

"Allison, I've grown in wisdom over the past two years. You're almost twenty years old now, and capable of determining your own fate. It's taken me a while to recognize you as an adult. I've made mistakes in my own life, and through them I've come to understand that learning by living is the only way to grow. From now on, I'll only tell you what to do when you ask me for advice."

"Thanks, Mom. It's good to know that. Would you like me to come home for the summer, rather than stay in North Carolina? We could spend some time together, which we haven't done in a long time."

"That would be wonderful," I replied.

At last, after two seemingly endless years, my daughter was back, and nothing would ever tear us apart again. What an unexpected surprise. What a joy. Then my thoughts turned to Ray and I wondered how he would deal with the news. Later that evening, I updated him. On hearing about it, he seemed melancholy and sad. I questioned him about his reaction.

"Ray, what are you thinking?"

"I'm so glad that Allison will be home for a few months. But will Danny and Allison ever be willing to spend time together in our home for holidays and celebrations? They say they'll always love each other, but will they feel uneasy, surrounded by us at the dinner table, now that they are no longer together? I'm worried about my son. Will he feel unwelcome here?"

"I don't know, but I'm relieved this chapter of our lives is over. I do know we must take one step, one day at a time. I released my anger long ago."

After the break up, Danny resumed life at the New Jersey shore. Although we reached out to him, he found it difficult to share his emotions and communicate with us. But at least he now lived within traveling distance to us, and we believed that maintaining the family connection would surely happen with the healing power of time.


**December 20, 1993**


It happened. The girls both left for college at the beginning of the fall semester, and now life had changed. Our home had become a quiet, uneventful place. The phone rarely rang, the bedrooms remained clean, daily arguments over school and curfews never happened, and teenagers no longer rang the doorbell every afternoon. Being a mother is who I am, the center of my being. Not having my children to talk to, to laugh with, to protect against the dangers of the world, brought a great emptiness within me. Did life have meaning without them surrounding me? It would take a while to adjust, to plan things with Ray and develop a social network to enjoy.

## December 21, 1993

My spirit filled with the anticipation of this special Christmas, with my children being home once again. Beautiful flashing lights surrounded my tree, artificial snowflakes hung over the windows, and I had finished shopping and wrapping the gifts. I couldn't wait for everyone to arrive. Allison would also be home for the holiday break. Danny had not yet informed us of his plans. Ray and I still wondered if Danny and Allison would feel too awkward to spend the day together with us.

Soon my bedrooms would be occupied again. My home would be the center of family life and activities. My daughters would be here, and my sister would join us for the Italian Christmas Eve fish dinner. The phone rang. It was Rebecca, and again I experienced the unexpected.

"Hi Rebecca. Are you all packed and ready to come home for Christmas?"

"Mom, I'm not going to hesitate to tell you this. I've been planning this call for weeks. I need to get everything off my chest, and I'm doing it right now."

"What is it? Are you in trouble or something?"

"Mom, I'm sorry, I don't want to disappoint you, but I'm not coming home."

"What are you talking about? Your flight leaves Los Angeles at 9:00 a.m. on Thursday, remember? I bought you that ticket months ago."

"You don't understand what I'm saying. Of course I know I have a flight scheduled, but I won't be on it. I just can't come there right now and face all of you."

"Why are you saying this? You don't want to be with us? I so look forward to our treasured time together."

"Maybe that's what you think, Mom, but I don't. You see, I've been so depressed since I came to California that I haven't been able to concentrate or complete my course assignments. I got so discouraged about three weeks ago that I just gave up and stopped going to my classes. I finally realized I needed help, so I started sessions with a counselor here and told him all about my family issues and the things I've been through. We talked for hours about your divorce from Dad, the endless fighting, and how my sister and brother fell in love and ran away together. The counselor told me that I grew up in a dysfunctional family. He believes that my trip home for Christmas would return me to an unhealthy environment, and contribute further to my depression. I'm so sorry, Mom. Right now I feel like such a failure. I know I've made some foolish decisions. But I've made some friends here at college, and we've decided to quit school for now and move together to the west coast of Florida, get jobs, and begin a fresh start. I don't know when, if ever, I'll see you all again."

I listened intently to Rebecca's final words. I could tell from her raspy voice that she spoke with great difficulty. Here she was, another child in pain. My first child had just returned into my life, and now my second had become lost. Lost and bewildered, wrapped up in the trauma of her childhood, my divorce and remarriage, and everything that had followed.

I tried to reason with her and have a discussion.

"Rebecca, I don't care about some judgments that a counselor in California has made about me and Ray. The truth is, he never met us, and knows nothing about who we are or what we stand for. Before you make this decision not to come home, I want to remind you that you are deeply loved. Yes, we've had problems in our family, like all other families. If you're in crisis right now, we need to be with you and discuss the options you have for dealing with your present predicament. Please, Rebecca, don't do this. Come home."

"No Mom, I can't. I just can't right now. I have too much going on, too much to handle. I'll call you another time."

In that instant, she was gone. It all happened so quickly. One minute I anticipated the thrill of her arrival, and the next minute I felt the anguish of my broken heart. More heartache. I walked across the room to gaze out the window. The cold and darkness of the

December days had already settled in. A thin layer of snow had fallen over our cars in the driveway. Through the pane of glass I could hear the echo of the frigid wind encircling my whole world. The world outside and the world within me, both bleak, empty, devoid of life and sunshine.

I kept asking myself, where did I go wrong? Why is this happening to us? Ray and I are now cast aside, discarded, tossed into the air and blown away. But why?

I dreaded bearing the news to him. He had been through enough with me. But of course I had to tell him. Dazed, I walked into the kitchen.

"Ray, I have something to tell you." Knowing me so well, he instinctively recognized my flustered look.

"Now what?"

"Rebecca's not coming home for Christmas."

"Why not? Is she alright? Is this serious?"

"It's serious, but she's not ill or hurt. She seems to be in an emotionally fragile state of mind right now. She dropped all her courses and sought help from a counselor on campus who advised her not to come home. In his eyes, we're not good enough as parents - too dysfunctional. How could any professional person say that about us when he has never even met us or spoken to us? Who is this man who inspired my impressionable daughter to delete her family from her life? She needs some time, I don't know how long, to sort things out in her mind. For now, she's quitting college and moving to Florida."

"Oh, no."

Ray stared at me, his eyes reflecting tenderness and sympathy. We reached for each other, and his warm, consoling arms wrapped around me. For the moment, I felt safe, protected, and loved.

**December 22, 1993**

I had stayed awake all night, thinking of Rebecca, thousands of miles away. How could I know if she was safe, free from danger, with the vast distance between us? Surely, she would feel alone and abandoned on Christmas. I looked at the clock. I had school today, the last day before the holiday break. I needed to get myself together and begin the drive to Staten Island. No time for makeup. I grabbed my purse and jumped into the car, not wanting to be late. Today will be the second grade holiday party with Santa coming to visit our classroom. The activities will definitely distract me from my problems. But as I continued the drive onto the New Jersey Turnpike, the relief I had looked forward to became short-lived. As my eyes filled with tears, I put on my blinker and pulled over to the side of the road. It took a while to regain my composure. Wrapped in my disappointment, it would not be possible to experience the joy and celebration of Jesus' birth.

But as I continued the journey to my school, I began talking to myself with the spirit of optimism.

*Hope, have you forgotten who you are, or what you have learned through your trials? You can do it. You can find the strength to deal with this, as you have so often done in the past. Give Rebecca the space that she needs. Remember, each one of us must find our own way through the darkness to find the light.*

I felt better. I arrived at school, ready for the festivities and the children that needed me.

## Christmas 1993

Christmas turned out to be better than we had expected. Danny and Allison chose not to see each other, so Danny spent the day with his mother, stepfather, and sister, Ashley. Although thoughts of Rebecca weighed heavily on my mind, we had the opportunity to bond with Allison and give her all our attention. We laughed, told stories, and made up for lost time. After Allison returned to North Carolina, we organized a family dinner for Danny, and included Ray's sister, niece, and brothers in our invitation. The dinner turned out to be a delightful occasion.

After the guests left, Ray and I talked.

"Hope, is this what the future holds for us? Our family separated and divided forever?"

"We certainly never imagined this happening. Only time will reveal what is to come."

***

# Chapter 31

## *One Last Attempt*

**April 5, 1994**

I TRIED TO heroically deal with my disappointments since the developments of last December. Some days I felt in control, stable and determined, and other days I became quiet and introverted, still seeking to analyze the meaning of life, and questioning my goals. I can recall that Saturday morning when I sat in the living room to escape from reality by engrossing myself in one of the new bestseller mysteries.

A short time later Ray came into the room carrying his legal newspapers, and joined me in my quiet solitude. We sat together for hours, side by side, our minds focused on things we needed to distract us from reality. Becoming bored, I interrupted Ray's concentration.

"Ray, do you want to spend the entire day sitting here, reading? What would you like to do?"

"I don't know, but I must be honest with you, my thoughts have been drifting to something that I want to discuss with you. It's something that's been weighing heavily on my mind for a very long time. I need your advice in making a decision."

"What is it?"

"It's Ashley. Ashley who had been my daughter, my sweet little angel, who had been snatched away from me. I've been looking at the calendar for months, waiting for this day to arrive. Ashley has now reached the age of eighteen. If you remember, Danny updated us about Ashley, and she's now living at Penn State. Like Rebecca and Danny, she is legally capable of making her own decisions now. I'd like to call and see if she'd meet with me. There is so much I would like to say to her. I especially want her to know that I never intended to abandon her. I've carried so much guilt all these years after I made that decision to request the paternity test. This is the one chance I have now to reconnect. Should I call her and try, or let it go forever?"

"I'm not really surprised to hear this because I also never stopped thinking about Ashley. I've wondered if she carries anger toward you or her mother for what had happened to her in childhood. I'd like to know what kind of person she's become, and if she has a happy, fulfilling life. You need to give it a try. You need to do it for yourself, to know that you took the opportunity to reach out to her. This will help you put aside your guilt. But most of all, you need to do it for Ashley. Even if she rejects you, she will never forget that you tried."

"The decision is made. I will call her tomorrow, and try to get in touch with her at the school dormitory."

## April 6, 1994

The next morning Ray anxiously called the dorm at 9:00 a.m., hoping that this would be a good time before most classes began. A female student answered the phone in the hallway. When Ray asked to speak with Ashley, she immediately recognized the name, and asked Ray to wait while she checked on her whereabouts. A few minutes later, Ashley walked out of her room.

"Hello, who is this?" she asked.

"Ashley, this is Ray Brooks. I realize it's been a long time since we've had any contact, but I'm reaching out to you because you've been on my mind. I would like to visit you at Penn State, to talk and spend some time together. Would you be willing to do that?"

"Oh, my God!" responded Ashley without hesitation. "Yes. When can you come?"

A plan was arranged for the next Saturday afternoon at 3:00 o'clock. Before Saturday arrived, Ray and I discussed whether or not I should accompany him. We decided he should go alone. This was something that had to be resolved only between Ray and Ashley, and I felt that my presence might be inappropriate.

**April 10, 1994**

After his visit, Ray recanted the events of the day.

It began as he sat quietly in the entrance foyer of the dorm. Many girls walked passed him as he waited for Ashley. As each of them approached, he studied their faces and features, reflecting on his reason for coming here. His eyes searched for the one he had once known as his daughter. He wondered if she would remember him, as they had not seen each other for more than a decade. He became filled with excitement as the day arrived that he had fantasized about for so long. He envisioned a new beginning with Ashley returning into his life, filling the gap of all the time that had been taken from them.

As he sat preoccupied, absorbed in his dreams, a young, blond haired girl approached him, wearing a bright smile. Ray instantly knew it was her. He rose from his chair, wanting to reach out with a hug. But feeling nervous and awkward, he withdrew and chose only to speak.

"Hello, Ashley. I'm so happy to see you again."

"Me too," she replied.

Ashley, also feeling uneasy, looked away from Ray and fumbled for words.

"Would you like to take a tour around the campus while we talk? I think you'd like that. This is a really cool, interesting place."

"Yes, I'd enjoy that."

The conversation began as they walked past many buildings on the huge, beautiful campus. It continued for the first hour while they shared impersonal information and stories to get to know each other.

"Tell me about yourself. What's your major at college, and what are your career goals?"

"I haven't decided yet. Maybe I'd like to get into social work."

"Helping people is always a rewarding choice. What's your favorite subject?"

"Reading and literature. How about you? Are you still a practicing attorney?"

"Yes, but over the past few years I learned to add enjoyment to my life as well as work. One thing I do regularly is windsurf at the Jersey shore. I also just bought a bike and plan on biking through the trails of the nature preserves. Ashley, I want to tell you how sorry I am about everything that happened. I just want you to know that I never intended to abandon you. Could you please tell me how you feel about me?"

Ashley looked at him with tenderness.

"You were my dad. My mom took me away and all I remember is I never stopped thinking about you. It happened every day. Every morning I opened my eyes and hoped. I hoped that I would see you. I believed that you would come. I would wait. And wait. And wait. But finally after a very, very long time, my hopes shattered. I finally accepted that it would never happen, and I believed that I would never see you again."

Ray stood there, absorbing her long awaited message. Yes, he thought, she had loved and remembered me, as I had loved and remembered her.

"Ashley, are you willing to try this again, and include me in your life? I'd like to know."

"Sure, I would."

Ray extended his hands as a final gesture of warmth. Ashley reached out to him in response, and they gently embraced. As Ray walked across the university parking lot, he turned his head for one last look at Ashley. There she stood, not really wanting to say goodbye. This had been the day he'd been waiting for.

**April 13, 1994**

Three days after Ray's reconciliation with Ashley, Danny called Ray and confronted him in a fit of rage.

"Dad, don't you realize what you've done? Why did you go to Ashley's college and uproot things that had been settled in the past? You've opened up old wounds that had healed, and now everyone will suffer because of it. My mother and stepfather learned about it, and they're both furious. They don't feel you have a right to be involved with Ashley. Dad, you've turned everyone's life upside down."

Although surprised to hear of Danny's feelings, Ray stood his ground. He had spent years processing his plan, and no one, not even his son, would stop him from enjoying that day he had waited for.

"Son, I'm proud that you care so deeply about your sister. But what happens between me and Ashley does not involve you, your mother, or your stepfather. Ashley is no longer a child. She and I have the right to make the decision to reconnect if we choose. I'm asking you to let go of your anger, and grant me your blessings. Please. For all of us."

"This is really hard for me, Dad, I just want it all to be over. Can't you understand that?"

"I can, but I've been through a lot too, and I'm still trying to deal with it in my own way. Let's both try to put our feelings aside and concentrate on what Ashley needs. She's been through a lot more than we have."

"You're right, Dad. Ashley should come first."

**June 1, 1994**

Ray approached me with frustration. After his visit to Penn State, he had tried unsuccessfully to contact Ashley. Whenever he called the dorm and asked for her, the student who answered would place him on hold, but always came back saying she was unavailable. He had tried calling different times of the day, asking for Ashley to return his call. She never did.

"Hope, I guess I just have to accept that things aren't going to work out between me and Ashley after all. She's obviously been avoiding any interactions with me. Why do you think she changed her mind?"

I tried to place myself in Ashley's situation.

"Maybe seeing you would just be too emotionally draining for her. Maybe she wanted to protect everyone, including Danny, from reliving the pain of the past. Maybe she just decided to accept the life that she had with her mother and her stepfather. But I can only guess. We'll never really know why. Ray, I'm so sorry."

In this moment we held each other once again, as Ray began to sob with sorrow and disappointment. As I held him in my arms, my thoughts took me back to the Easter of 1984, the time that Ray and I celebrated the holiday together with our four children. It had been a time to treasure, playing outdoors with sunshine, blossoming trees, and golden memories. A time when we were going to be a family. At least I have those memories, and they are something that no one can ever take away.

***

# Chapter 32

## *Wonders Do Happen*

**May, 1995**

THE PASSING OF another year. Despite our never ending concerns over the most recent child in crisis, Ray and I again managed to weather the storm. Relying on the skills learned in the past, I successfully blocked my daily fears by dedicating all of my energy to those little second graders. No longer being the mother of young children, it seemed that now, more than ever before, teaching had become the center of my universe. That's who I was, what I had become. The long and short vowels. The reading books. Elementary math concepts. Working with parents and co-workers. Being successful in the classroom, that's all that mattered now. And soon it would be the end of what had been a very inspiring school year.

Ray and I looked forward to a joyous occasion, Allison's graduation from North Carolina State University. She had worked hard, and dedicated herself to her studies with unremitting determination. After graduation she planned to pursue a graduate degree in the medical field, perhaps becoming a research scientist. Hundreds of chairs had been set up on the lawn of the campus for family members of the graduates. The graduation song, "Pomp and Circumstance," began playing, as the graduates slowly began their procession down the aisle, all dressed in the traditional cap and gown attire. I stood by my chair, awaiting my moment of pride, anxious to see my daughter make her entrance. As I waited, I looked across the crowds of people and noticed Drew, seated on the opposite side of the lawn. Thankfully, I thought, he and Ray were situated far away from each other, so there would be no opportunity for Drew to vent his relentless anger toward anyone. Closing him out of my mind, I returned my attention to Allison.

At last, I gazed at her, walking past me. Her exuberant smile and elated manner reflected her delight. I continued to look at her with fascination through the singing of the "National Anthem" and the endless speeches which followed. Finally, the graduates walked onto the stage one by one, to receive their diplomas. Clapping and cheers from family members in the audience followed the granting of each diploma. When I heard Allison's name announced and she proceeded across the stage, I clapped and cheered the loudest of all.

Once the moment of glory had passed, we had to face reality one more time. As Allison approached Ray and me, Drew moved toward us also. Suddenly we all stood there together. I looked at Allison with concern. For a brief moment, her smile disappeared and her eyes wavered back and forth from Ray to Drew, as she carefully weighed the situation. Finally, not allowing past incidents to intrude on this time of mirth, she took control and made an announcement.

"Family, I want to thank you and tell you how grateful I am that you made this day possible for me. I could not have reached this stage of my life without your love and support. I'll always remember the sacrifices you made for me. So tonight, I'd like to do something for you. Tonight, dinner is on me! We're all going to eat together at the restaurant where I've worked this year. Two of my friends and co-workers will be your waitresses. Please order anything you wish and don't look at the prices!"

"Allison, thank you so much for the invitation," I said excitedly. "You'll never know how much this means to me."

"I'm so proud of you," said Ray.

"You've matured into a wonderful young woman. Keep working hard to fulfill your aspirations, Drew added."

"Thanks, everyone," said Allison. "I have to return my cap and gown to the auditorium, and I want to say goodbye to some of my classmates. The plan is that we'll all meet at the restaurant at six o'clock."

As Ray and I walked to our car, I observed Drew as he strolled the other way. This was the first time I could remember all three of us were together without hatred or animosity. I hoped this step forward would at least be maintained for the rest of the night. When we all entered the restaurant, Ray and I sat next to each other, Drew chose a seat far away from us, and Allison situated herself in between. Still worried about a possible outburst from Drew that would ruin the day, I glanced at Allison. Her darkened expression returned as she carefully scanned her father's face.

Throughout the dinner, Drew kept his distance and avoided eye contact or conversations with Ray. The exchanges remained light-hearted, with Drew decisively placing consideration for Allison's needs above his resentments from the past. The next day when I had time with Allison alone, I asked her how she felt about us all being together.

"Well, Mom, to tell you the truth, I'm so glad that my graduation day is over. Having Dad and Ray in the same room was not easy for me. Sometimes I looked at my dad and felt like I never knew if a bomb would explode. Looking back through all the years since he left us, his wrath has effected every day, every hour of my existence. It would be really difficult for me to relive an occasion like this again."

Allison paused as she continued to evaluate another aspect of the experience. "But there is one more thing I'd like to say. Aside from my anxieties, this occasion has been mind blowing. I've been surrounded by all the people important to me, and my dad was able, at last, to put aside all of his issues about the past and enable me to enjoy the time we all spent together. Through all the days of my life, I will be grateful for the gift of today."

**June, 15, 1995**

With one daughter forging ahead in life, my younger daughter Rebecca now became the center of my attention. It had been eighteen months since she had announced that she could no longer deal with our family. Every day I drove to work and prayed to St. Jude for her return. I promised myself that I would persevere and never give up hope that I would see her again.

Another unexpected phone call came, Rebecca calling from Florida. I couldn't believe it, it had been so long. She sounded happy and upbeat, thrilled to hear my voice. Does she want to see me? Will she come back home?

"Rebecca?"

"Mom, it's me. How are you?"

"I'm fine, but really, how are you? What's going on? I'm so excited that you called."

"I'm good now, Mom. I'm over it. But I don't want to talk about it."

"Don't worry, neither do I. Is there a chance we can see each other?"

"Yes, Mom, I'm ready. Do you think you and Ray can come down here to Florida to visit me? I've missed you guys so much, and I have something to tell you. I've met someone and I'm planning to marry him. I really, really want you to meet him. When can you come?"

Somehow, in my mind, I had readied myself for this. I knew she would someday grow up and realize what she had left behind. I didn't have to think about it or consider my response.

"I can come as soon as I pack my suitcase, inform Ray of the plan, and start traveling."

"Then do it!"

"Yes, we'll get there as fast as we can."

Ray walked in the door and I ran to him.

"Ray, you're really not going to believe this. Guess what we're going to do right now?"

"I don't know. Have dinner?"

"No, we'll eat on the road. Rebecca called just a few minutes ago. She reached out to us, and wants us to drive to Florida. She sounds like she's really moved on. And she wants us to meet her fiancée, some young man she met there. I've already started packing. Are you in on this?"

Ray started laughing and couldn't stop.

"Will these kids every stop taking over our lives? I'm so happy, and I can't wait to see Rebecca, but do we have to leave tonight? Can't we get a good night's sleep and begin the trip in the morning?"

"Sorry, Ray, I'm in charge of this one. Can you be ready in twenty minutes?"

## June 17, 1995

We estimated the trip to Florida would take approximately twenty-four hours. Ray volunteered to be the first driver. We left at 6:00 p.m. and within two hours, the roads became dark and ominous, but he adamantly continued the drive with no reprieve. Surprisingly, I quickly fell into a deep sleep and remained undisturbed until the next morning, when Ray poked me and demanded that he needed his turn on the pillow. Not having any time together to talk or devise a plan for our reconciliation with our lost child, we arrived at Rebecca's doorstep exhausted and unprepared, but at the same time, ecstatic.

I jumped out of the car and waited for Ray to walk with me to the entrance door. We proceeded slowly, grasping hands. As we took the final step, Rebecca opened the door, threw her arms around me and screamed, "Mommy, Mommy!" Tears of joy streamed down our cheeks, as I held my baby, never wanting to let her go. Next she turned to Ray and hugged him tightly. "Ray," she whispered. "You are the man who's been the father in my life." Ray smiled, then we all laughed. It was such an overwhelming moment that I had not even noticed the young man standing aloof in the background, watching us.

Realizing that my eyes had focused on him, Rebecca motioned to him to move forward.

"Mom, Ray, I'd like you to meet Michael."

Michael reached out his hand with sincerity. He was a handsome young man, with a firm stature and dark, wavy hair. I had a positive first impression of him, although I knew that it would take time to know the real person inside. I had many questions to ask him. But more importantly, I wanted to know my daughter, who had been estranged from us for so long. It would take a while to become acquainted with the woman my child had become.

"Why don't we all sit together in the living room where we can talk and relax?" asked Rebecca.

Here our evening of disclosures and sharing began.

"Where are you working now, Rebecca?" began Ray.

"As soon as I got to Florida, I interviewed for a job in a Tampa brokerage firm. At first I knew nothing about stocks and bonds or buyers and sellers. But I gradually learned what I needed to know, and became proficient in what is expected of me. I wear a suit to work every day, I love my boss, and I just earned a $5,000 pay increase beginning next month. I can afford to pay the rent, buy food, and live independently."

I looked at my daughter.

"I'm so proud of you, Rebecca. You've come so far and achieved so much. You've definitely proven that you are capable of success at anything you choose. Do you think you want to stay in Florida, or is there a chance you'd like to move closer to us?"

"I'm good here for now, Mom. But Michael and I want to get married, and when we do, we might move to Nashville, where he can work for his father who owns his own construction business."

Noticing that Michael spoke with a slight Southern dialect, I asked, "Where did you grow up?"

"I lived in Nashville for a while as a child, but then my parents divorced and I spent most of my early years in South Carolina."

The small revelations were just the beginning. As we began to feel more comfortable, our exchanges continued and our hearts opened to each other. By the end of the evening, all our fears in coming to Florida had passed. Forgiveness had dominated. Joy filled the essence of my being as I was swept away by a newfound feeling of elation. Rebecca had returned to us and none of us ever mentioned or cared about what had driven her away. It was just another one of life's incredible events.

## June 28, 1995

After our trip to Florida, I returned to a hectic scenario at work. At the end of June, lots of paperwork had to be completed. It seemed endless. After the emotional month I had just experienced, I longed to find some quiet time for myself. I woke up to a beautiful Sunday morning, but just needed to be alone to process and relive all that had happened with Allison's graduation, our visit with Rebecca, and the progress of my life.

Nature always had the power to calm my spirit, so I went outside to our yard, as I often did, and sat on our bench swing, facing the nature preserve that encircled our neighborhood. I felt a cool breeze blow against my face, and noticed the leaves on all the trees swaying gently as they shadowed the morning sunlight. For the first time since Drew had left eighteen years ago, an inner tranquility soothed my soul. Dealing with their parents' divorce had been a struggle for my girls, but now I knew they would be alright. They had followed their own paths, not the paths I would have chosen for them. They had learned from their choices and mistakes, confronting all the trials of their young lives with stamina and confidence.

My thoughts turned to my stepson Danny. Despite his horrific childhood experiences and his reliance on alcohol to cope, he also has forged ahead and made a turnaround in his life. After earning his GED and working responsibly at a job for several years, he now earned a straight A average in a local four year college.

I took a deep breath. Things seemed so good right now. Have we reached the end of our turmoil?

✳✳✳

# Chapter 33

## *A Voice From the Past*

**August, 1995**

THE PHONE RANG.

"Hope?"

"Is this Grace?"

I couldn't believe it. A voice that I had not heard in eighteen years reached out to me. The voice of a person I had loved dearly, but who had rejected me in my most urgent time of need. It was Grace, Drew's sister, who had been my beloved sister-in-law through the ten years that I had been married to her brother. Grace, who had sheltered me in her basement the night I rang her doorbell as I sought a place to hide and cry after Drew had announced his plan to abandon me and the children.

"Yes, Hope. I'm calling you after so many years because it's taken me all this time to understand what a mistake I made when you and my brother separated. I don't know why but somehow at the time I felt obligated to stand by my brother, as if I really had to take sides with him against you. I regret my decision. I mourn the loss of our friendship. Our children, cousins, never had the chance to play and grow up together. Hope, can you forgive me for forsaking you in your time of need?"

I needed not even a moment's hesitation.

"Grace, I never understood it, but maybe now I do. You saw yourself in the middle, torn between me and Drew. I've missed you all these years, and a part of what we shared together has always remained with me. Would you like to meet and talk, and catch up on all the lost time?"

"We can never make up for what we lost, Hope. But maybe we can begin again and build from here. I'd love to spend time with you and get to know my nieces."

"We'll find the time, Grace. I promise."

## September 22, 1995

Grace and I kept our pledge to each other and planned a quiet reunion. I invited her to my home for lunch so we could talk and become reacquainted. It turned out to be a lovely, cool day, a perfect time to enjoy the colorful, falling autumn leaves. I anxiously made a suggestion.

"Grace, would you like to take a walk outside and enjoy this beautiful day?"

"Actually, Hope, I don't think I'm up to walking right now. There seems to be something wrong with my left foot. Take a look at this."

Grace sat down and showed me her shoe that appeared to be several inches too big for her foot.

"This foot seems to be shrinking. A size eight shoe always fit both of my feet perfectly, but now this one is much too big and always falling off. My right foot appears to be just fine. Have you ever seen anything like this before?"

"No, I haven't. Maybe you should see an orthopedic specialist to get his opinion. This might be serious."

"I already made an appointment for next week."

"Glad to hear that. Now it's time for an update. How are your boys? Have they finished college? Do they have careers or girlfriends?"

"David is still in school studying electrical engineering, and Pete is on his own, working for an accounting firm in Queens. Neither one of them has a serious relationship right now, but they date a lot of girls. I'd love to become a grandmother someday. And your children?"

"Grace, you wouldn't believe what an experience it's been for Ray and me, raising my daughters and his son in one household. I've taken out our family albums for you to see the most treasured photos of us. Come and sit with me on the couch while we talk and share."

Our conversation continued for hours, until darkness set in. When we hugged goodbye, we realized that the friendship we had lost had been renewed.

## October 1, 1995

More than a week passed, and I had not yet heard from Grace. Concerned, I called to ask about the results of her consultation with the doctor. She answered the phone sounding sad and emotionally disconnected.

"Thank you for thinking of me, Hope. But the truth is that I had some bad news from the doctor. He diagnosed me as having an onset of ALS, also known as Lou Gehrig's disease. He advised me that the nerve cells in my brain and spinal cord will slowly stop functioning. Within a short time I will be unable to move my limbs. I'll become immobilized, unable to walk, unable to have a life, and, finally, unable to care for myself. He said the disease is progressing more rapidly than usual, and soon I will die."

I sensed that she waited for my reaction, but at first I couldn't respond. I couldn't bear the news. It was worse than I had ever expected. How unfair. This young, beautiful woman. It couldn't be. Finally I spoke.

"Grace, believe me that I will be there for you, and help you in any way that I can. Thank you for coming back into my life. I love you."

"I love you too."

I couldn't talk any more, not yet. The news had been devastating. And another dream, the dream of our revived friendship in the years ahead, would never happen.

## February, 1996

The doctor's diagnosis had been correct. Grace slowly began her descent into suffering. At first she could longer walk, then could no longer sit. She spent her days motionless in bed. Next she lost the use of her arms and became unable to speak, losing the ability to communicate with the world and people around her. When she could no longer eat or swallow, even the simplest pleasures of life had been taken from her. I visited her often, realizing this was my last chance to be with her in this world. One afternoon I drove into her driveway, praying for the courage to ring the doorbell, fearing to see her anguish. But I never turned away. Sitting by her bedside, I held her hand, stroked her forehead, or stared at her as she slept. Sometimes I wondered if she was even aware of my presence.

Finally, the time had come for her to go.

Life is so unpredictable. Grace's presence had returned to me after so many years, but only for what seemed an instant. I am grateful for the time we shared, but a part of me holds deep regret for the time that passed us by. The loss of Grace has taught me a valuable lesson. Sometimes in life we only have one opportunity to be with those we cherish. We should all remember to never throw that chance away. With this awareness, I promised myself to hold my daughters dear to my heart. My daughters, who from this day forward, will be with me today and always.

***

# Chapter 34

## *September 11 in a Staten Island School*

**September 11, 2001**

THE STREAM OF life seemed to pass so quickly. Suddenly the year was 2001. When my alarm clock rang on the morning of September 11, I had no idea of what lay ahead for me, the children in my school, and the United States.

The school morning began like any other. It was 9:10 a.m. and my second graders sat at their desks, completing their morning work. We had just finished our daily salute to the American flag and singing of the national anthem. A knock on my classroom door. I looked up through the glass and saw my co-worker, Mary, motioning me to come into the hallway to meet with her with a look of panic in her eyes.

"Hope, did you hear?"

"What?"

"The World Trade Center. Terrorists hijacked two planes and crashed them into the Twin Towers, setting them on fire. Hope, my son Dan works in one of those buildings and now I don't know where he is or if I'll ever see him again."

I gazed at Mary, not understanding the reality of her words. Then within the next moment, standing together in sight of the classroom window facing Manhattan from Staten Island, we saw it. A huge cloud of gray smoke rose higher and higher into the sky, obscuring the clouds and spreading rapidly. We grabbed each other by the hand and ran past the seated children to the window. Yes, it was real. America had been attacked and we witnessed it.

I instructed my class to continue quietly with their morning assignments while Mary and I ran back into the hallway to summon our nearby co-workers. Susan approached us first. When we advised her of the dilemma, she quickly looked at Mary.

"Your son works there! Have you heard from him?" she asked.

Mary, with lips quivering, held her hands tightly over her chest.

"No, not yet. Hopefully he will call me here at school as soon as he can get to a pay phone."

Suddenly, I had a frightening thought. "This is all happening so close to us here on Staten Island. Do you think we're in danger right now, so close to New York City? Could there be repercussions of this headed our way?"

We all looked at each other, overcome with an awareness. Maybe we and all the children here with us were possible targets at this very moment. We became filled with fear as we recognized the severity of our plight, and the responsibility we held for the safety and survival of our students. An announcement from the principal on the loudspeaker redirected our attention.

"Teachers, I trust you are all aware of the crisis in our City. I ask all of you to remain calm, pull your window shades down, and lock your doors. A school lockdown is beginning. We will keep you informed of any information or instructions from the Board of Education."

Within a short time, radio and TV broadcasts reported the news of the Twin Towers collapse. There were reports of people jumping out of windows, attempting to escape from the burning buildings. Hundreds of firefighters appeared at the scene, risking their lives and doing their jobs throughout the shocking tragedy. As the news spread, the Staten Island parents began to flood our school office, coming to retrieve their children and bring them home to a safer place.

One after another, the announcements continued. "Mrs. Brooks, please send Jessica White to the office for dismissal." "Mrs. Brooks, please send Thomas Dooley to the office for dismissal." The calls seemed endless. By 10:30, all but two of my students had been picked up by their parents, and all teaching that day came to an abrupt end.

All morning I kept thinking about Mary. I had no news, and I wondered if she had heard from her son yet. I stepped out into the hallway to find her, as she came running past me.

"Yes, yes. Dan just called the office and I spoke to him. He had to walk with hundreds of people across the Brooklyn Bridge to get out of Manhattan. He said that bridges were shut down and driving was impossible, but he made it! He's safe now."

"Great news, Mary. I'll see you tomorrow."

I almost didn't get home that afternoon either. Alerts had been issued that terrorists had plotted to blow up all the bridges in the City, so teams of police and security personnel blocked the highways while they searched for explosives. I sat in traffic for hours, attempting to drive across the Staten Island Expressway and over the Goethals Bridge, back to New Jersey. Thinking of my own children, I was grateful that none of them lived anywhere near the center of attack in Manhattan.

## September 12, 2001

School resumed the next day. I looked forward to a day without incident, but September 12 proved to be more challenging than I ever imagined. Before class began, I signed in at the office and picked up my daily mail from the teacher's mailbox. In it I found a devastating letter from the mother of one of my second graders, Ryan.

Dear Mrs. Brooks,

It is extremely difficult for me to write this letter. I want to inform you that my husband, Ryan's father, was one of the firefighters who lost his life yesterday in the Twin Towers disaster. Ryan will not be in school for the remainder of the week. I would like to meet with you and the guidance counselor some time before he returns, to develop a plan to help him deal with this earth shattering loss.

Sincerely,<br>Lois Johnson

I stood motionless with the letter in my hand, trying to grasp the meaning of it all. An innocent child's life destroyed. Why has the world come to this? I had no answers. In a few minutes, I would be standing before my students with the aftermath of the day before. Gather your strength, I told myself. You will need it.

The morning bell rang and the children entered the classroom. No one spoke, silence reigned. Usually they were full of life, talking and giggling. But not today. They hung up their sweaters and book bags in the closet, then returned to their seats, eyes focused on me. I could sense that they needed me to say something that would make them feel better.

"Good morning, boys and girls. I'm so glad to see you all back in school today. Yesterday was a tough day for all of us. Do you all know what happened, and do you want to talk about it?"

At first no one responded, but finally Joey summoned the courage to raise his hand.

"Mrs. Brooks, the bad people killed Mr. David, my soccer coach. He was in the airplane that they stole and crashed into those Towers. My mom told me about it after I ate my breakfast this morning. I can't believe they did that to Mr. David, and now I feel sad and don't know what will happen to our soccer team. I'm going to miss him a lot."

Again, I needed a moment while I searched for the right words. His classmates stared at him in their unusual silence. Then out of nowhere, another child, Tara, called out.

"And my Aunt Millie died in the fire. That's where she worked. She tried to get out of the building by running down the stairs, but it was too late. The fire had already blocked the stairs, and she couldn't get out. Aunt Millie was my mom's sister. I heard my mom crying all night, and I couldn't sleep."

Finally, Daniel raised his hand. I nodded my head, giving him permission to speak, but dreaded the heartbreaking story he might add to our morning discussion.

"Mrs. Brooks, did you know that Ryan's father died in the fire yesterday too?"

It was time. Time to take action. I had to deal with this. I had to address what had happened in a way that could bring peace. I invited the children to come out of their seats and sit closely together on the comfortable corner rug that had been provided for our classroom for intimate story time. I sat down on my chair with them surrounding me.

"Boys and girls, I am so sorry that you had to witness the events of yesterday. I wish I had the power to change things so that yesterday had never happened, but I don't. Many of you are afraid and hurt, and this has impacted your lives in so many ways. Joey lost his soccer coach, a wonderful man who loved working with children. Tara lost her Aunt Millie, an important part of her family whom she loved. And Ryan, who is not here today, lost his dad, a brave American who gave his life for his country. None of this is fair or just.

We are all asking ourselves why people from another country would want to hurt or kill us. Throughout history, people have always fought against those who are different. And that is the source of all the evil in our world. White and black people have fought against each other. People of different religions have battled over their understandings of God. During the Civil War, our country was torn apart, with Americans fighting Americans, over their views on slavery. Not long ago in our country, women were not allowed to vote until Congress passed the Nineteenth Amendment in the year 1920.

How can we fix the world to put an end to this injustice? Boys and girls, only you can do it. You and your friends and your generation will someday be our leaders. One of you in this room might be the President of the United States, or the Vice President, or our Governor. If you lead with love and acceptance of others, you will make the world a better place for yourselves and the generations that follow. And you should start right now and right here in this classroom. Be kind to your classmates, share your crayons and markers. Do not ridicule someone because they are short or tall, thin or overweight, or come from a different culture. Be compassionate with others, and include them in your activities, sports, and play time. Accept others as they are with respect, and you will establish the path that is needed to take us to a better place in the years to come."

The children listened intently, and seemed more relaxed as their expressions changed. Maria raised her hand and asked, "Mrs. Brooks, is it snack time yet? I'm hungry."

Everyone laughed, and their silence broke at last.

## November 10, 2001

Two months had passed, and life resumed. But the effects of 9/11 would remain within all of us. Each day it seemed that some child had a question or an issue relating to that unforgettable morning. Once I gave them a writing assignment and asked them to describe what they had learned from the experience. Then they shared their ideas by reading them to each other. One boy, Richie, drew a picture of a man jumping from the Twin Towers. Showing it to his classmates, he announced, "This man is my father. He jumped off the building and died that day too."

This had never happened, but his fears had intruded into his understanding of reality.

The most touching memory that I hold of the World Trade Center aftermath occurred on a Friday afternoon, during our scheduled show-and-tell period. On this Friday, Ryan anxiously raised his hand as he waited for his turn. When I called on him, he asked if he could get something out of the coat closet that he had brought to school for us to see. Ryan exited the closet carrying a New York City firefighter's helmet in his hands, and proceeded to stand before us. He held an expression of pride in his eyes.

"This is my father's helmet that he always wore at his job. When I see or hold this helmet, I feel like he is still here, next to me. Every night when I go to bed, I make sure that the helmet is on the night-stand, close enough for me to touch it. As long as I know it is there, I can sleep. My Dad is a hero who gave his life for us and America."

At the end of Ryan's presentation, his classmates cheered and clapped their hands with incredible exhilaration. I joined them as we all stood together to honor this child and the hero he held in his heart. I went home that day with a great feeling of serenity. Although the world had changed on 9/11 and Americans would live in fear for decades to come, I came to believe that the future will someday lead us to a better place. These children in my class could love and understand the meaning of life better than the leaders who had brought us to our present circumstances. Yes, there was hope.

# Chapter 35

## *The Last Mountain*

**March, 2002**

THANKFULLY, OUR THREE adult children continued to progress in both maturity and independence. In the six years since her college graduation, Allison had completed her Master's degree and announced that she had fallen in love. Her fiancée, Spencer, was a bright, enterprising young man from a successful family. We made plans and scheduled the wedding for the following September. But there was one more mountain to climb that I had not anticipated.

With the gala event only six months away, we began the endless preparations. We met with the photographer and made arrangements for bouquets and floral centerpieces. We visited banquet halls and helped with honeymoon arrangements. Then without warning one day, the doorbell rang, and it was Allison visiting unexpectedly.

"Mom, I can't go through with it. I can't go through with the wedding. It's not possible. I want to call it off."

"What do you mean? Did something happen between you and Spencer?"

"No, I love him. But we can't have a wedding reception with both Dad and Ray being there at the same time. I'm still nervous about them being in the same room together. I know we survived my college graduation, but I still have no idea what my father might say or do. He has never, ever gotten over his anger. I can still hear it in his voice when I talk to him. I just can't face the possibility that my wedding will be ruined. Mom, we have to cancel it. What other choice do I have?"

I had never seen Allison so distraught.

"Don't cancel anything yet. Give me a few days to see if I can resolve this."

She seemed agreeable to my request, calmed down, and left.

The next morning I had to do it. I had to call Drew and attempt to have my first real conversation with him in more than twenty years. But I dreaded talking to him. I told myself I had to find the right words so it wouldn't seem as if I was attacking him.

I walked downstairs to the lower level of the house, closed the doors and lowered the window shades. Sitting in the dark, I placed my hand on the telephone receiver, but did not yet find the courage to lift it. Five minutes passed. Then ten. Finally, I raised it to my ear and dialed Drew's number. He answered.

"Hi Drew, it's Hope."

At first there was a prolonged silence, then a cautious response, "Hi Hope. How are you?"

My mind searched for how I would greet him. He actually spoke to me, and didn't hang up the phone. I wondered what would happen next. Maybe there was hope. The words began to stumble past my lips.

"Drew, it's been a long time. I hope you are happy and doing well now. I know things had been difficult for you in the past, but that's over now. Our daughters are grown and support themselves. I thank you for making it possible for me to have them in my life."

At that point I planned on discussing the wedding, but the conversation came to a halt with the sound of Drew's sobs. Within moments, we cried together. I knew then that this was a time of healing and reconciliation, one that had been delayed far too long. Pulling myself together, I continued to address the reason for my call.

"Drew, I'm calling to talk to you about Allison's wedding. Can you and I and Ray all be present and share in the celebration of her marriage to Spencer? Can we bestow on our daughter that memorable gift without hard feelings and animosity? I need to know, I need your word that we can do it."

"We'll do it, Hope. I'll call Allison and reassure her. Thanks for calling. I'm sorry for everything. I'm so sorry."

With those parting words, I collapsed on the nearby chair. I felt weak, as if all my energy had been drained from me. But it had been worth my efforts. My daughter would have her wedding day, and it would be a time to rejoice.

The next day Allison received that promised call from Drew. After they talked, Allison ran to see me and burst through the front door.

"Mom, I have wonderful news. The wedding is on and I'm so excited!"

We cradled each other and laughed. Nothing would stop us from enjoying this day.

1

***

# Chapter 36

## *In Conclusion*

**The Present**

THE EXPERIENCES OF my life have led me to wisdom and knowledge. Looking back at the many crises I had to face beginning from childhood, I now know the answer to survival is forgiveness. One must learn to let go of the fury that interferes with every aspect of our existence. Without forgiveness, we lose the power to love and be happy. I found the path to forgive my father for his years of domination that had driven me away from him. I forgave my sister-in-law Grace for abandoning me, which enabled us to share precious family time together before her unexpected, early demise. Finally, after what seemed a lifetime of fear and anger, Drew and I had the opportunity to reconcile.

The moment that I arrived at Drew's doorstep in Michigan to help with his terminal pancreatic cancer, I realized there was where I wanted to be. During my visit, we spent hours together viewing videos of Allison and Rebecca as preschoolers that I had treasured and saved. That day, we were taken back in time and relived the life we had shared so many years ago. A week before he passed away, we talked. He also sent me an email, the last communication we ever had.

Dear Hope,

Please don't cry. We both did the best we could. It took me a long time, but now I'm changed. At last, in my final days I have released my outrage for the things that drove us apart. As I leave this world, I cherish our friendship and I thank you for your kindness from the bottom of my heart.

Love always,
Drew

An emotional chapter of my life, closed. But closed with gratitude for having been able to say goodbye as we did. During the forty-five years that I knew him, I had witnessed his misery. He had an illness, but never sought proper treatment. Unable to deal with the demon within him, he repeatedly married and remarried, blaming others for his despair. Being so intimately involved with Drew has led me to compassion for those in our society who suffer from the misunderstood, devastating effects of mental illness.

Another loss affected me when I learned that Aunt Ava died at the age of ninety-four. I attended her wake and sadly stood over her casket. I was grateful that her exit from this universe had been quick and painless. To me, she will always remain the most beautiful person that had ever walked this earth. Knowing Aunt Ava has made me understand that the good we do in this world lives in the minds and hearts of people we touch, and is never forgotten. As I stood there gazing at her lifeless body, an uncontrollable joy overcame me, as I realized that I had done it. I had kept the promise I had made to myself. I had kept the secret. She never knew.

The only person I have not been able to forgive until this day is Uncle Scott, who robbed me of my childhood. But I'm still working on it, hoping to understand why he turned out to be the kind of person he was.

I do regret what I was unable to give my daughters and stepson. I lacked the power to protect them from the consequences of their parents' divorces. I wish they could have grown up with an intact family, like the kind of family I had envisioned long ago in those memorable days in Brooklyn. Today the children Ray and I raised together are marvels. Allison, the dedicated mother of two, devotes her time and energy to researching cures for diseases rampant in society. Rebecca has a daughter and has been working successfully for many years in the field of law. In her spare time, she volunteers as an advocate for children in the public schools and health care systems that have special educational and medical needs. Danny graduated from college in the field that he loved, environmental studies. He is now a firefighter who cherishes his role in life, being there for those in need and saving people's lives. Ashley remains removed from our lives. She has chosen to close the door that would have connected us, but we have never forgotten her, and never will.

For anyone contemplating divorce, just promise yourself one thing. Do not hurt your children or manipulate them to satisfy your own needs. Put them first, and remember that they will strive for the love of both their parents through the remainder of their lives. The choices you make and the example you set will influence their attitudes, their futures, and the kind of people they choose to become.

Thank you, Ray, for being my soul mate, for riding with me through the storms, until the sunlight made its way through the clouds. We did it together. You kept the promise that you made to me on our wedding day. You stayed with me for better or for worse, and taught me the meaning of commitment and love.

***